Acclaim for Elisabeth Hyde's

THE ABORTIONIST'S DAUGHTER

"Hyde's account . . . is fascinating and complex."
—*The New York Times Book Review*

"[Hyde] thoughtfully explores the illusion of choice and spins a tale rife with tragic consequences. . . . What a pleasure it is to read this well-crafted novel with complicated characters and interesting ideas."
—*The Boston Globe*

"A gripping thriller that will entice even those not particularly fond of the suspense genre, *The Abortionist's Daughter* delivers a rare but successful breed of multifaceted morality and adrenaline-infused action that purely satisfies."
—*Bookreporter*

"Hyde does a terrific job fleshing out her characters and dissecting all their problems."
—*USA Today*

"This is ferociously paced, up-all-night suspense, an exquisitely wrought murder mystery that's also richly layered and morally complex, as intelligent and provocative as it is impossible to put down. Elisabeth Hyde is a master."
—Joseph Finder, author of
Company Man and *Killer Instinct*

Elisabeth Hyde

THE ABORTIONIST'S DAUGHTER

Elisabeth Hyde is the author of three previous novels, including *Crazy as Chocolate*. Born and raised in New Hampshire, she has since lived in Vermont, Washington, D.C., San Francisco, and Seattle. In 1979 she received her law degree and practiced briefly with the U.S. Department of Justice. She has taught creative writing in public schools as well as through Naropa University. She currently lives with her husband and three children in Colorado.

THE ABORTIONIST'S DAUGHTER

THE
ABORTIONIST'S
DAUGHTER

———————

ELISABETH HYDE

VINTAGE CONTEMPORARIES

Vintage Books

A Division of Random House, Inc.

New York

FIRST VINTAGE CONTEMPORARIES EDITION, JUNE 2007

The Library of Congress has cataloged the Knopf edition as follows:
Hyde, Elisabeth.
The abortionist's daughter / by Elisabeth Hyde. —1st ed.
p. cm.
1. Women physicians—Crimes against—Fiction. 2. Mothers and
daughters—Fiction. 3. Mothers—Death—Fiction. 4. Abortion—Fiction.
5. Secrecy—Fiction. I. Title.
PS3558.Y38A64 2006
813'.54—dc22
2005044487

Vintage ISBN: 978-0-307-27641-4

Book design by Robert C. Olsson

www.vintagebooks.com

Printed in the United States of America
10 9 8 7 6 5 4 3 2 1

For Jane, Sara, and Sue

PART ONE

———————

DECEMBER

CHAPTER ONE

————

T HE PROBLEM WAS, Megan had just taken the second half of the ecstasy when her father called with the news.

Earlier that day, her roommate had bundled up and trudged out into a raging Front Range blizzard to buy two green clover-shaped pills: one for herself, and one for Megan, as a kind of pre-Christmas present. Natalie had meant to wrap them up in a little box. But the day got a little hectic, what with exams and all, so after dinner, when they were back in their dorm room together, Natalie simply dug in her pocket and took out the little pills and without any fanfare set them on the open page of Megan's biology text. "And don't wuss," she warned.

Megan screwed up her face. The green pills reminded her of those pastel dots you got when you were a kid, the kind you peel off a long strip of paper. She didn't have time for this tonight. She scooped up the pills and put them into a clay pinch pot that sat in the back corner of her desk. Lumpy and chipped, the pot looked as though someone had stuck his elbow into a ball of clay. Which is exactly what Ben, her brother, had done, eleven years ago. A major accomplishment, for Ben.

But Natalie wouldn't let the matter go, pointing out that they could start with just half. And so instead of studying for her biology exam as planned, Megan Thompson, pre-med freshman at the university, found herself giving in to something larger and decidedly more fun that evening. Not only that, but she gave in with no clue as to what had transpired earlier that evening two miles west, in the two-story stucco house she'd grown up in—the house that had been on the Home Tour three years in a row, the one that backed up to Open Space, with the model solar heating panels and the evaporative cooling system that kept the temperature inside a mere seventy-five when outside it soared above a hundred. She had no suspicions, no worries, no funny feelings that might have caused her to think twice, to resist the temptation and opt out of what she knew from experience would be another evening of all-night bliss. Forgetting about everything else—her exam, the argument with her mother earlier that morning, that last *very* strange e-mail from Bill—Megan placed half the pill on her tongue, washed it down with water, and waited.

That was at eight o'clock.

At eight-thirty they weren't feeling much different.

At quarter to nine Natalie wondered if they should take the other half.

And it was right after they split the second pill that the phone rang. Natalie recognized the number on Caller ID. "It's your mother again," she announced.

When Megan didn't reply, Natalie said, "I think you ought to straighten things out. Maybe she changed her mind. Maybe she'll buy you the plane ticket. I'm answering it." She picked up the phone, singing "Yell-*low*?" before even bringing the phone to her ear.

Seated cross-legged on her bed, Megan slumped against the wall. The reason she didn't want to talk to her mother was simple. That morning they'd argued over whether or not Diana would buy Megan a ticket to Mexico for spring break. Mean things were said—by both of them—and Megan shuddered when she recalled how pleased she'd felt with that last wicked remark about killing babies. Why did it make her feel so good to make her mother feel so bad?

Speaking of feelings, the drug was kicking in and she was beginning to feel pretty good—so that when Natalie told her it wasn't her mother but rather her father on the phone, she felt a welcome surge of love and affection.

"That's my dad," she said fondly, "wanting to play the guy in the middle. He's always doing that, you know? Whenever Mom and I get into a fight, there he is, Mr. Mediator. It wasn't even a big fight," she went on. "He just wants everything perfect, since it isn't with him and Mom. Freaks him out to think that she and I—"

"Take the fucking phone," said Natalie.

Megan took the phone and cradled it to her ear. "Hi, Dad."

"Sweetheart," he began.

"It wasn't a major fight," she told him. "Did she tell you? A bunch of people are going to Mexico. I'll pay for the ticket, I'll pay for everything. I didn't mean to lay it all on Mom." She heard her father clear his throat but felt a rush of apology coming—not just for things said earlier that day but for all the wrongs she had committed over the course of her nineteen years.

"I was rude," she said. "I shouldn't have yelled at her. Jesus, it's Christmas. What was I thinking? I hate it when I yell."

"Megan," her father said.

Megan stopped. There was something black and buggy in his voice that made her heart skip. And it took her less than a second to realize why. It was the voice he'd used ten years ago, when he'd called her at summer camp with the news about Ben.

"Megan," he began.

Frank Thompson couldn't tell if it was the reflection of pool water bouncing off the windows, or the shriek of his daughter over the phone, or the flapping sound of the sheet as the paramedics covered his wife that made his legs begin to wobble and shake. All he knew was that the ground beneath him was falling out from under, and he had to get down, fast, or he was going to be sick.

He squatted, set the phone on the slate floor that Diana had chosen when she put in the pool, and covered his face with his hands. He listened to the pool pump as it sucked and squirted from somewhere underground, and breathed in the moist, chlorinated air that filled the solarium. A few feet away a young woman in a police uniform was conferring with the paramedics. Next to him lay Diana's peach-colored bathrobe, along with a pair of purple flip-flops with the darkened imprints of her heels.

A shiver passed through him, and he turned his gaze to the water in the pool, which continued to dance as though some ghost were out there sculling in the middle. It was a small elevated pool, framed in by blond birch panels—not much bigger than two hot tubs end to end, really, with a motorized current that allowed Diana to swim nonstop without having to turn. Although he hadn't wanted to put the pool in, he'd later conceded to one of his colleagues that it was a worthy investment, since it gave his high-strung wife a chance to come home and mellow out. After twenty years of marriage, he knew that a mellow Diana was a cohabitable Diana.

Frank lifted his head, and a sparkle of light caught his eye from underneath the ficus tree across the room. Broken glass, needly shards—and Frank cringed as he recalled how earlier that afternoon he'd thrown the glass across the room to get his wife's attention. It was wrong of him, he knew that. But after coming across the pictures online—pictures that no father should have to imagine, let alone see—well, everyone has a breaking point, and it was the way Diana was so oblivious to the problem at hand, the way she assumed he was upset because she'd skipped out on lunch earlier that day: he felt his shoulders clench, and the glass just flew.

Three clicks.

It would seem that a man in Frank Thompson's position, with over twenty years' experience as a prosecuting attorney, would know better than to start tampering with things in a room with a dead person. A man in his position would get out of that room and call his own attorney. But Frank didn't have his wits about him at the moment, certainly not his professional wits, and all he could think was that broken glass would convey the wrong impression about his marriage. (Though *lord* it felt good to shatter a glass like that; the gratification was unmatched, like saying *shit* or *fuck* in front of small children.)

Rising stiffly, he walked over to a little poolside closet to get a broom and dustpan. Nobody seemed to notice him; the patrol officer was on her cell phone and the paramedics were conferring with each other. As if making up for all the times during their marriage that he hadn't cleaned up after himself, he knelt down and swept up the ficus leaves and shards of glass and emptied them into a wastebasket. He didn't want people to have the wrong impression.

Outside, a blast of grainy snow pelted the sliding-glass doors. Now the cop and the paramedics were kneeling beside Diana's body.

"That's not good," the cop said, glancing up. She was new on the force, blond and blue-eyed like someone straight off a farm in Minnesota; but she already had that bossy, black and white air that you find in cops, and older siblings. "Did you know about this?"

"Know about what?" asked Frank.

"Come see," said the cop. "If you get down, you can see better."

Reluctantly, Frank squatted. He hadn't looked at Diana since the paramedics had arrived. They held the sheet away from her head, and Frank, who'd harbored the lay belief that maybe it was all a mistake, now forced himself to look.

For all the times he'd seen a dead body—and there were plenty, his having been with the district attorney's office for twenty-four years—nothing could compare to this. His wife's dark corkscrew curls fanned away from her face, Medusa-like. Her skin was white and waxy, her lips the color of plums. Her eyes stared up, flat and fishy. He looked away.

"What concerns us is this," the cop said, and she nodded to the younger of the two paramedics, a man with a long straggly ponytail. Gently taking Diana's head in both hands, he turned it slightly and splayed the hair above her ear.

"Right there," said the cop. "You see?"

What he saw made him choke. The bruise was huge and ripe and living, a fat, blue-gray slug in her tangled hair.

"Any idea how this happened?" the cop asked Frank.

Numbly Frank shook his head.

"Well, it's some bruise," the cop said. "Hard to imagine what could have made a bruise like that. And look at those knuckles."

Frank heard himself suggest that she'd perhaps fallen.

"Maybe it's that simple," said the cop, "but I'm calling the coroner."

Frank stared at the cop, and for the first time he recalled that on two separate occasions he'd had her on the witness stand; both times she'd not flinched when the defense attorney had implied she was a forgetful, inattentive liar.

"—crime scene from now on," she added. "Frank, you need to have a seat."

"You mean you think this wasn't an accident?"

"Frank," she said, "your wife is a national figure. There are a lot of people out there who don't like what she does."

"Could she have been swimming too fast?" the older paramedic asked. "Maybe she swam into the edge of the pool."

"This is two-four-oh-five," the cop was saying into her radio. "Where's Mark? I need backup *now*."

Frank just stared at the three of them.

"Or maybe she tripped and hit her head and fell into the pool," suggested the paramedic.

Frank couldn't answer. It wasn't sinking in. He looked at his wife's face. The night before, she'd been complaining about the frown lines between her eyebrows; now her forehead was perfectly smooth and unlined. The night before, she'd informed him that for the past five years she'd been coloring her hair without his knowing; now for the first time he noticed that, yes indeed, it was a shade darker.

He wanted to tell her how beautiful she was, how young she looked, but the words kept catching on little fishhooks in his throat. What had he said earlier that afternoon? Something about photo ops and Ben? *The great Dr. Duprey,* he'd said. Now he cringed, recalling his words, and he bent down and rested his cheek against hers, wanting to take back everything he'd said that afternoon.

He might as well have tried to take back his wedding vows.

"I'm sorry," he whispered into her ear. "I'm so, so sorry."

His name was Huck not because of any affinity his parents had for Mark Twain but for the color of his eyes, which reminded his grandmother of the huckleberries that flourished throughout Michigan's Upper Peninsula, where she'd grown up. Blue as a huckleberry pie, she'd said when she first saw the child. Blue as Lake Superior in October. And so Huck it was, even though his parents christened him Arthur Harold.

Only two people in the department knew his real name: Deb in

Payroll, and his partner, Ernie. Ernie was a happily married man who spent his weekends coaching Little League and watching his daughter play soccer, and he liked to tease Huck about his name. So where are your glasses, *Arthur*? he would say. Where's your bow tie, *Arthur*? But Ernie never let it go beyond their private company. At the department, with the rest of the guys, it was Huck, and nothing but.

Which Huck appreciated.

He and Ernie didn't see eye to eye on everything. They carefully avoided the subject of religion, for example, since Ernie was Catholic and the last time Huck had gone into any church was for his grandmother's funeral eight years ago. Yet they worked well together, for the simple reason that their thoughts consistently dovetailed, making every investigation move just a little bit faster. Which is not to say that they were equals. Ernie had a good ten years on Huck and clearly saw his role as that of mentor. "Trust your instincts, Arthur," he would advise, as though Huck had never thought of this himself. "Nine times out of ten, what you're looking for is staring you in the face."

Ernie's advice extended into the personal sphere as well. "Don't go looking for love," he'd warn. "It'll come looking for you." This he said while undertaking a near-mythic search himself by fixing Huck up with every single woman who crossed his path—colleagues, neighbors, friends, his wife's friends, even his dog trainer. It became a joke; as the social occasions mounted, Huck began asking for a dossier before the fact so that he and the woman could skip over the basics. It was well on its way to becoming a Very Bad Joke when Ernie introduced Huck to a woman from his wife's office named Carolyn, who upon meeting Huck made no comment whatsoever about either his name or his eyes. That was one year ago. This spring, when Carolyn's lease was up, Huck and Carolyn were going to move in together—a development for which Ernie had volumes of wisdom. "The key to a good relationship is you gotta have more than just good

sex," he advised Huck. "Do stuff together. Crosswords. Movies. Anything. Above all don't screw around. I guarantee you, complicating a
good thing is a bad thing to do." As usual, Huck listened to all of this
with the dutiful appreciation of a good son who needed a little advice
now and then.

"And put your sunglasses on," Ernie would growl. "You're gonna
kill people with those eyes."

———————

Tonight Carolyn was on her way to Minneapolis, because earlier that
day, as the snowstorm raged, she'd received a phone call from her
father, telling her that her mother had had a small stroke. Although
her father assured her it was not that serious, nevertheless Carolyn
felt bound to go back and help. And so late in the afternoon, as the
snow continued to pile up, Huck drove her to the airport.

"I'm not ready for this, Huck," she said in the car.

Huck tried to be reassuring, but his words sounded generic and
cowardly. This troubled him, because he prided himself on his ability
as a cop to comfort people in frightening situations. Why not here?
Why not now?

"You'll take care of the cats?" Carolyn was asking.

"I'll take care of the cats."

"And the mail?"

Huck reached over and took her hand. "Your mother is going to be
fine," he promised.

"I'm sure I'll be back in a few days," she said, adding, "because I'm
really not ready for this."

By the time he got back in town, it was after seven, and the snowplows were barely keeping up with traffic. He picked up some Chinese takeout, stopped at a 7-Eleven for orange juice and throat
lozenges, then headed home.

Huck lived in a remodeled outbuilding that sat tucked behind a small neighborhood fire station. Originally used by the firemen to store worn hoses and whatnot, it had been Sheetrocked and painted but still occasionally smelled of mildew, which explained why Huck was able to rent it from the city at a reasonable price. (After living in the house for several years, he'd noticed something odd about the smell: it grew noticeably worse whenever a fire raged in the hills nearby. This he didn't like to ponder too much.) It also had a faulty heater that on these cold nights refused to kick off. Several times he'd mentioned it to the building manager, assuming that, since the city was paying for the utilities, they'd be financially motivated to fix it. Yet they didn't, and on nights like these he simply opened up the windows and let the heat blast out, an act of environmental lawlessness that could get a man banished in this town.

At nine o'clock he stepped outside for some air, and it was then that he experienced what would be the first in a series of odd coincidences that evening. The wind was blowing everything sideways in great angry gusts, and he was in the process of gauging how much snow had fallen, when he caught sight of a yellow VW Bug idling out in the parking lot of the fire station. The driver's window was down, and the driver seemed to be rummaging around inside. Without bothering with a jacket, he waded through the snow to see if whoever it was needed help. It was his nature; he was a cop.

As he approached the car, he was struck by a moment of recognition: the driver was the daughter of Frank Thompson over at the district attorney's office. She wouldn't have recognized him, because they'd never been formally introduced, but he'd been present at a swearing-in last year at which Frank had introduced the judge, and his wife and daughter were up there at the podium with him. Like mother, like daughter—the two of them looking so foreign, with their Arabian eyes and wild dark curly hair. Huck remembered how nervous everyone had been, worrying that Frank's wife, Dr. Diana

Duprey of the Center for Reproductive Choice, would take advantage of the opportunity to make a speech about the latest incident, in which their walkway had been coated with fresh tar. (Dr. Duprey, scheduled to perform a midterm abortion at eight-fifteen, had simply glopped through the sticky sludge as though it weren't there; upon reaching the door, she calmly removed her heavy Swedish clogs, left them by the door, and stepped inside.) But up there at the podium that night, Dr. Duprey had remained quiet. Frank made his speech, the judge got sworn in, and everyone went home happy.

Huck didn't envy Frank, being married to a woman like Dr. Duprey.

"Do you need any help?" he asked, bending down to the girl's level. She shook her head and mumbled something. He noticed her windshield was icing over and offered to get her some de-icer, but she refused that too. She seemed awfully jumpy, in fact, and he contemplated telling her he was a cop to put her mind at rest—but then he realized he didn't have any identification on him and why should she believe him, a man in a T-shirt who came wading out of nowhere through the snow on a cold dark night? He knew the kinds of things that could happen to a young woman alone with car trouble on a night like this.

Nevertheless he pressed, worried that she might drive off with poor visibility. She ignored him, though. As soon as she got a small circle cleared, she drove off with a quick pop of the clutch.

Fine, he thought. Not my problem.

Returning to his house, he unloaded clothes from the compact washer in the hall closet and stuffed them into the dryer above. He opened a beer and put on some music and settled down onto the sofa. It had been a long day, and he was looking forward to a day off tomorrow. He could get the oil changed. Do a little Christmas shopping, find something for Carolyn.

He was flipping through the channels when the telephone rang.

Now: Huck Berlin wasn't the spookable type. He didn't believe in ghosts and he didn't believe in ESP, and except for that strange thing with the mildew smell, he really didn't believe in crystals or seances or any of that New Age stuff this town was so full of.

Tonight, though, when he picked up the phone and heard Ernie informing him that Diana Duprey was dead—just minutes after her daughter had been stalled in his driveway with a fogged-up windshield—Huck felt an unmistakable chill run down his spine. He turned off the television.

"The abortion doctor?"

"That's right, my friend."

"How?"

"She drowned in her pool."

"They have a *pool*?"

"One of those little indoor jobbers. You swim against a current."

It sounded like Ernie was eating something. Huck opened the door to let more cold air in. "When?"

"We don't know exactly. Sometime after five this afternoon. Frank found her about eight-thirty."

"How can you drown in a pool like that? What'd she do, bonk her head?"

"Something like that."

"And they don't know how she did it—"

"—and that's why they called us," Ernie finished. "You got it. Anyway, the coroner's on her way over there now. What are you doing at the moment?"

"Laundry."

"Where's Carolyn?"

"Off to Minnesota."

"Why?"

"Her mother had a stroke this morning."

"Bad?"

"No. I just got back from the airport. Long day, bud."

"Well, not as long as Diana Duprey's. Pick you up in ten."

Huck hung up the phone and rubbed his eyes. Truth be told, he really wasn't a big fan of Frank Thompson's. It was a personal thing that had to do with an old case. Three years ago one Sally Templeton had been found dead in a frat house on a Sunday morning with a blood alcohol level of .38 and multiple semen stains on her legs. Huck and Ernie had gotten matching DNA samples from five different boys, but Frank wouldn't go forward because of one arguable screwup with chain-of-custody issues. Huck always felt that Frank's decision had had more to do with one of the frat boys being the son of a prominent businessman than any chain-of-custody issues; this was a huge mistake, in Huck's view, and it was compounded when the press started hinting that the police department couldn't be trusted to collect so much as a fingerprint without screwing up.

So there was no love lost between the two of them. Still, it was wrong to hold a grudge. And in the end, whatever the professional gripes, right now they didn't matter. Frank Thompson had lost his son a while back, a terrible thing, one of those kids with Down syndrome. And now to lose his wife, right before Christmas? Huck had seen stable, well-adjusted men at the height of their careers spiral into a ruin over things like this.

And the girl. What was she, a freshman in college?

He pulled a gray sweatshirt over his head and waited for Ernie.

The Reverend Steven B. O'Connell got the news as he and his family were negotiating over the appropriate pose for the annual Christmas photo. Emotionally drained from his own day's unfortunate events, Steven was in no mood for a picture, but his wife Trudy had booked the photographer months ago. For their part, three of the four children were disgusted with both parents for operating on the assumption that they'd be able to pose with smiles, for they all felt that the world at large would be better off if their respective siblings would go off and die in a plane crash. And Scott, the fourth, had his own set of problems—big problems, nasty problems—that made any notion of smiling into a camera seem ludicrous to all.

Steven took the phone call in his study. One of his friends was a reporter for the local newspaper, and he listened now as the reporter told him that Diana Duprey had drowned in her lap pool. Her husband had discovered the body. An autopsy had been requested. Did he have any comments?

"I don't understand," said Steven. "How did she drown in a lap pool?"

"Might have bonked her head. They don't know. But hey, people drown in hot tubs," the reporter said. "It's nothing new."

Steven sat down in a daze. "I just saw her this morning. She was fine." Trudy poked her head in. Steven waved her away.

"What, like you had coffee or something?" said the reporter.

"Or something," Steven said. "How do you know about this?"

"I'm outside the house as we speak," said the reporter. "Freezing my butt off, I might add. But they just carried out a body, and it wasn't Frank."

Trudy poked her head in again. This time Steven pivoted in his chair. On the wall behind his desk was a framed photo of himself standing alongside the Reverend Jerry Falwell, both wearing grins as wide as collection plates.

"So I was wondering if you had any comment," said the reporter. "On the record, as spokesman for the Coalition."

He was referring to the Lifeblood Coalition, an anti-abortion group Steven had founded six years ago. In the past two years the Coalition had stepped up its protests at Front Range abortion clinics; some suspected it was behind the bombing of a clinic down in Colorado Springs last summer, which had left a twenty-three-year-old student in a wheelchair. Steven O'Connell, of course, denied any involvement and continued to maintain that his organization did not condone violence of any kind.

Right now Steven felt too stunned to say much of anything, let alone something for the record. But as spokesman for the Coalition, he groped for the right words.

"This is terrible news," he finally said. "Dr. Duprey and I had our obvious differences, but this is a terrible tragedy and I extend my heartfelt sympathies to the family. May the good Lord bless them with the strength and courage to get through the coming days and months."

"Some people in the Coalition have made threats," said the reporter. "Is this the work of an activist?"

If Steven had been less drained, he would have bolted up and vehemently denied the suggestion. As it was, he wearily reiterated his position that the Coalition did not operate in that manner.

"Some of your members do," said the reporter, referring to a young man who had gone to jail for firing three shots through another doctor's window a few years ago.

"We never condoned that," said Steven. "We do not condone the taking of any life—that of a fetus or a doctor."

"Some people think that if you kill the abortion doctor, it's a net gain for mankind," said the reporter.

"Well, that is not our group," said Steven.

From down the hallway came the sound of a scuffle. "Flamer!" someone yelled.

"You'll have to excuse me," said Steven.

"One more thing," said the reporter. "Did you have any kind of a personal relationship with Dr. Duprey?"

"Excuse me?"

"Were you having an affair?"

Steven was dumbfounded. Diana Duprey was certainly an attractive woman, with her bright smile, her jangly bracelets, and that wild mane of curly black hair. But to suggest—

"Don't you have better things to do?" he said icily.

"I was just asking," said the reporter.

"Well, you have my denial," said Steven. "Now if you'll excuse me, I have family obligations." He hung up the phone and swiveled around to find Trudy with her arms folded tightly across her large breasts. Behind her the photographer fussed with his camera.

"Send him home," Steven said wearily. "This is no day for pictures."

The rest of the town wouldn't find out about Diana Duprey until the next morning, when big black headlines announced her death all over the state. Jack Fries, a local divorce attorney whose daughter Rose lay recovering in the hospital, learned about it on public radio, while shaving. Bill Branson, Megan's ex-boyfriend, got the official news when he walked past a newspaper machine; the size of the headline alone caught his eye. The chief of police, who'd been notified the night before but was unable to get over to the Duprey house because his son was spiking a fever of 104, immediately assigned their public relations person to the investigation full time. And Dixie LaFond, the receptionist at Diana's clinic, learned about it only when she arrived at the clinic at seven-thirty the next morning and found the building cordoned off with yellow crime tape.

"My goodness! What happened?" she asked the security man.

He raised his eyebrows. "You didn't hear? Why, somebody killed the abortion doctor."

CHAPTER TWO

DRIVING FROM THE DORM to her house, all Megan could think about was the argument with her mother that morning. In hindsight it seemed unbearably foolish and petty. Did she really expect her parents to hand her everything on a silver platter? Just send her to Mexico at the drop of a hat? But no, she'd had to blow up and stomp out of the room, and those last words—*Have fun killing babies*—seeped like a poison through every vein in her body. Twice she had to pull over, she was shaking so badly. Outside the snow was blowing sideways; the plows hadn't been around for a while, so the road ahead was blanketed in white, the tire tracks a mere shadow, like collapsed veins. According to the time and temperature sign at the Ford dealership, it was five degrees. And that didn't account for any windchill.

Compounding the problem was the fact that her VW Bug had no defroster. Or rather, it had a defroster, but the defroster didn't work; and although she kept wiping the glass with an old shop towel, the moisture from her breath quickly refroze on the glass. Soon the windshield was so frosty that she could no longer distinguish between road and curb, so Megan—who was a very cautious driver, especially when under the influence of any recreational drug—

steered into the driveway of what turned out to be a neighborhood fire station. There she put the car in neutral and took a plastic scraper and started vigorously scraping at the ice on the inside of the windshield, sending out little showers of frost dust.

Having cleared a ragged hole, she was about to put the car in gear when she noticed a man standing outside a little house just behind the fire station. He was watching her. Despite the frigid temperature he wore no jacket, just a white T-shirt. One of the firemen? Just a guy? She couldn't tell.

Shit! He was walking toward her. She didn't want to talk to anyone! She was high! Her mother was dead! Shit! Fuck! She would have rolled her window up, but it was impossible for her to do so in any quick manner, because the threads inside the roller were worn, and to get the window up she'd have had to crank with one hand and force it up with the other, which would have taken too long. She let out the clutch. The car stalled.

The man peered down to her level.

"You okay?" The shadow of a beard, a tiny gold hoop in his left earlobe. "Car trouble?"

Megan quickly averted her eyes. She wanted to say, No, I'm fine, or, No, it's just my windshield, but she seemed to have lost her voice. She wished she'd brought along a water bottle.

She restarted the engine, only to find Saran Wrap forming on the windshield. Trying not to appear jumpy, she took the towel and began rubbing the glass, which only served to smear everything into a blurry mess.

"Got any de-icer?" he asked.

Megan paused. She could smell the man; he smelled like laundry detergent, or too much deodorant—she couldn't put her finger on it. She resumed her polishing.

"Sorry?" he pressed.

He's fucking with you, Megan told herself. Answer him and he'll go away. With great effort she managed to shake her head—meaning to communicate three things: one, that she didn't have any de-icer; two, that she was fine and didn't need his help; and three, that she was onto the fact that he was fucking with her.

But the man seemed bent on a mission. "I can go check," he said. "I might have some." But then he paused, watching her, as though waiting for permission. She stole a quick glance at him, and jesus his face was moony in the light of the snow and how did he get that scar on his chin? It suddenly occurred to her that here she was, talking to a strange man in an empty parking lot at nine in the evening, someone who might *not* just be fucking with her. Her heart took a little riff. This town was not the safe little place people thought it was. Had the cops gotten that man who was sneaking into women's bedrooms? She tried to remember the sketch she'd seen in the local section of the newspaper—hadn't the guy been wearing an earring?

Megan popped the clutch. The car lurched forward, and the man gave a clumsy little hop off to one side. She didn't care. She pulled out onto the road. Maybe now she would have to keep poking her head out the window to see where she was going, but at least she wasn't hanging around like a sitting duck, asking to get mugged.

Conscientiously watching her speed, Megan managed to navigate up the main street and turn at the light. To make up for lost time, she decided to take the shortcut to their house, even if it did go up and then down a steep hill. When she stuck her head out the window, icy needles spat against her face. All you have to do is get home, she reminded herself. There's just this last hill. She floored the accelerator, but as she neared the crest, her wheels began to spin. She took her foot off the gas with the intention of simply coasting back down to get another start but instead found herself gliding quietly off the road and down into a little ditch, finally coming to rest against a sprawling juniper bush.

It was as soft a landing as any car could possibly make, but when

Megan tried to open the driver's door, the boughs of the juniper bush elbowed back. She would have climbed out through the passenger door, but it had been jammed shut since last summer, when Bill kicked it in.

She was stuck.

She'd forgotten her cell phone, and the horn didn't work because she'd disconnected it last summer when it started honking continuously. All she could do was wait until someone drove by. And so in this sheltered ditch, with her windshield frosted over and the snow falling gently and the juniper boughs pressing up against the window, Megan sat. And waited. And tried not to think about the last words she had said to her mother.

———

When Frank answered the door and saw Detective Huck Berlin standing on his porch in the pale glow of the streetlight, he cringed inwardly. Not that Detective Berlin wasn't top notch. He was one of the best, even if he was relatively young. But Frank had exchanged heated words with Detective Berlin back when they had decided not to go forward in the Templeton case. Berlin was pissed. Frank didn't blame him. The guy had done a lot of good work. But since that time, whenever he had had to deal with Detective Berlin—when Berlin presented him with a positive ID in a rape case, for example—Frank sensed a naked skepticism on the younger man's part, as though he would have gone into shock if Frank had followed through.

And of course, Berlin was accompanied by Detective Vogel. Frank had always suspected that it was Ernie Vogel who was responsible for the chain-of-custody fuckup in the Templeton case, and he wished Ernie would have admitted as much. Vogel had responsibility issues, in Frank's view. Plus he could just be a real asshole. His older daughter had played on Megan's soccer team, and Frank had never much appreciated the way Ernie stalked the sidelines, huffing and yelling at the ref every chance he got. Some parents got way too worked up over these games, and Ernie was one of them: he was an embarrassment to the team.

The two detectives exchanged glances, then wiped their feet on the mat and stepped into the house. Detective Berlin wore a gray hooded sweatshirt and stood in the hallway with his hands stuffed into the kangaroo pockets. His nose was red, his eyes bleary and moist. Detective Vogel followed—quiet for once. (Though why wouldn't he be? There was no ref to yell at.)

"I'm sure sorry about this," said Detective Berlin.

Frank merely blinked. All manner of graciousness, all manner of protocol had suddenly escaped him. He had no idea what to do next.

"Maybe you could show us the pool," Huck offered, and Frank dutifully led them down the hall to the solarium, where the patrol officer and the paramedics were kneeling over Diana's body. They all looked up.

"Hey, Jen," said Huck.

"Huck," said the patrol officer. "Ernie."

"What happened? If I may ask," said Ernie.

Frank said, "She drowned."

"She *hit her head* and drowned," Jen corrected him. "Frank, I asked you to sit over there. Please sit over there. Please don't go wandering around. Come take a look," she told the two detectives.

Huck and Ernie squatted by the body and looked at the area where the paramedics splayed Diana's hair.

"Yowsers," said Ernie.

"Did you call the coroner?" asked Huck.

"Piper's on her way," said Jen.

"When did backup get here?"

"About half an hour ago. They're outside," said Jen.

Huck stood up and surveyed the room. "Any signs of forced entry?"

"Not that I can tell."

"Any struggle?"

"Just the bruise. A few scratch marks."

"Was your wife on any medication?" Ernie asked Frank. "Any chance she'd been drinking?"

Frank snorted.

"It might be a simple explanation," said Ernie, shrugging. "Maybe she fell."

"She wasn't drunk," said Frank.

Ernie walked over to the pool. He leaned down and swished his hand through the water. "How do these things work?"

"You swim against the current," said Frank.

"And how fast does it go?"

"You set the speed. As fast as you want."

"What, like two miles an hour? Five?"

"I don't know," Frank said, growing irritated. "It's got a dial."

Just then two other police officers arrived, and Huck sent them back outside to start taping off the house. "Make sure you get the entire yard," he said. "Plus the garage. Does anybody have a key?" he asked Frank. "Housekeepers? Workers?"

"Just my daughter," said Frank. Which reminded him. He checked his watch. It was ten past ten. Where was Megan?

"Anyone come in to feed the pets?"

Frank shook his head, although now that he thought of it, it was certainly possible that Diana had given a key to the housecleaner. Though whoever that was, Frank didn't know. Diana went through housekeepers like paper towels.

But before he had a chance to correct himself, a small athletic woman came striding into the room. Piper McMahon was the county coroner. Her son Brian had been a classmate of Megan's. During his sophomore year Brian had gotten heavily into hallucinogenics, and instead of graduating he went off to live on a commune in the Arctic Circle. Piper hadn't had it easy, Frank thought.

Though neither have you, he reminded himself, flashing on Ben. Amazing, how parenting could age a person beyond his wildest expectations.

Piper unzipped her puffy black parka and dropped it onto the floor and stepped forward to hug Frank. "The whole drive down I kept telling myself it wasn't true," she whispered. She knelt down beside Diana's body. She pressed her fingers against Diana's neck. She glanced up at Frank, then shifted her weight and pressed in another spot. Frowning, she smoothed back Diana's thick curls and examined her head, turning it this way and that. She palpated the area around the bruise. She lifted Diana's eyelids and shined a tiny light in her eyes. She rolled Diana to one side and examined her back, then rolled her back again and gently straightened her arms by her sides and brought the sheet up over her head.

"You're right, we're going to need a full autopsy," she said. "What time did you find her?" she asked Frank.

"Eight-thirty."

"In the pool?"

Frank nodded.

"And you dragged her out?"

Frank nodded again.

"Wish you hadn't done that," Ernie murmured.

"And when did anyone last see her?" asked Piper.

"I did," said Frank.

"What time?"

"Five, five-thirty."

"Well, we definitely need an autopsy," Piper declared. "I can't tell a damn thing here except she hit her head and drowned. Let's get her over to the morgue," she said, snapping off her gloves. "I'll call John, and we'll get started."

"Tonight?" said Frank.

"No reason to wait," said Piper.

Meanwhile Huck was over by the sliding doors, inspecting the doorjambs. "Did you say the door was unlocked?"

"The lock's broken," said Frank. "She was supposed to call someone."

"You leave all your doors unlocked?" asked Ernie.

"No, we don't, detective. I just told you. This one was broken."

Huck bent to inspect the lock. "Broken indeed. Nice ficus," he said, glancing around. "Hard to keep alive, aren't they?"

"I don't take care of the plants," said Frank.

"Must be the moisture in here," Huck remarked. He knelt down to examine something.

"What is it?" asked Ernie.

"Broken glass," Huck said. Frank watched as Huck slipped on a pair of gloves and picked up the glass and placed it in a Ziploc bag and sealed it. He watched him put the bag in his pocket. He saw the two men exchange glances and suddenly put things together. They thought it was him! But of course! You always suspect the husband! He should have thought of that by now.

As though Ernie had read his mind, he now approached Frank's side. "Listen, Frank," he said in a low voice, "do you have somewhere to go tonight?"

"Why's that?"

"It's just that we have to treat this as a crime scene," said Ernie, "and we need to preserve things."

"I'm not going to tamper with anything," said Frank, "if that's what you're saying."

"I'm not saying that," said Ernie. "But we've got to follow procedure. And I think you know that your staying here could cause problems later on."

"You mean when you want to name me as a suspect?"

"I'm not saying that."

"Good. Because I'm not leaving. I'm waiting here for my daughter."

"Where is your daughter, by the way?" Huck asked.

"She's on her way over here," said Frank. "I called her. She should be here." He looked at his watch again.

"Doesn't she have a cell?" asked Ernie.

It hadn't even occurred to him to call her cell. There was a phone on the wall by the door, and he picked it up and dialed Megan's number. There was no answer.

"She drives a yellow Bug, doesn't she?" asked Huck.

"Why?" said Frank.

"I think I saw her on her way over here," Huck replied. "She was having trouble with her defroster. I'll call Dispatch." He left the room. Frank was left standing there alone with Ernie, who glanced at him and then jingled the change in his pocket.

"Look, Frank," he finally said. "I'm very sorry about this."

Frank wasn't yet ready to start receiving sympathies. He cleared his throat and asked where Ernie's older daughter was these days.

"Up north," said Ernie.

"Is she still playing soccer?"

"No. How about Megan?"

Frank shook his head, and Ernie gave a sigh. "They were all going to get soccer scholarships," he said. "Remember those days?"

Frank managed a smile.

"Mia wannabees," said Ernie. "Everywhere you looked."

His wife dead—and here they were talking about soccer! Frank started to pick up his wife's robe, but Ernie stopped him. Frank dug his hands into his pockets.

"Our house was on the Home Tour, you know," he told Ernie. "Somebody might have scoped it out."

"Certainly possible," said Ernie.

"Somebody from the Coalition, did you think of that? They could have just walked through the house and gotten the layout of everything."

Ernie shrugged and agreed that there were a lot of people who didn't like what Diana did. "Lots of avenues to explore," he said. "We're just getting started. Look, Frank, I hate to say this, but you should—well, you should call your attorney."

For the first time that evening Frank felt himself stand erect. It was surreal, being on this end of the telescope, but he was not going to give anyone the satisfaction of watching him act like a suspect at this point. He would have liked a cigarette right now, to tell the truth. He would have liked a good stiff drink. He would have liked to fall fast asleep, and wake up in the morning to find it was all a dream.

"Thanks for the tip," he told Ernie, "but I'm more concerned about my daughter right now."

It was probably the only time in her life when, while under the influence of a recreational drug, Megan would be glad to see the police.

The two officers wrenched open the passenger door, pulled her out, and helped her into the back of the squad car. For a few seconds she forgot why she was there—the car was warm and she was warm and her neck was no longer spazzing up. But as soon as they crested the hill—as soon as she looked down and saw the ambulance, the police cars, the yellow tape already strung up all around her house— a fish flopped in her stomach. The Big Thing that they'd always lived under the shadow of had happened. It was real. It didn't seem real, but it was.

She let herself in and walked straight to the solarium, where her father met her, looking rumpled in the day's workclothes: white shirt, dark trousers.

"Dad," she said as he hugged her, "Daddy," and she was glad he was holding her because her knees went wobbly and she saw zigzag lights and she knew it had nothing to do with any green clover-shaped pill.

She glanced around the room. There were people milling around, and they all looked at her. There on the green tiled floor was the long white-sheeted form. Suddenly Megan felt herself splitting into two people, the girl with the wobbly legs versus the girl watching it all unfold on TV.

"Come on, I'll make you some tea," her father was saying, but Megan broke free from his arm and went and knelt by her mother. The only other time she had been in the room with a dead person was at Ben's funeral, and Ben certainly hadn't been covered with a white sheet; he'd been plumped and rouged and laid down to sleep in his Superman pajamas, and everybody who walked by the coffin seemed to want to touch his face, which had pissed her off, for reasons she couldn't put her finger on.

Megan turned back the sheet. Her mother's face was puffed and gray and froggy-looking. The girl with the wobbly legs went fuzzy and sat down while the girl watching TV took over.

"How did it happen?" she asked.

"We don't know," her father said. "It looks like she had a nasty blow to her head."

"By someone else?"

"Possibly."

"So, like, someone did this to her?"

"Let's wait for the autopsy, honey," said her father.

Megan stood up and looked at all the people standing around her. "You guys think someone killed her?"

"That's what the detectives are here for," said her father. "This is Detective Berlin," he said. "And Detective Vogel."

Megan looked at the detective with the blue eyes. The gold earring. The shadow of a beard. She looked away. How the fuck?

The detective stood there with his hands awkwardly on his hips, and she willed him not to say anything about the fogged-up windshield, because her father would get on her case for not getting the defroster fixed.

"I lost traction," she explained. "I slid into a ditch. I could see fine." Shut up, she thought. Who needs to know?

"I figured as much," the detective said. "In any case I'm glad you made it home. Of course, I'm terribly sorry," he added.

Megan went over and sat by the edge of the pool, looking at her mother's form. The girl with the wobbly legs had vanished by now, and Megan found herself wondering if her mother had been frightened. Or did she even know what was happening? Maybe she just slipped. Then again, maybe somebody sneaked in and hit her over the head. She told herself it didn't matter, her mother was dead either way, and she wondered if her mother had forgiven her for the things she said, for her *attitude*, that morning.

"Come on," her father said, taking her arm. "We'll go out to the kitchen."

"Actually," Ernie began, "actually, Frank, the two of you really need to find someplace else to go. You've got a lot of friends."

Her father's face hardened. "I certainly do have a lot of friends," he said without any trace of a smile, "but it's my house, and I'm going to go and make my daughter a cup of tea."

Ernie glanced at Huck. "Actually we just want to prevent this from turning into another—"

"You think I'm going to fuck with things?"

"It's a question of following procedure, Frank," said Ernie.

"Fine. I'm following procedure. I'm being a father."

Ernie was about to say something back, but Huck caught his elbow and drew him aside. Frank and Megan walked out into the hall.

"What was that all about?" said Megan.

"Our house is a crime scene," said Frank. "They don't want us contaminating the evidence. In fact, we're not even supposed to be here right now, but too bad. I'm making us some tea."

Suddenly Megan remembered her mother's stash. She hurried ahead into the kitchen and opened up the spice cupboard, spun the lazy Susan, and took the jar of thyme, which was not thyme at all, and dumped the dried buds and leaves down the garbage disposal and turned on the water and ran the disposal. Her father looked on.

"We don't need to cloud the issues, Dad," she told him. "It's okay. Really." She dried the jar with a paper towel, replaced the lid, and put it back in the cabinet. "*Really*, Dad. So what happened?"

"I came home around four," her father said. "We had a brief exchange."

"You mean a fight?"

"Something like that."

"Over what?"

Her father looked at her strangely then, as if to imply that she shouldn't be asking, and she wanted to say, *You're going to keep me in the dark?* But something in his eyes told her that it wasn't anything to press at the moment, and she kept silent and watched as her father set the teakettle on the burner, opened the tea drawer, rummaged around, opened the cupboard, got out cups. She had a vague sense that the two detectives would go ballistic if they could see everything she and her father were touching here in the kitchen, but she was reassured by the fact that her father was a prosecutor. He would know what was right and what was wrong, in circumstances such as these.

Besides, if there were clues to be found, they wouldn't be in the kitchen. She glanced around, trying to view the room as the detectives might view it. A pile of unopened mail lay recklessly tossed on the center island, and a basket of white laundry sat unfolded on the floor. Other than that, the kitchen was relatively tidy. A queer feeling came over her as she suddenly realized that she no longer felt like this was her house.

"Are they going to make us leave?"

"They're going to try." He was pawing through the tea drawer; half the boxes were empty, and he began tossing them angrily into the trash. "Doesn't she keep any plain old Lipton's around?"

Megan was about to warn him about certain medicinal teas her mother kept on hand, when Detective Berlin appeared in the doorway. "You guys have a dog?"

"No," said Frank.

"Because there are a bunch of paw prints out back."

"What about human footprints?"

"Not that we can find. Then again, it's been snowing all day. It doesn't surprise me." The detective looked troubled, and Megan felt her heart begin to race. Between her mother's pot and Natalie's ecstasy, she had a lot of things that she would rather keep to herself at the moment.

"Here's the thing I don't get," he went on. "Diana was a lady with a bounty. She had a direct line to the police station. Why would she put her house on the Home Tour?"

Frank didn't mention that that was another thing they'd fought about.

"Just seems weird," the detective went on. "Because if I was getting threats on my life, I wouldn't want all these strangers tromping through. Can you shed any light on this?"

"No," said Frank. "No I cannot, sir."

The detective waited, then shrugged. "That and the broken lock. Oh, well." He glanced around the room. "Hey look, between you and me, I know you're not going to mess around with things but see, Ernie gets pretty uptight over stuff like this."

"We're not messing with things," Frank said.

"I know that."

"This is weird," said Megan, glancing from one man to the other.

"It's just Ernie's a real stickler for procedure," the detective said. "So if you could call—"

"Excuse me," said Frank. "Did you just lose your wife?"

"I did not," said Huck.

"Did you just lose your mother?"

"I did not."

"Then give us a little peace in here, okay?"

("Really weird," Megan murmured.)

Huck scratched the back of his head.

"Thank you," said Frank.

"What's going on?" Megan demanded as Huck left the room, but her father didn't answer. He was flipping through the Rolodex on Diana's kitchen desk, and when he came to the number he was looking for, he picked up the phone and dialed.

"Dad?"

Her father shook his head. "Yeah, Curt," he said, straightening up. "It's Frank Thompson. Look, sorry to bother you at this hour, but I'm going to need a little help.

"No," he said. "It's not about Megan."

———————

Upstairs Megan closed the door to her bedroom. She was glad to be alone at this point. She thought it strange that her father was calling an attorney for help. Then again, maybe there were will issues. Or maybe that's just what you did when someone died: you called your lawyer.

She leaned against the door. Since she'd gone off to college, her mother had been using the room for storage. Summer clothes lay folded and stacked on the bed, old computer parts sat on the floor, an ironing board waited with a shirt over its nose. Megan set the stack of clothes on the floor, turned back the comforter, and slid between the sheets. Staring at the ceiling, she tried to recall just exactly which words had triggered the fight with her mother that morning. She had a way of pushing her mother's buttons. And oh my god, push them she had.

She lay there and felt her heart pound against the wall of her chest. She took her pulse, calculated a hundred beats a minute. She never should have taken the second half of the ecstasy. She assured herself that her father was clueless; he was way too preoccupied, and besides, he never suspected anything with her. (Worried about, yes; suspected, no. Unlike her mother, who didn't worry but suspected everything.) The detective, on the other hand . . .

There was no way she was going to sleep. For someone whose mother had just died, she felt awfully numb. She waited for a flood of emotion, but it didn't come. Outside it continued to snow, and she watched it through her window, big fat flakes spinning and swirling. She tossed and turned. She was thirsty but didn't want to risk running into her father out in the hallway, so she just stayed in bed and was thirsty.

Around two in the morning she heard her mother's voice in the hallway. *Frank? Is Megan back yet? Are you coming up to bed, Frank?* Immediately Megan recognized this as the hallucination it was. She forced herself to take some long, deep gulps of air, at which point she finally began to cry.

And lying there in the dark, Megan Thompson cried without stopping, in chopped, rocky sobs that terrified her: for even a girl who had lost a brother at the age of nine had no idea just how devastating it could feel to lose a mother at the age of nineteen.

CHAPTER THREE

MEGAN HAD ALWAYS had a lot of boyfriends in her life. When she was three it was Bo, who lisped; when she was four it was Tyler, who wheezed. At the age of five she shared her first brief kiss with a boy named Nick, who parked himself in front of her and then tipped forward like one of those magnetic kissing dolls. It was a huge letdown.

Throughout grade school there was always one boy or another calling the house. Because Megan was not just pretty but smart and responsible as well, boys called under the pretense of needing help with their math, spelling, geography—anything to talk to her. Boys who in their all-male groups made gagging faces at the mere mention of a girl's name would secretly invite Megan to their private family birthday dinners at Casa Bonita down in Denver, where the bland Mexican food took second billing to the teenage cliff divers who daringly plunged from faux cliffs into bubbling pools *right beside your very own table*!

In junior high there was Matt, who skied, and Brendan, who snowboarded, and Kyle, who skateboarded. Nobody lasted more than a month or two. Not that she meant to be cruel; she just lost interest after a few movies and make-out parties. Mostly Megan saw the boys as an equal opportunity for cross-gender education, so that when Kyle stuck his hand up her shirt and ran his fingers over her budding nipple, she stuck her own hand down into his pants and touched the soft tip of his penis. To Megan, breast buds and penis tips felt about the same.

Yet by the time she reached high school, Megan decided she was ready for something more serious. She scouted out the older boys (who were also scouting her out), and when Homecoming rolled around in October of her sophomore year, she had narrowed her choice to two boys: Duane, who played soccer and logged onto his e-mail account every night as "nutkicker22," and Bill, a more studious boy from her Advanced Placement U.S. Government class, who had been urging her to join the debate team since September.

Bill Branson was outspoken about everything. He called the president a liar. He called Fox News a bunch of liars. He called the school board narrow-minded and the city council a bunch of weenies. And in their government class one day, he made a point of calling Justice Blackmun a hero for writing the *Roe v. Wade* decision.

Megan didn't catch on at first that he might be expounding on this last issue for her benefit. But over lunch one day, as Duane desperately juggled a soccer ball nearby, Bill told her that he admired her mother's courage.

"Not that I'm advocating abortion as a means of birth control," he said between cheesy bites of a thick calzone. "It's just that mistakes happen. Condoms break. And you shouldn't have to pay for it the rest of your life."

Megan did not respond. Without knowing it, Bill was opening up a very big can of worms here; her personal feelings about abortion were far more complex than he could have known. She'd first seen the products of her mother's work when she was in middle school. Every day she walked over to her mother's clinic after school to do her homework; usually there were no signs of the business at hand around, and she found an empty examination room to work in. But one day she happened to walk through the lab and made the mistake of glancing into a white bucket on the counter. She stared in horror. There were tiny fingers with miniature pearls at the tips, noodly little legs and bean-shaped heads, all mixed together in a thick bloody soup. She continued to stare until one of the nurses happened to come in for something else; when she noticed the bucket, she whisked it away, swearing under her breath.

Megan hadn't talked about the incident with her mother, but it haunted her. At home that night she'd watched her mother julienning red peppers before dinner, and she couldn't help but envision those same hands tugging on baby parts. What an awful way to earn a living, she thought. She began to see her mother in a vaguely diabolical light, and worried that she might be carrying around her mother's karma.

So Bill had no idea what he was stepping into, commenting on Diana's courage. But sitting there in the school cafeteria, Megan made the very practical decision that it was not the time and place to try and explain her very conflicted feelings. Instead, she changed the subject—sort of. Boldly she asked Bill if he'd ever gotten someone pregnant.

"No," Bill replied. "Have you?"

Megan laughed nervously.

"You know what I mean. Have you ever *been* pregnant?"

"No," Megan said, feeling her neck flush—an unusual feeling, for rarely did she flush, or feel any kind of nervousness for that matter, in a boy's company.

"We're lucky, aren't we," said Bill, wadding up the calzone wrapper.

The implication of this short conversation was that the worry of an unwanted pregnancy was something Megan might already have experienced; and the implication from *that* was that she had already engaged in the sexual intercourse that would have given rise to the worry in the first place. Neither of which she corrected. She left their lunch with a strange thrill knotting up her stomach, a feeling that tightened on and off that afternoon, especially whenever she thought of Bill thinking of her having sex.

Duane took the Homecoming decision hard. She'd led him on! She'd jerked him around! When these accusations didn't change her mind, he called her a cockteaser, which bothered Megan far more than she let on. It was an ugly word, and it made her feel conniving and dirty and mean, when in fact she'd simply been undecided.

Sometimes she wished she could talk to her mother about such things. But hah! Never in a million years would that happen! Megan hated talking to Diana about love, or sex, or the changes her body was going through. Back in the sixth grade Diana had made one off-hand remark about Megan's tiny puffed nipples beginning to poke through her T-shirts, and that was enough to shut Megan up for the rest of her life. When Diana asked if she was interested in shopping for bras, Megan leveled a stormy, silent gaze upon her mother, and her mother never mentioned it again. (Ditto with tampons, a word Diana seemed unable to mention without also mentioning the word *hymen*. Megan cut her off in mid-sentence and made it very clear that she would figure everything out for herself. And she did: after a few months of dealing with bunched-up napkins, she went out and bought a package of SlimFits on her own. Following the illustrated directions, she quickly figured out how to lift her knee and shoot up the little torpedo, and thereafter she didn't so much mind being female. The only thing she needed from Diana was cash, plus a little brandy when the cramps got so bad she couldn't get out of bed in the morning.)

The night she told Bill she would go to Homecoming with him, she could not get to sleep. She felt an unbearable pressure building inside, more energy than she knew what to do with. She'd read of people with autism who needed to be squeezed, who in fact built elaborate compression devices to meet their needs, and she lay there imagining how good it might feel to climb into one of those machines and get pressed from all sides.

But she had no such device, and so on that night, with the sound of Bill's voice in her ears and a warm iron ball swelling between her legs, she lay in bed as the moon crept across the sky, and drew up her knees, and tugged relentlessly at herself. Mystified, she rocked back and forth in agony: for as much as she knew about the U.S. government and tangents and tampons and how to flirt with a boy, she knew very little about her body, or the things it could do when touched in the right spot.

And she certainly wasn't going to talk to her mother about *that*.

———————

As a sophomore, Megan wasn't eligible to be Homecoming Queen; that plum position was reserved for juniors and seniors. But she might as well have been Bill's queen on that chilly October night. She wore a low-cut green taffeta gown that cinched her waist and lifted her breasts. When her father saw her, he gave a long, low whistle—embarrassing enough in its own right, but pale when compared to her mother loudly reminding her that she hadn't yet gotten fitted for a diaphragm and shouldn't rely upon condoms given their ten percent failure rate.

"Diana! They're going to Homecoming, not—" He turned his glare upon Megan. "You're not sleeping with him, are you?"

"Oh my god," said Megan.

"Look, you've embarrassed her," Frank said to Diana. "Why do you have to be so explicit about everything?"

"Oh, for Christ's sake," said Diana. "They teach this stuff in school. Teachers talk about it. Kids talk about it. Why can't *I* talk about it?"

Megan looked upward and asked God to shoot her parents.

When Bill arrived, he presented Megan with a pink corsage. She had a white boutonniere for him. They pinned them on each other while Frank took pictures. After numerous poses—Megan alone! Bill alone! Now Megan and Bill! Now Megan and Frank! Now Megan and Frank and Diana!—Frank asked Bill what time he intended to bring Megan home.

"One o'clock, sir," Bill said.

"That sounds reasonable," said Frank.

Diana eyed Bill up and down. She had delivered him into this world, actually, back before she opened the clinic. She'd also circumcised him, she recalled now. Involuntarily she glanced at his crotch.

"I actually don't like to stay out too late," Bill was saying.

Diana rolled her eyes. "Bill, one thing you've got to understand. Don't Eddie Haskell me, ever. Look, I'm well aware that kids stay out all night, and if you guys have a cell phone, you might as well—"

"One o'clock seems very appropriate," Frank said, guiding them to the door. "No drinking. No drugs. Am I clear?"

"And no sex," Diana added. "Not until I fit you with a diaphragm."

"Oh my god," said Megan, slamming the door behind her.

Megan and Bill didn't spend much time at the Homecoming soirée. After a few perfunctory dances, they retired to Bill's car, where as soon as they closed the doors they fell upon each other, kissing long and deeply, their hands gliding up and down each other's bodies. It was a far cry from magnetic kissing dolls, and again Megan felt that warm iron ball inside, which tonight made her so dizzy that when she pulled away for a breath, she found herself gasping for air. Bill, for his part, wore an expression of anger, or so she thought; but then he pulled her close with an urgency that convinced her that it was not anger he was feeling but raw lust, a word she'd read about and heard about but never really known about until now.

They sped up into the foothills. Bill drove with one hand on the steering wheel and the other hand up her dress. At the first turnoff—just before the Overlook Restaurant, where her parents were dining that night—she ordered him to stop the car, and before he'd even had a chance to pull up the emergency brake, she unzipped his pants. His penis popped out, and she took it in her hand; it felt like a little zucchini, smooth and slightly curved. He groaned, then yanked the bodice of her dress down around her waist. After an eternity, he slipped his finger up inside. Megan gasped. She wondered if people passed out during sex. Fleetingly she thought of condoms.

But then, when he lowered the seat and parted her legs and she felt the first awful, wonderful thrust, when she felt him pressing into her, the last thing on her mind was condoms, or passing out. She had crossed over the line tonight. She was no longer a virgin, and that, under her logic, meant she was no longer her parents' child.

It was the coolest thing that had ever happened to her.

———————

After that first night Megan was willing to have sex whenever they could find the time: during lunch period, after school, in the evening at Bill's house when they were supposed to be studying. She didn't worry about pregnancy, because along with her adolescent belief that she would not live past the age of thirty lay a deep conviction that her so-called periods were in fact the beginning stages of some kind of cancer, and that she was, in short, infertile. Since she could never have babies and was going to die in the next decade, she might as well enjoy herself.

Mostly they had sex at Bill's house. It gave her a thrill to think of his parents upstairs watching TV as she and Bill coupled on the nubby, soiled sofa in his basement. She went to the mall and stole a lacy black bra to lift her cleavage, along with a black thong, which, granted, felt like the old sanitary napkins she'd tossed aside but which, again, made her feel happily alienated from her parents.

Bill, for his part, thought this was all a pretty good deal. He wasn't sure if he loved Megan, but she wasn't asking for love, it seemed to him. So who was he to turn down her advances? Sometimes he worried that he should be using something, but since Megan didn't seem concerned, he just assumed that her mother had put her on the Pill. There were a lot of advantages, he figured, to dating the daughter of the local abortionist—one being a certain freedom from narrow-minded notions of teenage abstinence.

Within five weeks Megan skipped a period.

The nightmares began soon afterward. She dreamed she was in a Chinese restaurant, but rather than hot and sour soup, she was served a thick red broth with tiny feet floating about. She awoke drenched in a cold sweat. Together she and Bill agonized over what to do. Bill pressed her to steal a pregnancy-testing kit from her mother's office, but Megan felt the risk of getting caught was simply too high. She waited and waited. Every hour she went to the bathroom and scrubbed herself raw with toilet paper, searching for the tiniest faint twinge of red.

But it never came, and after seven weeks, convinced she was not only pregnant but evil as well for putting herself in this position, she went to the drugstore and bought a home pregnancy kit. If it was negative, great. If it was positive—

She thought of the white bucket.

Following the directions the next morning, she peed onto a little stick. There was only one red line in the window. She waited a little longer. Still just one red line. She held it under the light. When she realized it was negative, she wanted to leap, she wanted to turn cart-wheels, but instead she ran downstairs and gave her mother the first hug she'd initiated in three years. Then she rushed off to school, where in that one morning she aced a math test, read three chapters ahead for U.S. Government, and volunteered to help out at the upcoming College Night. She bought a box of condoms and a giant tube of spermicide. As for Bill, he felt that the experience had uni-fied them as a couple. He felt bonded. And he wanted to tell Megan that he loved her, because for the first time in his life he found him-self waking up in the night with that torn-apart, ragged feeling that comes partly from feeling loved but also from the fear that this newly discovered sense of himself as someone worth loving could vanish in the morning, that it was all maybe a big joke, a silly dream, a bucket of air.

From Megan's hug that morning, Diana intuited a couple of things about her daughter. One: the girl was in love. This she knew because it was an established medical fact that love could turn sulky adoles-cent girls into sentimental and affectionate daughters. Two: not only was her daughter in love but she was sexually active as well—for the pheromones in their house were so thick you could wipe them from the walls. Every room smelled of mushrooms and musk; Diana couldn't even *look* at Megan without being transported back to her sixteenth year when she, too, carried around a constant steely ache between her legs.

One night she stood in the kitchen chopping vegetables. Frank was sitting at the island, reading through a pleading file, his glasses perched crookedly on his nose. The news was on, and outside a neighborhood dog was barking. But the smell! Megan had just walked out of the room, and her aroma had even managed to overpower the sweet Vidalia onions Diana was slicing. Diana was certain that Frank would notice. How could he not? They could go upstairs, make love, and eat dinner late. She kept waiting for him to put down the pleading file, but when he did, he took off his glasses and picked up the remote control and changed news stations.

Diana went back to chopping onions, and wondered how it was she had gotten so old, so quickly.

That spring, when Bill turned seventeen, his parents gave him a digital camera. The first thing he wanted to do was use it with Megan.

"Forget it!" she exclaimed when she realized just what he meant. They were upstairs in Bill's room, a dark messy alcove with an unmade trundle bed and shuttered windows. Bill had gotten a new sound system for his birthday, and the boxy components lay scattered on the carpet like oversize blocks.

"What, you think I'll show the pictures to someone?"

"Uh, *yeah*," said Megan. "Frankly."

"They'd never leave my possession."

"What about when your mom goes on the computer?"

"What do you think a password's for? You don't trust me," he said.

"That's right," she said. "Not with a digital camera. God, what happens if someday I want to run for Congress?"

"Are you planning to run for Congress?"

"Who knows? Who *cares*? God, I'm sixteen. I don't need photographs in cyberspace. You could lose them. You're not the most organized person, you know."

Bill thought about this. "Okay then," he said, "we don't ever download anything. You can delete everything yourself. No pictures, no files, nothing."

"Then why do it at all?"

"Because it turns me on," he said gruffly.

Megan eyed the camera warily, as though it were a loyal pet that would automatically have sided with Bill. Wanting to capitalize on her hesitation, Bill took a picture of his unmade bed, showed it to her on the screen, then told her to push the delete button. She pushed it. The picture disappeared.

She bet her mother had never done anything like this.

"This is *really* kinky," she said, unbuttoning her jeans.

"We're consenting adults."

"Not adults," she pointed out.

"Lie down," he told her. "Not there. Over here. Good. Oh," he breathed. "Wow."

He adjusted the shutters so that slivers of light fell across her hips. She turned her head away from him. She could feel the hairs rise on her lower back, and for a brief moment she imagined the photograph as it might appear if printed: her skin pale below her bikini line, the downy blond hair, the mole just south of her navel, shaped like California.

"Turn," he said. "Good. Now don't move."

That night he took sixty-five pictures, all of Megan in various stages of undress. After the first dozen or so clicks, she found herself able to look straight into the lens. She turned herself in ways that she thought might be suggestive, like kneeling with her back to the camera and looking over her shoulder. She sat cross-legged. When she told Bill it was her turn with the camera, he shyly agreed, but it wasn't much fun. His hard-on just looked like a lumpy little sausage on the screen.

"Now we're finished," she said. "Now I delete. You tell anybody about this and you're dead meat, by the way."

"You are so fucking sexy," said Bill.

In the meantime Megan had graduated from condoms to birth control pills, which she got at the local Planned Parenthood and only after they assured her they would not tell her mother. As a result of the Pill, her acne cleared up; as a result of her acne clearing up, her grades went up and her running times went down and her sleep habits stabilized. She and Diana began fighting less and less— although to say that they were "getting along" would be an exaggeration. Megan never volunteered anything, and still gave vague, noncommittal answers when Diana probed. "Are you and Bill having intercourse?" Diana might ask, to which Megan would reply, "Mom, I know how to take care of myself, *if and when* I decide to have sex." (It wasn't a lie.) And Diana, who if Megan were a patient rather than a daughter would have asked the question again and again, directly, until she got a definitive answer, let the matter go. Theirs was a fragile peace.

One summer night Bill handed her a small box that he had wrapped in childish dinosaur paper. Megan, who loved dangly earrings, suppressed her excitement. But when she opened the box and lifted the cotton batting, she found two small green pills.

"Where'd you get these?" she asked.

"It doesn't matter," said Bill. "Are you interested?"

"I don't know," said Megan. Up until now she'd only smoked a little pot, which merely made her hungry and thus resulted in severe sugar hangovers the next morning. She'd heard about ecstasy mostly from word of mouth: how it made you fall in love with the entire world, how it could make you so thirsty you could drown yourself.

Like anyone her age, she was curious. "Have you done this before?"

"I have." Bill spoke very thoughtfully, as though someone had just asked him if he'd ever considered the meaning of life. "It's a nice, friendly drug."

"How do you feel the next day?"

"Perfect."

Megan thought for a moment. "Okay," she said.

And so that night they took the pills. Megan felt good, but not as good as she'd expected to feel, after all she'd heard. They listened to music in Megan's room, went out for some food, and ended up at Bill's house, watching old videos of Bill as a toddler. Megan thought the first five minutes were cute but soon grew bored. It was a hot night, and she went outside to his backyard for some air. Crickets chirped loudly, and white hydrangeas bloomed like soft luminescent faces at the yard's edge. Next door, in the neighbors' backyard, there was a swimming pool. Moonlight bounced off the surface. The house was dark.

She went back inside and found Bill fumbling with his camera. "Where are your neighbors?" she asked.

"Up in Steamboat," he replied. "Let's play with the camera again."

"Oh, that is getting so cheesy," sighed Megan. "I've got a better idea." She went outside and kicked off her flip-flops and ran through the dry grass to the side of the pool. Quickly she pulled off her tank top and stepped out of her shorts. Then, after swishing her foot through the water, she slipped quietly into the pool.

"Come on," she sang in a low voice, sculling in the middle.

But Bill, for whatever reason, couldn't be persuaded. He went and got a blanket from his house and came back and spread it on a patch of grass near the hydrangeas and sat down and waited. After a while she hoisted herself out of the pool and ran naked and laughing across the lawn to the blanket.

"Oh, put that thing away, Bill," she said, collapsing beside him.

Bill ran his fingertips up and down her thighs. She lay back and shivered in the night air.

"No," he said. "Sit up."

"Oh, Bill," she sighed. "You've really gotten kind of obsessed, you know."

Bill knelt on the grass, about three feet away from her. She sat up on her elbows. Her hair was wet, and she leaned back and pointed her toes. Suddenly a star streaked across the sky. Then another, and another. Bill took a picture.

"It's too dark, you know," she told him.

Bill scrambled to a new angle. Suddenly Megan felt very tired. She imagined herself on a beach by a turquoise sea, and lifted her head to the warm tropical sun. Then she lay back down, and stretched her hands above her head, and turned her head to one side. Someone would bring her a piña colada. Wild parrots would squawk. Dark men would walk the beach, offering rainbow hammocks.

She was sailing across the equator when Bill lay down beside her.

"You're so beautiful," he whispered.

She heard herself murmur something about the pictures.

"Trust me," he whispered.

Or so she would later recall.

———

During junior year things were on again, off again with Bill. He had a jealous streak that both irritated and flattered her, but in the end he would come around with flowers and tears and maybe a hit of ecstasy or two, and they would reconcile. By the fall of her senior year, though, Megan was looking for change. Harshly critical of herself for devoting so much time and energy to a boy, she threw herself into college applications. Her dream was to get as far away from town as possible—Princeton, to begin with, and then points east: France, Italy, Budapest, Moscow. The only thing wrong with this plan was that her parents approved of it.

That fall she served as editor in chief of the school newspaper, under the tutelage of a young language arts teacher named Michael Malone. Often they worked late together in the small room on the third floor, subsisting on PowerBars and Cokes. One evening he suggested that they get a latte.

It was a warm evening in late October, and they sat at an outside table at a nearby espresso vendor. Mr. Malone rolled up his sleeves and leaned back and crossed his hands behind his head and closed his eyes. He was contemplating something important, Megan assumed, but then, out of the blue, he said her name.

Startled, Megan said, "What?"

Mr. Malone smiled. "Megan Thompson," he said again. "What do you plan to do with your life, Megan Thompson?"

The question caught Megan off guard. She knew where she wanted to go, but not what she wanted to do.

"Medicine, law?" he asked. "Journalism, business?"

"Well," Megan began. "Well, I don't know."

Mr. Malone chuckled at this. Although still in his twenties, his face had craggy lines when he smiled. A tuft of dark hair sprouted from the collar of his denim shirt.

Megan didn't like it when people chuckled at her. "How about you?" she asked. "What do you plan to do with *your* life?"

He tipped his head back and laughed loudly. "Touché," he said.

Megan relaxed. She was about to tell him she wasn't looking much further than acceptance letters at the moment, when Bill happened to walk by with a group of friends. He almost didn't notice them, but when he did, he executed an exaggerated about-face.

"What's this?" he exclaimed. "Student and teacher having coffee together? Just kidding!" he laughed. "Like it matters these days. Hey," he said to Megan, "I'll see you tonight?"

"I don't know," said Megan. "We're under deadline."

"Sounds sexy," said Bill. "Come over afterward. In case you're wondering," he told Mr. Malone, "we've been going out for two years, you know."

Michael Malone held up his hands. "Wasn't wondering," he said.

Bill excused himself—he backed away, coyly leveling his index fingers at Megan, like pistols—and Megan and Michael Malone returned to the high school, where they did, in fact, work through the dinner hour. The room was cramped, with two desks pushed together, and because he had grown suddenly quiet, Megan wondered if he was angry with her for something. The tension continued to mount until Michael Malone finally stood up to get something from the file cabinet (just behind Megan's chair); softly he traced a line across the nape of her neck before opening the file drawer.

"You're making me nervous, Megan," he said quietly.

Megan didn't need much more than that. The impetus was not her parents, as it was when she first slept with Bill; it was Bill himself, who needed to be told, if not in words, that he could stake no claim on her. As Mr. Malone closed the drawer, she set her pencil down and lifted her hand, and one thing led to another and they didn't bother turning out the light or locking the door or even making their way out from between the desk and the file cabinet onto a cleaner part of the carpet.

"I want to feel your knees shake," he whispered, just before entering her.

It was a one-time thing; what would later amaze Megan was the ease with which they continued on in their assigned roles: Michael Malone as adviser, Megan as editor. This must be how grown-ups manage it, she thought, reflecting on television shows where everyone slept with everyone else. It's not at all difficult. And the situation pleased her; it proved something to her, although just what, she couldn't quite put her finger on. She knew it had a lot to do with Bill, though. She never told him about Mr. Malone, but she made a point of letting him grow suspicious, which made her feel at once very powerful and very, very Machiavellian in her young ways.

But by the year's end she forced herself to admit that things with her high school boyfriend were, in fact, over. Just after midnight on New Year's, Megan officially broke things off. Seated cross-legged on her bed, she explained that with college on the horizon, she didn't want to be tied down anymore. (Bill had applied to Princeton as well, though he had no chance, as far as she could tell.) Regardless of what happened with Princeton, she said, they'd be better off making independent decisions. She did not expect him to take the news well; still, she was surprised by his response, which was silence.

"Say something," she finally said.

Bill, sitting in the swivel chair by her desk, just looked at her blankly.

"Look, I'm sorry," she went on. "I really care about you, but I think it's time we went our separate ways. What do you think?" She hated herself for asking that—she didn't care what he thought, frankly, but he was being so quiet and she just wanted to *get him to talk.*

Finally he began swiveling back and forth. "What do I think? What do you *think* I think? You're the only person I've ever loved, Megan."

"There will be others," she offered.

"Oh, that's helpful."

"We can still be friends." *Lame.*

Bill stood up. "If you think we can still be friends, then you, my dear, are seriously out of touch with reality. In fact, you are stupid in a way I never could have imagined."

The words, pretentious as they were, stung. "I'm just trying to make things easy," she said.

"Well, guess what, Megan," he said, pronouncing it *Megg-Ann*. "You're failing big time. Tell me something, though. Did you fuck that guy Malone?"

She told him no, she did not fuck that guy Malone.

"And I should believe you?"

"Yes."

"Why?"

"Because I don't lie."

Bill regarded her with what seemed to be liquid hate. "Well, good," he said. "I'm glad to hear that. I wouldn't want to think that I spent the last twenty-four months of my life fucking a liar."

Now Megan stood up nervously and folded her arms across her chest. "Maybe you should leave now."

"That's probably a good idea," he said, although he didn't move. Awkwardly she leaned around him and pushed the door open, and he finally walked out. Downstairs in the front hallway, she asked him if he was going to be all right. *LamelameLAME*.

Bill grinned. "I'll be fine," he said. "Just dandy. Happy New Year, Megan Thompson." And with that he slung his jacket over his shoulder and opened the front door and walked down the rock path to the sidewalk.

Snowflakes collected on his shoulders, and as the wind picked up, he put his jacket on and turned up the collar. Watching him walk away, it seemed like a dramatic occasion for Megan, cinematically so, with the snow swirling down and the man heading off into the dark and the woman standing in the doorway watching him go; and she might have felt like Scarlett watching Rhett walk off into the fog, except their situations were so completely the opposite—*she* was the one who didn't really give a damn anymore. Plus Scarlett O'Hara was such a flake with men.

She stood in the doorway until he drove off, then went back inside. Best not to try to invent all this meaning and melodrama, she told herself. You're just a girl breaking up with a boy, no more, no less.

It amazed her that he could disappear so completely. But he did, and over the next several weeks she saw him all of two times outside of their classes together. He seemed to have a new girlfriend, a mousy sophomore known for giving blow jobs. He withdrew his application to Princeton, she learned, and decided to go to the state college up north. She wrote him an e-mail saying she hoped he'd be happy up there. It was a good school, she wrote. WHOOP-TE-DO, he wrote back.

Things with her mother deteriorated even more after that. Diana wanted what Megan refused to give, which was access to her inner thoughts and feelings. How could she tell her mother that she'd been right to call Bill obsequious? (Megan had had to look up the word.) She just wanted to be left alone. Diana would come into her room at night, just before bed, and start talking about her own escapades in high school and college, which Megan didn't want to hear.

In March she began to find things in her locker. Chocolates. Roses. Unsigned cards. Somehow she got on a pornographic e-mail list and found herself barraged with lewd suggestions that seemed more personal than most. She changed both her screen name and her server, and the messages stopped.

Then in April she received a thin, business-size envelope from Princeton. This came as a shock, and she wished now she'd applied to some other colleges. But with her only backup the local university, she realized she was going to be spending the next four years of her life here in this town. She could either feel sorry for herself or make good of it. Being a pragmatic sort, she opted for the latter and negotiated a written agreement with her parents that she wouldn't be coming home every weekend and they were not to just drop in unannounced. Diana and Frank thought it was an act of maturity on her part, and signed proudly.

And so late in August Megan moved into her dorm, and Bill moved fifty miles to the north. The e-mails stopped. The flowers stopped. The chocolates stopped. Megan began a rigorous schedule that left little time for a social life; she might blow off a Saturday night with her roommate, but other than that she studied just about every evening.

It surprised her, how easy it was to start a new life.

CHAPTER FOUR

A T TWO O'CLOCK on Wednesday morning, Frank struck a match to the first cigarette since Megan was born. He'd bummed it earlier that night from one of the cops, had tucked it into his breast pocket as a kind of security blanket. But the craving had grown until it paralyzed him, and now, standing in front of the kitchen sink, he inhaled slowly and deeply, tipping his head, letting the smoke tickle the back of his throat before drawing it deep into his lungs.

He looked at the clock. Piper would be finishing up soon. He trusted Piper, but part of him worried that merely by cutting open the physical body, Piper would be able to detect what Diana was thinking at the moment of death.

I hold you responsible.

Frank drew deeply on the cigarette and recalled with grim objectivity the fury he'd felt the day before. He'd been livid, absolutely livid as he sped from his office back to the house. The fact was, he *did* blame Diana for what he'd seen online. If she hadn't always been so permissive with Megan! Letting her wear a sundress in the middle of winter, or pierce her ears at the age of six, or stay up past midnight on New Year's Eve—whatever Megan wanted, Diana always said it was up to her. When Megan was young, none of it had really mattered. But as Megan grew, the stakes grew, and suddenly there was his wife letting Megan make decisions that no child should make. Such as which middle school to attend, for example! Wasn't that a decision for parents to make? That, and curfew, and your punishment for breaking curfew? *Well, Megan, what do you think the consequences should be?*

And then there was the whole issue of sex. In Frank's opinion— well, not that he was expecting Megan to remain a virgin until marriage, but sex was a big commitment, with big consequences, and teenagers by definition were not ready. And he'd always wanted to tell Megan just that. But Diana! Diana maintained that anything they said at this point was going to go in one ear and out the other, and they might as well bypass the *oh my god sex is such a big deal* route and get straight to the matter of contraceptives and HIV protection. And he'd bought into it.

In the dim light of the kitchen, Frank leaned against the center island and took another long draw on the cigarette. Diana could never face up to the fact that she was a parent, not a pal. Maybe there'd have been less animosity between mother and daughter, he thought now, if Diana had taken her parenting role more seriously.

He flicked his ashes into the sink, conscious of the police officer standing just outside the door, of the muffled voices and footsteps of the detectives out in the solarium. He knew that any recriminations he might have at this point against his wife were the stuff of fancy; he knew too that their wretched, petty disagreements were a luxury he'd be lucky to have. Yet anger at his wife continued to boil up as though she weren't dead. What kind of a girl went and posed like that, anyway? he still wanted to demand. Someone who didn't have enough guidance growing up, that's who.

"I'll go buy you a whole pack, if you want."

Startled, he glanced up to see Megan standing in the doorway.

Her hair was disheveled, and her face was so puffy and swollen that for a fleeting moment she resembled her brother, Ben. (Except for the eyes. Nobody had eyes like Ben's, wide apart and slanted, flush with his forehead. Ben's face had always seemed to him as flat as a piece of construction paper, and he used to imagine a troop of gods in a kindergarten class, armed with scissors and paste, cutting and folding and fringing a new race of people.)

"Never would have guessed it, Pop," she said flatly.

Frank, embarrassed, ran the cigarette under water and dropped it into the disposal. "Did you sleep?"

She shrugged and straddled a stool at the island and tilted her head to finger-comb her curls in a manner that recalled the picture online.

"Did Piper call yet?" she asked.

"No."

"So what happens tomorrow?"

"We make a lot of phone calls," he said.

"Do we get Mom's body back?"

The blunt edge of her words dug another hole in his stomach. "After they finish the autopsy," he said.

"I guess we're going to have a funeral," she ventured.

"That's usually how it works." He intended it as a light reply, but it came out snide and sarcastic. A shadow crossed her face, and once again he felt something quicken in the bottom of his chest, in that space where dead air collects. He reminded himself there was no room for mistakes like this; it was just the two of them now. They *were* the family. He flashed on Christmases to come: not bothering to wrap their gifts, maybe a pizza or two, Diet Cokes, store-bought cookies.

How was he ever going to parent this girl all by himself? For as much as he resented Diana's leniency, he also knew it had provided a necessary balance to his strictness. If it hadn't been for Diana,

Megan would have grown up shackled by his rules, a churchy Girl Scoutish type who would have rebelled either by shooting heroin or signing up with the Moonies and he'd never see her again.

"Didn't she want to be cremated anyway?" said Megan. "Why do we even need a funeral home? And why is it called a home? Whose home are they talking about? Not Mom's, that's for sure."

"Yes, she wanted to be cremated," said Frank, "but we still need a funeral home for a service."

"Well, they better not make any references to God," said Megan. "Mom would hate that."

"We'll make sure," Frank said. He didn't point out to Megan that since Diana was an atheist, it wouldn't much matter what they said at her funeral, as far as offending her. Gone was gone.

Just then the phone rang, and Frank picked it up before Megan could reach for it. It was Piper. He turned away from Megan.

"This is just preliminary," Piper warned.

"And?"

"Is Megan with you?"

"Does it matter?"

There was silence on the other end.

"Look," Piper finally said, "this is pretty difficult for both of us."

Megan was trailing him like a puppy, parking herself directly in his gaze no matter which way he turned. Frank waved her away, Megan crossed her arms.

"Go ahead," he told Piper.

"Well," she said, "first of all she had a blood alcohol level of point-oh-nine. That's legally intoxicated."

"I know the numbers."

"So on the one hand, I'm tempted to just say that she got a little drunk and fell and hit her head."

"But?"

"It's this bruise," she said. "It's just not the kind you'd get from a fall. There's too much trauma. On the other hand, it doesn't really look like it was made by some kind of blunt instrument, either," she said. "Like I don't think we're talking crowbars here."

"Gee."

"Sorry. Do you want me to stop?"

"No," said Frank.

"You sure?"

"Just go on," he said.

Piper took a deep breath. "Now, the bruise looks like something that could have happened if someone threw her down with some extra force," she said. "Have the cops found any other signs of a struggle?"

Frank thought of the shards of glass he'd swept up.

"Okay, I guess it's a little early for that. Well, in any case, she died about six p.m.," said Piper. "What time did you get home?"

"Eight-thirty."

"Working late?"

"No," said Frank.

Piper waited, but Frank didn't feel like elaborating.

She said, "And you found her floating in the pool?"

"Right."

"God, Frank," she said. "I'm sorry."

Megan was scribbling on a piece of paper, which she then handed to him. He read it and frowned. "Megan wants to know if there were traces of Valium," he told Piper.

"No. Why? Does she have a scrip for Valium?"

"I don't know."

"You don't?"

Frank bristled. "Look, Diana has been on a lot of medications," he said. "I don't keep track of them all."

"Well, she didn't take any Valium tonight," she said. "This is all I have. Blood alcohol of point-oh-nine and severe head trauma. Look,

Frank," she said, "I need to tell you something else. I'm going to have John perform the complete autopsy and write up the report. I've got to be professional here," she said. "You and I are friends. I don't want the report thrown out for bias."

"What, so you think I killed her?"

"No, Frank," she said. "But I've been in court. I know what they can do with a written report. Let's just take steps to make sure everything's above board here."

"Jesus, Piper."

"Frank, you're tired," she said. "You're tired and about as stressed as anybody can possibly be. It's no big deal, John writing the report. It won't say anything different from what I would say. It's just that John's not a good friend of yours."

"So?"

Piper was quiet for a moment. "We go back a bit, Frank," she reminded him.

Frank looked up. Megan was watching him closely. He scribbled the words *nothing final* on a piece of paper, then stepped out onto the deck and huddled back against the door, where the deck was barren of snow. The sky had cleared, but the air remained frigid.

"What are you saying, Piper?" he said in a low voice. "You suddenly feel like telling the whole town we slept together a couple of times?"

"It was more than a couple of times," said Piper, "if you remember. And I wouldn't have to tell anyone; the whole town knew. Look, Frank, I don't think you realize something. This isn't just some accident in a pool. And Diana's not Marcus Welby. The press is going to be all over this tomorrow. Now, I'm your friend, but I've got two kids in college and I'm up for reelection next year. Do you see what I'm saying?"

She was right, but Frank felt a strong sense not only of abandonment but of accusation as well. Having once been intimate with him,

Piper knew a lot of things about his relationship with Diana that most people didn't know. And she knew *him* too: how under the right set of circumstances, his temper could flare.

"So fine," he said. "Have John write up the report."

"I will. And Frank?"

"What?"

"You're going to need an attorney," she said.

The children who lived on Hill Street were crushed to learn that after fourteen hours of blizzardlike conditions, school authorities still refused to declare a snow day on that cold Wednesday morning. Particularly crushed because, having had no major snowstorms in three years, they'd spent the previous night waxing sleds and tying up phone lines as they debated the relative merits of every hill, every slope in the neighborhood. Given their high expectations, the disheartening news from the radio that morning gave them no recourse but to crawl back into bed and groan and complain until their parents (who felt quite the opposite about snow days, who hated them with a vengeance for the hole they dug into daily routines) threatened to withhold television privileges if the kids didn't snap to it and get moving.

So the kids got up; they got dressed; they ate their breakfasts with morose faces. But then they opened their doors and saw the yellow tape stretched all around the Thompson-Duprey yard—the people who'd put a friggin' *pool* in their house and never invited anyone to try it *out*!—and their long gloomy faces lit up. A crime! In their neighborhood! Wow!

Even the parents got excited: by the time the yellow school bus came lumbering up the street, five or six of them stood huddling together, unwashed, unshaven, holding steaming mugs of coffee as they speculated on the possibilities. Only one of them had seen the ambulance the night before, the others having closed their drapes to insulate their great rooms from the bitter cold; but the one who saw the ambulance was consumed with problems of her own, namely her eighty-six-year-old mother out in California who'd just that evening wandered out of the nursing home in another Alzheimer's fog. Now this morning, with the yellow tape suggesting a slew of dark possibilities, everyone's mind was racing, and as they waited for the bus, they began to call their children back, ostensibly to check for mitten clips but in fact to reassure themselves that they were in control in the face of unknown evil.

While parents and children were waiting for the school bus, Huck and Ernie were heading into a nearby coffee shop. Having been up all night, Huck was ready for a plate of eggs and hash browns; the coffee shop was known for its baked goods, so he ordered a blueberry muffin as well. Ernie, whose bad cholesterol had peaked out at 153 during his last checkup, opted for plain oatmeal, but when the waitress set down a volcanic sugar-crusted muffin, Ernie reached across and broke off a good-size chunk.

"Do you mind?" Huck demanded.

"Leigh never makes them this big," Ernie said through a mouthful. "And she doesn't put sugar on top, either. What did Piper say, exactly?"

Huck relayed what Piper had said. "She's handing it over to John," he added.

"Whoa. Piper McMahon giving up a high-profile autopsy? How's that happen?"

"I don't know. I don't want to know, either. I have other things to wonder about."

"Did Frank find a place to stay?"

"Yeah."

"Because the chief's not too pleased we let him stay at the house last night," Ernie said.

"Well, the chief wasn't there. He didn't see Frank. We can be human once in a while."

Ernie braced his forearms along the edge of the table. "Okay, so what do we got? Besides a woman with a smashed-up head and a blood alcohol of point-oh-nine?"

"Broken glass. Fingerprints. Possibly a few footprints, if we're lucky. No sign of forced entry."

"And no weapon."

Huck felt a sneeze coming on. What was the deal with echinacea, anyway? On Carolyn's advice he'd started taking it since the first itchy tingle in his throat two days ago, but the virus seemed unstoppable. "I'm still not entirely convinced she didn't cause the injury herself," he said. "She was drunk, remember."

"Point-oh-nine isn't exactly smashed."

"It's enough to make you slip. Take the whole thing why don't you," he said as Ernie broke off the remaining top of the muffin.

"Want some oatmeal?"

"No thanks."

"Good stuff."

"So quit eating my food," said Huck.

Just then his cell phone rang, and he turned away from Ernie to answer it.

"Where have you been?" Carolyn exclaimed. "I tried calling until midnight!"

"On a new case," he said. "Look, can I call you later?"

"All night?"

"It's a big one," said Huck. "How's your mother?"

"Okay. What happened?"

Huck briefly explained the circumstances. "I'm here with Ernie right now," he said. "I'll call you later."

"I love you," she said.

"I love you too," he told her. He hung up. Ernie wore a smug look on his face.

"So," said Huck. "Where were we?"

Ernie brushed crumbs onto the floor. "Okay," he said, "maybe she fell. Doctor comes home after a long day at work, has a drink before her daily swim and slips on the floor and her glass goes flying across the room as she falls and bonks her head. Kind of stretching it, I'd say. And why would she be having a drink *before* working out? Isn't it usually the other way around? I'm with Piper," he said. "Somebody did this to her. Whoever it was, maybe they meant to, maybe they didn't, but this isn't a slip-and-fall."

Outside on the sidewalk a man in red Gore-Tex straddled his bike and tore off bits of croissant and fed them to his dog.

"Fine," said Huck, turning back. "Let's start a list."

Ernie opened up his notebook. "Well, we start with the obvious," he said. "There's Frank. Domestic argument. Top of the list. After that there's the Coalition. Motive is pretty obvious."

"Someone from the Home Tour," Huck suggested. "Yes indeed," he added when Ernie cast him a quizzical look. "Three years in a row, according to Frank."

Ernie shook his head. "This is a woman who because of all the threats on her life has a direct line to Dispatch—and then she goes and opens up her house to strangers?"

Huck too found this unsettling. It didn't make much sense, unless she had a massive Martha Stewart kind of ego.

"What about the girl?" Ernie asked.

Huck gave a hoot.

"Just because she's young and pretty?"

"You'd have to be pretty pissed to kill your mother."

"Girls fight with their mothers all the time."

"Forget it," said Huck. "You can write it down, but there's no way. Let's go back to the Coalition. Any statement from the reverend?"

"Not yet. It's not exactly their tactic," said Ernie, "going in and bludgeoning someone. Seems to me that if they'd wanted to kill Diana Duprey, they would have hired a sniper. Or wired her car. Doesn't seem the most efficient way, going into her house and smashing her head against the pool. Hey"—he tore another packet of Sweet'N Low into his coffee—"did you read that editorial he wrote a while back?"

"Comparing abortion to genocide?"

"I don't get it," said Ernie. "He says he doesn't condone violence, and then he goes and writes something like that. Who's he trying to win over with an argument like that?"

Huck glanced at his watch. The restaurant was filling up, and they had to get back up to the house.

"What about jilted lovers?" he said.

"Piper McMahon doesn't strike me as the type. Plus that thing was over a decade ago."

"Maybe Diana had a lover," said Huck. "Maybe she dumped him, and he was pissed."

"We'll check it out," said Ernie. "Hope you didn't make any plans for Christmas, my friend."

"Just dinner at your house," said Huck.

"As long as you bring the beer."

"What are you getting the kids this year?"

Ernie's face darkened. "Snowboards. Know how much a snowboard costs?"

Huck shook his head.

"Too much for what I make, that's for sure," Ernie declared. "Finish up." He nodded at the rest of the muffin.

"Be my guest."

Ernie finished the muffin in one bite. "How come you can eat like such a horse?"

"I don't," said Huck, "when you're around."

By noon that day a group of press trucks from the major networks had settled themselves in front of the Thompson-Duprey house. Already the chief of police was fending off speculation by an increasingly cynical press corps: Was this going to turn into another Templeton debacle? Didn't Frank's position with the DA's office pose a conflict of interest? Would they bring somebody neutral in? The chief of police tried his best to respond with professional dignity, but when a reporter asked point-blank how he was going to avoid another screwup, he snapped—according to the reporter, he used the F-word, as referencing a certain act that that certain reporter might perform upon himself. Afterward it was agreed that certain biases ought to be toned down and a semblance of objectivity maintained. The department, after all, was under new leadership. The sins of the past were the sins of the past. Et cetera.

Inside the house, trained investigators were busily taking photographs and searching for fingerprints, fibers, hair samples, handprints, footprints, pieces of glass, paint chips. A thorough vacuuming turned up hair and fibers—promising, but they would have to await further analysis. Outside they were looking for tire tracks and footprints mostly, but their efforts were largely hampered by the ongoing snowstorm, which had picked up again with a vengeance and long since covered up evidence of any activity the night before. And the snowplows had been out before dawn, before anyone could stop them, thus obliterating any possible tire tracks that might have remained on the side of the street.

Huck's job was to make sure that every square inch of the house was examined—that every fiber, every shard of glass was properly bagged and labeled, that every surface was carefully dusted for fingerprints. While this was being done, he went outside to talk with the neighbors, many of whom were milling around outside the cordoned-off area. Most had little to say, but one of the neighbors, a young mother, revealed that around four o'clock the previous afternoon, just after she finally managed to get her son down for a nap, she'd heard a car go *thwump* out in the street. Huck took out his notebook. Because it had been snowing all day, the woman went on, she was afraid someone had had an accident, so she hurried to the window, only to see Frank's car parked at an odd angle, half up on the curb; and there was Frank himself running up the walkway, and he had no coat on, which she thought was a little odd, but she didn't dwell on it, because she knew her son would only sleep for half an hour, and in that half hour she had to return three phone calls, truss a chicken, and mop up the apple juice that her son had flung on the floor in an effort to avoid getting put down for a nap. She had been in the middle of the second phone call when she heard Frank and Diana arguing.

"There must have been a window open or something," she said, "and it got so loud that it woke my son up, which frankly ticked me off, because without a nap he's like a *monster*. Got kids?"

"No," said Huck.

"Just wait," said the woman. "Anyway, I almost called them up and told them to respect their neighbors but then I heard a glass break and thought, Oh god, here we go again."

"Meaning?"

"They're *always* throwing things," the woman said. "Once Dr. Duprey threw an entire television out their bedroom window! How do I explain that to my child? I'm always saying, Use your words, honey, and then he sees the neighbor throw her television out the window!"

"What time was that, do you think?" asked Huck.

"What?"

"When you heard the glass break," said Huck.

"Four-twenty," the woman declared. "Which I know, because my son was wanting to watch cartoons, and although I normally don't let him watch television until five, I had to get this chicken in the oven and so I told him he could watch *Yu-Gi-Oh!* for special, in ten minutes."

"Were they yelling before or after the glass broke?"

"Before. After. Maybe both. I don't know. They're a noisy family, that much I know. Well, Diana's noisy. Frank, he's the quieter one. But this isn't any of my business, I suppose."

Huck wrote down her name and thanked her. He talked with a few other people; one man revealed that it wasn't at all unusual for Frank to come home in the afternoons.

"He's a runner," said the man. He was white-haired and tan, gir-dled head to toe in slick black Lycra. "So a lot of days he comes home around three and heads off on the trail for an hour or so. Then he goes back to work."

"Did you see him go running yesterday?"

"Nope."

"Did you ever run with him?" Huck felt confident making this assumption, considering the man's build. He looked like Spider-Man, only with white hair.

"Oh, sure. He was a good partner, kept a steady pace. In spring we trained together."

"Did he ever talk about his personal life?"

"*Whoa* no. The guy was *very* private. Just the opposite of Diana. Now *she* was talkative. She'd be working in the yard and I'd be out for a run and she'd nab me and start asking how my grandkids are doing. I'm about to become a great-grandfather, you know," he said with pride. "Any day now."

"That's great news," said Huck.

"As long as I don't have to babysit," the man warned.

"Did you ever see or hear them fighting?" Huck asked.

The man gave a long sigh and shook his head. "You guys are going to be focusing on Frank, aren't you? You're thinking this was a domestic dispute that got out of hand. Actually, Diana was the one who provoked everybody. You probably know this. She was a very opinionated woman. They'd have these dinners out on their back deck, fire up the grill, and maybe she drank a little too much but some nights you could hear her hollering like she was up on a soapbox."

"About what?"

"Oh, you name it. Money, kids, the right-to-lifers outside the clinic. Very strong feelings here."

Huck suspected that, given the chance, the man would gladly have offered up his own views on the right-to-lifers outside Diana's clinic. Not exactly a direction he wanted to take. "What do you know about the daughter?"

"Oh, she's a good kid. Very smart. She put all her bets on Princeton but didn't get in, so she's here at the university."

"Did she get along with her parents?"

The man smiled. "Not my domain, detective. All I can say is mothers and daughters, they all have their issues. Diana and the girl weren't any different. There were a few times, you'd see them in the morning, hurrying out of the house together, screaming at each other, but—Hey: you don't think the girl had anything to do with this, do you?"

Huck looked over his shoulder to where Ernie was beckoning him. He glanced at his watch and saw that it was close to three o'clock.

"Because that's absurd," the man said with reproach. "Don't waste good taxpayers' money on that one. Please."

"We're just trying to get a complete picture," said Huck.

"Then focus on the anti-abortionists. Tell the truth, I doubt Frank had anything to do with it. But certainly not the girl."

Huck assured him once again they were covering all their bases and thanked him for his time. He walked over to one of the vans that was serving coffee and pastries out of its rear door. Ernie was eating some kind of sticky bun, claiming how this was going to have to count as dinner. Huck poured himself a cup of coffee and told Ernie about his conversations with the neighbors.

"Well, get this," said Ernie. "You know how Diana was a twenty-four-seven kind of gal? Guess how? Pharmaceuticals," he said proudly.

"Who'd you hear this from?"

Ernie indicated a young man wearing a black leather jacket with the collar turned up.

"How does he know?"

"He's friends with the daughter. Name is Branson."

"So what, you're thinking this could have been drug-related?"

"Money owed, a deal gone sour, could be lots of things."

The coffee was vile. Huck flung the remainder into a snowbank. It always amazed him that here were these expensive houses in expensive neighborhoods, and the stuff going on was the same as in South Central L.A. Glancing at the house, he wondered what the asking price might be. Against the snowy hills, its taupe exterior looked dead and undistinguished; the shrubbery that presumably burst into color during warmer months now merely smudged the architectural lines. He pictured the Thompson family over the years raking leaves, planting bulbs, stringing Christmas lights. He pictured one of those wooden swingsets, kids flying in the air. *The tire swing in his grandmother's yard, the vast blue lake beyond, whitecaps, a red canoe on the horizon. Too far! his grandmother shouted. Come back to shore!*

Huck dug his hands into the pockets of his sweatshirt. He thought about how life goes on in a normal fashion and then in the blink of an eye something happens. A girl walks down the wrong street at night. A car skids. A whitecap flips the red canoe. A woman goes for a swim.

"Hey," said Ernie. "Did you hear anything I said?"

"Sorry," said Huck.

"I said go home. Catch some sleep. I'll set up a time to talk to the reverend. And see what I can get out of Frank."

"I guarantee you he's hired an attorney," Huck said.

"So I'll talk to his attorney."

By now Huck's throat felt as though someone had sprayed it with Tabasco sauce. He hadn't slept in thirty-six hours, and all he'd had to eat were those eggs and a few muffin crumbs, and he needed a shower and a shave and some time to himself to make some kind of sense out of this. Plus he'd forgotten to deposit his paycheck yesterday, plus he kept having some vague recollection of a doctor's appointment that had been on the calendar for months. Ernie was right. He was entitled to a break.

But before he could leave, one of the reporters stuck a microphone in his face.

"Do you know the cause of death yet, detective?"

"We're waiting for the final autopsy report," said Huck.

"Is it true that Dr. Duprey had a drug problem?"

"No comment," said Huck.

"Is it true that Reverend O'Connell was seen at the clinic yesterday?"

"No comment."

"Would you characterize the reverend as a suspect?"

"No comment," said Huck. "Excuse me now."

"One last question," the reporter said. "Have you seen the photos?"

If Huck had learned anything from seven years on the force, it was how to bluff. "Look, guys," he said, "when we have some news, we'll let you know."

"Was she paid?"

"Was who paid?"

"Megan. For the photos."

Huck felt the blood rise in his neck. As a cop, he felt there were worse things than having a reporter know more than you, but right now he couldn't think of any.

"Good day, gentlemen," he said.

CHAPTER FIVE

————————

WHEN HUCK GOT HOME, he found a slew of messages on his answering machine, all from Carolyn. Immediately he called her back. She answered from her mother's hospital room. She said that her mother was sitting up, alert, talking—Huck instantly sensed the relief in her voice.

"When are you coming back?" he asked.

"I'm going to stay a while," she told him. "My dad's got to go back to Philly. I'm just going to stay a few days. She's going home tomorrow. I'll get some groceries and help her get settled." Carolyn's parents had been divorced for over twenty years, but neither had remarried, and like blood relatives they still depended on each other in emergencies.

"What about your sister?"

"She's so busy with the girls. I don't mind. I'll take some of my leave time. How are the cats?"

Huck had forgotten all about the cats. *Cats!!!!* he scrawled on a piece of junk mail. "Fine."

"So what's going on?" she asked. "This is big, isn't it. Any leads?"

"Not really. The press is going apeshit."

"Do you think it was political?"

"Could be. Could be a lot of things, though. I can't really talk about it."

"God," she said. "I liked Diana."

Something in her voice made Huck wonder if Carolyn had ever been a patient of Diana's. She had never mentioned it. There were a lot of things they still didn't know about each other, he thought.

"Well, I guess you either loved her or hated her," he said.

"What will happen to her clinic?"

"I'm just a cop," he reminded her.

"Well, be a cop," she said. "Be a good cop. I have to go. My mother's lunch is here. They still serve Jell-O in hospitals," she said. "Did you know that?"

"Call me tonight," said Huck.

"I love you," she said.

"I love you too," he said.

He hung up and called a florist and ordered a hundred dollars' worth of flowers to be sent to Carolyn's mother in Minnesota. That's what you did when someone was sick. Then he called back and ordered another hundred dollars' worth of flowers to be sent to Carolyn, at her mother's home. What did he want to say on the message card? the florist asked. Just, I miss you, said Huck. That's so sweet, said the woman.

Huck and Carolyn had met at Ernie's Super Bowl party the year before. Huck wasn't much into football, but Ernie used the annual event as an occasion to invite a lot of people over and drink beer and eat Kentucky Fried Chicken. Carolyn, it turned out, liked football a lot, and Huck watched with interest as this woman with short spiky blond hair booed and cheered, beer bottle in hand, shrieking at the ref over any unfavorable call. Within a month they were seeing each other regularly, alternating nights between their two houses. She thought his little house was frighteningly bare, and found occasions to bring in plants and ruffly placemats and baskets of potpourri, which mystified Huck, why people spent good money on dead flowers. Still, he appreciated her gifts, and spread them about the house.

When they made love, she did this thing with her knees, a trembling squeeze, a quiver he could feel in his loins for the rest of the day.

———————

After ordering the flowers, Huck stripped down, showered, dried off, pulled on a pair of sweats, and went out to the kitchen to see what he might find in his refrigerator. His kitchen was small and dark, with scallopy veneer cabinets and avocado-green appliances. A chipped Formica table butted up against the wall; there was only one chair, its match having collapsed from Ernie's weight one evening back before Ernie started Atkins. Carolyn had given him two quilted placemats with flowery napkins to match, and these he kept on the table all the time, even if they weren't exactly his style. He was meaning to get the other chair fixed soon, so they could dine together.

Now he poked through the refrigerator in search of something to eat. Not much. On one of the lower shelves he found half a meatball sub. He ate it, regretted it, washed the taste out of his mouth with a beer. On the table was a scrap of paper on which he'd scribbled the address of the Web site, which he'd gotten from Ernie. He threw it in the trash. He clipped his nails, stacked the newspapers, opened another beer, turned on the television, turned it off, flossed his teeth, dug at the specks on the mirror. He went on a long search for a pair of slippers he'd been missing for over a year. He took out the trash. He lay down on his bed. He called Carolyn, but she didn't answer. He lay back down again.

Finally at eleven-fifteen he stormed back outside to the trash bin, where he hauled up the damn bag, unknotted it, dug through the gunk to find the damn scrap of paper with the Web address, took it back inside, and sat down at his computer.

With three clicks he brought up the picture.

For something taken at night, it was awfully clear.

Quickly he shut down all emotions. He was a cop, after all; this was a case he was investigating, and if he couldn't maintain a sense of professionalism, then what good was he? He glanced at the other two shots—yes, her hair was definitely wet—then closed out the window. He'd just commended himself for keeping his cool, however, when he flashed on Megan sitting in the Volkswagen last night, and crap if he couldn't see her profile as clearly as if she were sitting here beside him, with the slight bump on her nose and the chiseled upper lip and the stray curl that corkscrewed over her forehead.

Huck Berlin felt a light sweat break out on the back of his neck. Suddenly the girl's presence was everywhere—sitting at his table, lying on his sofa, curled up on his bed fast asleep. It upset him enough that he grabbed his jacket and fled the house to a nearby all-night deli, because although he didn't believe in ghosts, he certainly did believe that some people had the power to dig themselves into the very deepest part of your brain and stay there until you paid them the attention they demanded.

Early the next morning he found a fresh memo in his mailbox from the chief of police.

It has come to my attention that the Duprey investigation
may require staff members to log on to certain websites
that could portray certain family members in compromising
positions. Such websites may or may not be relevant to the

case, but we are not in a position to rule anything out at this point. Thus we must all accept the need to investigate these sites as they might pertain to motive, etc.

I have no doubt that everyone will remain professional about this matter. *Jokes will not be tolerated.* Pleased be advised that an inordinate number of hits on said websites will be viewed as presumptively inappropriate and dealt with accordingly.

Ernie wasn't in the office yet, so instead of going to his office, Huck went down to the lounge, where someone had brewed a fresh pot of coffee. Two officers coming off the night shift were sitting at a table. One was a woman named Gretchen who'd been on the force eight years. The other was a man named Brad, still young enough to have acne. In the middle of the table was a plastic tray of Christmas cookies, seventy-five percent eaten except for the powdered nut balls.

Huck sat down.

"Busy night?" he asked.

"Ask Gretchen here," said Brad.

"You do look kind of wasted, now that I think of it," Huck said to her.

Gretchen leaned back, closed her eyes, and folded her hands behind her head. Twin pockets of sweat darkened her underarms, like Muppet mouths.

"Kid puked in my car," she said grimly.

"Not just a few cookies, either," Brad added. "We're talking eruptions. We're talking Vesuvius. We're talking *whales.*"

"Joke all you want," said Gretchen. "You're hosing it, bud. Better get on it."

"The kid was lucid," Brad said defensively. "Blew point eleven. Who knew he had a virus?"

Huck popped a nut ball into his mouth. Big mistake. He went over and spat it into the wastebasket.

"So I heard about the Web sites," said Gretchen when he got back. "This is going to be a fun little case."

Huck supposed that she hadn't seen the chief's memo yet.

"So what's the theory?" Gretchen continued. "Frank saw some Internet pictures and flipped?"

"Don't know," said Huck. "Could be anything."

"How old is the girl?"

Brad said, "Nineteen."

"How do you know?" Gretchen demanded.

"I check things out," said Brad. "I'm a cop on the ball. God, I hope I never have a daughter."

"I hope you don't too, but not for your sake," said Gretchen. "So what else are you finding?" she asked Huck.

"Right now, not a whole lot."

"Think it was Frank?"

Huck shrugged.

"How ironic," said Gretchen. "Guy wouldn't go forward with Templeton and this is how it comes back to haunt him."

"Karma," said Brad, nodding.

Gretchen rolled her eyes. She'd grown up in rural Colorado, and her notions of spirituality and world harmony did not extend to the Far East.

"Are you guys even sure it was a murder?" she asked. "Maybe she just fell."

"Not likely," said Huck. "Not with that kind of a bash."

Gretchen leaned forward. "Here's what bugs me, though. Of all the DAs I've worked with, Frank's the most level-headed. Never snapped. Never lost his temper. It's just very hard for me to imagine."

"Everyone's got a breaking point," said Huck.

"Not the kind where they kill their wife."

Huck looked at his watch. He wished Ernie would get here. He wanted to know if Ernie had seen the pictures, if they had stayed in his mind too. Or was it just him?

"The funeral's tomorrow, I hear," Gretchen was saying. "Are you going?"

"It's up to the chief."

"It'll be huge."

"*Huge,*" agreed Brad.

"Lot of bigwigs, I'll bet."

She was right. There would be the NOW people, and probably their congressman, and maybe even one of their senators would show up. Huck found himself stifling a yawn. He hadn't left the deli until four that morning, at which point it had been futile to try to sleep. Instead he'd gone home, put the music on loud, showered, and come straight in to headquarters. Without decent coffee, he was going to crash before the morning was over.

"They keep you up all night?" Gretchen asked.

"I was home," Huck said. "Just couldn't sleep."

"Take Benadryl," advised Gretchen.

Huck stood up. He threw out his coffee and left Gretchen and Brad arguing over chemicals versus herbal sleep tonics and went off in search of Ernie. If he was going to go to the funeral tomorrow, he was going to have to borrow something decent to wear; a black hooded sweatshirt wouldn't cut it.

He found Ernie at his desk in the office they shared. They greeted each other grimly, knowing that long days and sleepless nights lay ahead of them for the next month. Two, possibly. Even three or more.

"Here's a list," said Ernie, handing him a yellow pad. "Start calling."

Huck sat down. He didn't want a list; he wanted to hear from Ernie that someone had come forward and confessed. He wanted to hear that they had found an open door, footprints leading to tire tracks leading to an abandoned but identifiable vehicle; or that Piper had looked again and found a bloodless bullet wound for which the anti-abortionists were claiming responsibility. He wanted to hear that Frank had a foolproof alibi.

Most of all, though, he wanted to hear that Megan had a secret twin, a look-alike halfway around the world who was of legal age and who had received millions for what she did. That the pictures he'd seen were not, after all, of Megan Thompson.

He flipped open his wallet, took out a picture of Carolyn, and propped it against his phone.

CHAPTER SIX

THE FUNERAL WAS HELD that Friday at the largest funeral home they could find. Hundreds attended. Those who knew Diana as a public figure wept; those who knew her personally were too numb to shed tears at this public event. Neither Megan nor Frank got up to speak.

Afterward Megan was heading across the parking lot when she felt a light touch on her shoulder. She turned to see Bill, dressed in a dark green windjacket and baggy black pants. She hadn't noticed him at the service—in fact, the last time she'd seen him was over Thanksgiving break, when she ran into him at the video store.

"Well *hello,* Megg-Ann," he'd said, and first off she'd noticed he was growing a beard, although it was a pretty measly beard, just a few blond bristles on his chin. She'd glanced at his stack of movies and remarked that he must be planning a movie marathon that weekend. "Oh yes indeedy," he said. "Want to join me?"

"No, thanks," Megan said, "we've got plans—"

"*We,* meaning?"

She was going to tell him she was referring to her parents, but he clucked and moved forward in the line. Later she heard through classmates that he was transferring schools, some private college in the Northwest, and she thought that would be a very good idea. If you told her she'd never see or hear from Bill Branson again, she would have been just fine with the idea.

Now, though, here they were, face to face within a foot of each other in the parking lot of McPherson's Funeral Home. The beard was gone and his chin was raw with shaved pimples.

"God, I'm so sorry," he said, opening his arms. "I am so, so sorry."

Megan accepted a light embrace but pulled away quickly. She wished her father would come so they could leave.

"Such a cool lady," Bill said. "Such a cool *doctor*. Any leads?"

Megan shook her head.

"I hope they're looking into the Coalition group. That's where I'd put my money," Bill said. "Those are some wacko dudes."

Megan shrugged. "I heard you were transferring."

"I was," he said, "except that things have gotten a little complicated."

"How's that?"

A bashful smile crept over his face. "I met someone."

Megan leaned against the car. "That's great, Bill," she said. "Where's she from?"

"That's the problem," Bill said. "She's up at the college, and so now I have to see if I can re-enroll."

"And not move to Washington?"

"Right."

Even in a state of grief Megan found herself tallying the pros and cons of this news. On the one hand, his having a new girlfriend lifted a heavy burden. On the other hand, she'd gotten used to the idea of him being far, far away.

"How long have you known her?" she asked politely.

"All semester," he said. "But we didn't hook up until right after Thanksgiving."

"Well," she said, "I'm very happy for you, Bill. What's her name?"

"Amanda."

Hearing this, Megan felt an unexpected tug, which unsettled her. Why should she feel anything, hearing his new girlfriend's name? She guessed she had a lot to learn about love, and breaking up, and moving on.

"Well, good for you, Bill," she said. "I'm sure you'll be able to re-enroll."

"How's the U?"

"Hard," Megan said. "Pre-med is a bitch."

"You'll be a great doctor. As good as your mother ever was—and that's saying a lot."

Megan's eyes welled up.

"You'll get through," he said, fingering a strand of hair back from her face.

Megan recoiled. "There's my father," she told him. "I have to go. Thanks for coming to the service. That was a nice thing to do. Good luck with Amanda."

She already had her hand on the door handle when Bill said, "So how come Mister Michael Malone didn't show up?"

Megan turned around and stared.

"Weren't you two kind of, you know?"

"Excuse me?"

"Actually I heard he was being forced to resign," Bill said. "I heard he was sleeping with a student. I didn't say *you*," he added innocently. "Why do you look at me? *Was* it you?"

She jabbed her key in the lock.

"Was he good?" he asked loudly. "Was he better than me?"

She wrenched open the driver's door.

"Did you swallow?" he called.

She didn't look to see who might have heard; instead she slid into the seat and slammed the door shut and started the engine. Her father, hearing her rev the motor, broke from a group of people and came over. Megan saw him shake hands with Bill, give a curt nod, shake his head. Then he opened the passenger door and settled himself into the seat.

"That was nice of Bill to come," he remarked, buckling his seatbelt.

They headed back to the Goldfarbs', friends of the family who had persuaded them to come stay at their house the day after Diana's death. The Goldfarbs had a large multilevel house in the same neighborhood, with lots of spare bedrooms, and Megan had welcomed the chance to stay in a place that was neither home nor dorm.

All afternoon people stopped by. Megan stood by the fire in the living room most of the time, making small talk with her parents' friends. Everyone seemed to need to touch her, like she possessed some kind of religious shroud. She was aware that she was still in shock; the fact of her mother's death kept slipping in and out of reality, and at times she found herself acting quite normal—unemotional, even, as though she were in an audience, watching a play about a girl whose mother had died.

In a quiet moment she held her palms out to the fire and let her thoughts skitter about. She wondered if her father would have thought it was so nice of Bill to come to the funeral if he knew about the e-mails they'd exchanged earlier that fall. Can't we try again? he'd written. It's over, Bill, she wrote back; You need to accept it and move on. Don't give up, he typed; You know you really love me. Please do not e-mail me anymore, she wrote back, to which he retorted: GIRL YOU HAVE TAKEN A **SLEDGE HAMMER** TO MY HEART AND SOUL!!!

Megan turned her back to the fire and faced the roomful of people again. It seemed as though the entire town had passed through this house in the last several hours; there'd been city councilmembers and state representatives, and even their U.S. congressman had stopped by, bearing a basket of fruit. People were drinking beer, wine, scotch, soda, water; they were eating cake and pie and lasagna and fruit salad and chicken wings and chips and salsa. It might have been a New Year's Eve party, for all you saw on the tables.

Her back began to sting from the heat of the fire. During a burst of laughter in the background, she found her coat and slipped unnoticed out the back door. It was dark but the moon was out, its sharp clear light illuminating the blanket of snow that remained from Tuesday's storm. She walked up one street and then down another, then asked herself who she was kidding and beelined it to her own house.

Still such a shock, all that yellow tape! There were police cars, and news trucks, and people going in and out of the front door like partygoers. She scanned the faces, and there on the front walkway was the detective with the blue eyes, writing in a notebook. Someone in the house shouted something, and he looked up and spotted her. She gave a little wave with her fingers. Tucking his notebook into the kangaroo pocket of his sweatshirt, he walked over to her.

"Ms. Thompson," he said.

"Oh please," Megan sighed, "don't call me that."

The detective smiled. "I didn't really expect to see you over here right now."

"It looks like a movie set."

Huck glanced around. "I guess you could say that. By the way, I was at the service this afternoon," he said. "Your mother certainly had a lot of friends."

Megan felt herself in the theater again, watching the girl on stage act out her grief. "She had a lot of enemies too," she remarked.

"She did at that."

"Which you're looking into?"

"We are."

"Pretty closed-lipped, aren't you?"

Huck smiled wanly.

"Sorry," said Megan. "I'm in a pretty shitty state these days. Can I go inside and get some clothes?"

The detective shook his head. "Nope. We're still collecting evidence."

"Like what? Fingerprints? I'm sure mine are all over the place," she said. "Does that mean you're going to think I did it?"

Huck frowned. "It's not just fingerprints. We're looking for a lot of other things."

Megan watched a man walk out carrying a large box. He seemed to be struggling with the weight. "Oh darn, they found my gun collection. Just kidding," she added quickly, when Huck looked alarmed.

"Not the best time to kid," Huck advised. "Look, do you want some coffee? We can go sit in my car."

She didn't want any coffee, but she did want to sit in his car. She wanted to tell him about the girl in the play, how by pretending she was in the audience, she was able to keep herself from falling apart. She wanted him to know that she wasn't some kind of monster for being able to joke around with him (gun collections!) when she'd just lost the most important person in her life. None of this would she actually say, of course, but she found it comforting, just being with him.

He led her to where he'd parked his car and opened the door for her. It didn't look like a cop car. "Where are all the bells and whistles?"

"I'm a detective," he said, "not a patrol officer."

"So this lets you sneak around undetected?"

"Correct."

The undetected detective, she thought. "So," she said after a moment. "Aren't you going to ask me questions about my mother?"

"If you want."

"Then ask."

Huck turned down the blower. He glanced at her, then sniffed and cleared his throat and looked out the front window of the car. "Okay. Your mother was an outspoken woman, and she got a lot of threats."

"I know that," said Megan, "but how do you know that?"

"She had a contact at the department, someone to call in case of emergency. We do the same for any public figure who's at risk. So if there's a bomb threat or a phone call, we can check it out ASAP. But my point is, we found some things we didn't know about in the house."

"Like what?"

"Like videos, under the VCR," he said. "Right-to-life material. Pretty graphic stuff." He paused for a moment. "Did you know about these?"

"Sure. She got them all the time."

"Why'd she keep them?"

"Just a pack rat, I guess. Actually I have no idea. Maybe she was going to write a book someday."

"Did they ever arrive with any letters?"

"There were always letters. Threats. Little notes. Smiling pictures of others who died."

"Other what? Abortionists?"

"Abortion *providers,*" she corrected him. "Don't use that word."

Huck took out his notebook and made some notes. "Did she keep any of the letters?"

"I don't know."

"When was the last time she got a package?"

"No idea," said Megan. "I don't live at home anymore."

Huck made another note.

"I know this must be very hard for you," he said, "but when was the last time you saw her?"

Megan felt something catch in her throat.

"I'm sorry," he said. "We can talk about this later."

"No. It's fine. The last time I saw her was Tuesday morning."

"The day she was killed?"

"Yes."

"Where?"

"At the clinic."

"What were you doing there?"

Megan cleared her throat. "We had breakfast together."

Huck nodded.

"But I didn't stay long," she added. "My mother had a busy day ahead of her. As if every day of hers wasn't some kind of marathon."

Huck, who'd been writing, glanced up then, and she immediately looked away. Even in the dim light of the police car she could see how blue his eyes were—blue as the lapis stone in the necklace Bill had given her one Christmas. She was going to mention it but quickly realized that commenting on the color of someone's eyes was an inappropriate thing to say to a cop.

"Well, I should get back," she told him. "No one knows I'm gone. My father will freak out."

"Yes, he does seem the type," Huck said, which jolted her a little; what did he base that observation on?

"But one more thing, if I may," he said. "Can you think of anyone else who might have been upset with your mother? Even over something that had nothing to do with the abortion issue?"

Megan had to think. Mrs. Beekman next door didn't like either of her parents because they let dandelions go to seed in their yard. Diana's friend Libby was mad at her because Diana had been too busy while Libby was going through her divorce. Then there was that thing with Piper six, seven years ago. But Piper and Diana weren't mad at each other anymore, and besides, Piper had come over that night. Why would she do that, if she'd killed Diana just a few hours before?

Megan didn't think any of this was his business. She told him she would think about it.

"Here's my card," he said, reaching into his breast pocket. "In case anything comes up."

Megan inspected the card. All it said was Huck Berlin, Detective.

"I have a friend named Suzannah Berlin," she said. "Any relation?"

Huck shook his head.

"What's your real name?"

Huck reached up to readjust his rearview mirror. "Just Huck," he replied, which suggested to Megan that it was probably something dorky, if he didn't want to tell her. Harvey, maybe.

She looked at the card again, then opened the door to get out of the car. "So are you like head cop on this case or something?"

"No," said Huck. "That's the head cop." He pointed to a man in a heavy leather bomber jacket, who was holding a doughnut between his teeth while pouring himself a cup of coffee from the back of the van. Megan recognized him as the chief of police. Of course. Who else would be head cop on a case like this?

All the way back to the Goldfarbs' house, Megan skidded and slipped on the black ice. By now it was seven o'clock. Soon the long day would be over. She would go back now, maybe even go on stage; she would make more small talk with whoever was lingering too long, and eat more junk, and then she would go upstairs to the Goldfarbs' guest room and shut the door. She would get out of her clothes, put on a sleep shirt, and brush her teeth, because that's what you do, even when your mother has died. Then she would take a Xanax and climb into bed under Sandy Goldfarb's pillowy comforter and try not to think about how shitty it all was, until the drug took over and her jaw relaxed and her shoulders sank and she could return to that time and space—was it so very long ago?—where taking a good hard honest look at the world always came up roses.

———————

When Huck saw Megan Thompson approaching the house, his hope had been counterintuitive. Which is to say that he'd hoped that she would walk right by. He had a lot of questions he wanted to ask her, and he knew that her input would be crucial to the investigation, but he was not prepared to stand face to face with the woman he'd seen online last night.

But she hadn't walked by; she'd seen him and waved, and he knew it would seem rude if he didn't talk to her. So he'd gone over, and they'd sat in his car, and he'd really gotten no information from her, except that she'd last seen her mother the morning of the murder. Actually he had the sense that she got more information out of him than he got out of her. She was good at asking questions.

After she left, Huck went over to the van, where Ernie was drinking coffee and eating a doughnut.

"So what'd the girl say?" asked Ernie.

"Not much. She knew about the videotapes. She said there might be some letters lying around the house."

"Well, get this," said Ernie. "You know that shirt we got out of the hamper? The one that was damp? Turns out it had traces of chlorine in it."

"What size?"

"Fifteen and a half."

"Frank's size."

"That's right. And the long dark curly hair on it belonged to Diana."

"That'll stun a jury."

"Don't get fresh. The shirt was balled up and stuffed under a bunch of towels in the bottom of the laundry basket."

"So?"

"So he was hiding it, Arthur. Come *on*. Tell me more about the girl. Did she say anything about her parents' arguments?"

"I didn't get into that," said Huck. "This wasn't anything formal."

"You get what you can get, when you can get it," Ernie said.

"Well, this isn't the last time I plan on talking to her, you know. Has Frank come up with any kind of an alibi?"

"I think the guy probably had other things on his mind today," Ernie said. "All we know is everyone saw him leave the office pissed off. The neighbor saw him running into the house around four, heard them fighting, heard a glass break. And nobody else went into the house."

"So she says," said Huck.

"Who?"

"The neighbor. She has a little kid, though. It's not like she can stand there watching the Duprey house for three hours straight. Did they get a cast on the footprints?"

"There wasn't anything to cast. Why are you holding back on Frank? He's presumptive to begin with. Then there's all this evidence of a fight. Add in the pictures online, and they'd cause anyone to snap."

"At his wife? Why would he hold her responsible?"

"Apparently you've never been married," Ernie said.

"Apparently so," replied Huck. "Fine. Maybe Frank's at the top of the list. But I wonder if there's anything else going on with all of us here."

"Like what?"

"Like Templeton. Like let's stick it to Frank." As soon as he said it, he hated himself. The Templeton case was viewed as Ernie's baby, really, and now for him to imply that Ernie couldn't set aside an old grudge was—well, it was a bad thing to do to a friend.

"What are you getting at, Arthur?" Ernie asked in a low voice.

"Forget it."

Ernie narrowed his eyes. "I have to say, you must have a pretty low opinion of me, if you think I'm settling scores."

One thing Huck was working on these days was correcting a mistake before it got too big. He shook his head and looked Ernie in the eye. "I didn't mean it," he said. "It was just words popping out."

"Yeah. It happens." Huck couldn't tell if Ernie was accepting the apology or not. "It's okay," Ernie said. "Anyone who's a friend of Frank's is going to be thinking the same thing."

"But I don't," Huck said firmly.

"Fine. Fine!" he exclaimed when Huck continued with his woeful look. They both turned, embarrassed, and hunted intently for the right kind of doughnut, which wasn't there.

"Well," Huck finally said, "we'll have to look into all the threats she got."

"The reverend does not advocate violence," Ernie reminded him. "And say he is behind this. Why isn't he taking credit? What's the point of killing someone for a cause, if you're not going to make your cause clear?"

Huck sighed. Whatever common wavelength he and Ernie usually shared seemed blocked at the moment. He was glad that they'd been able to put the apology behind them, at least. "I don't know," he said.

"You see? It just doesn't make sense."

Huck dumped his remaining coffee into the snow. "What about the videos?"

"Kind of bizarre," Ernie agreed. "Why she saved them, I can't tell you. If it were me, I wouldn't even open the packages; I'd turn them right over to the police." He pulled the string on a pack of Life Savers and popped one into his mouth, glancing down as he did so. "Hey pup," he said, for a dog had trotted up and was now sniffing the ground at their feet. "How come you're not on a leash?"

The dog, an overweight husky, sat down and began to howl. Ernie threw him a piece of doughnut. The dog vacuumed it and sat back down, panting.

"That's enough," said Ernie. "You're fat. No. Bad dog. Go on. This is my doughnut." He threw the dog another piece.

Just then Stan Wolfowitz, the chief of police, walked up to the van. "Hey, chief," said Huck. "What's new?"

"Well, I'm cold and I'm tired and I've got an upset stomach," he said. "But I just got a phone call from the coroner's office. Guess what."

"Is it good?" said Ernie.

"It is good," said the chief. "There's a bunch of skin under Diana's fingernails."

Skin meant DNA analysis, scientific evidence, certainty.

"There you go," said Ernie. "In another week Frank'll either be on the bus or off the bus."

"Yeah, and my guess is he's on."

"Who's going to handle things over at the DA's office?" Ernie asked.

"I don't know," Stan said. "They might even refer out to another county. Hey!" he shouted, for the husky had lifted its leg by his car. "Get outta there! Whose dog is this? We don't need a dog around here right now! Where'd this dog come from?"

A woman in a red fleece jacket came up and shooed the dog away. "You guys better come inside."

"Whatcha got, Jane?" said the chief.

"You have to hear it," Jane said. The three men followed her up the walkway and into the house and down the hall to Diana's study, a tiny room dominated by a large wooden desk and three walls of books. On the desk, beside the neat rows of carefully marked plastic bags, was an ancient answering machine.

"I thought we went over all the messages," said the chief.

"This machine was in the back of a junk drawer. Listen." Jane pushed the play button. There was a hiss. They all waited, hands on hips, eyes cast downward. Then a woman's voice came on.

You're next, Dr. Duprey.

"Southern drawl," the chief noted.

Jane held a finger to her lips. They heard the sound of a baby crying. *Do you hear that sound?* the woman asked. *Do you know what it is? Maybe an embryo? Or what you call a protoplasm? Oh my goodness me, why, that's the sound of a fetus, Dr. Duprey—the sound of a little live human being, born at thirty-five weeks.* The voice paused. *You will answer to God.*

There was a long silence as the tape continued to hiss. Finally Jane shut it off. The four of them looked at one another with raised eyebrows.

The chief gave a low whistle. "Well," he said. "There goes the simple Frank theory."

PART TWO

———————

JANUARY

CHAPTER SEVEN

T HE FIRST TIME Diana performed an abortion, she was twenty-six years old and so nervous that she performed the entire procedure without uttering a single word. The attending physician stood by, waiting to answer her questions, but Diana—normally a gregarious person—didn't even clear her throat. Who could ask questions with all the voices hollering in her head? *Don't miss any tissue! Don't perforate the uterus! Don't traumatize the patient!* There was so much noise she was afraid that if she tried to talk, she would end up shouting just to make herself heard, and that would scare everyone, herself included.

So she kept her mouth shut In order to concentrate. The girl was sixteen, a little overweight but not fat, with soft freckled skin and coppery hair. She came with her mother, a thin straggly woman who stood by her daughter's side the whole time, wiping the girl's forehead with a damp cloth and murmuring soft words of encouragement. (Diana was grateful that *someone* was talking.) Afterward, when the color had returned to the girl's face and she was sitting up in the sun-washed recovery room sipping apple juice, the mother followed Diana out into the hall and thanked her.

"Don't thank me," said Diana. "Thank Harry Blackmun."

From the beginning Diana had a special touch, a kind of sixth sense for doing the things an abortion doctor has to do. The attending physician had noticed this even that first day, the way her long slender fingers were able to slip the plastic cannula in through the cervix, the way she guided it around while the vacuum aspirator pumped out the contents. She wouldn't come to understand what he meant until she herself was training medical students and saw how some of them pushed too hard or pushed too little or angled it the wrong way, causing the woman to cry out not so much in pain as in fear. "Guide with your fingertips, don't push with your whole hand," she would tell them. "Don't hold it in one place for so long. Keep it moving. Good."

As time went by, the voices that had first been so loud in her head quieted down, and she found herself able to chat through the procedure. She told the patient exactly what she was doing, step by step: injecting the anesthetic, removing the laminaria, emptying the uterus. "You'll feel some cramping now," she would say, "but we're almost through. Everything's going just fine . . . There you go."

"It's over?"

"Not only that," said Diana, straightening up, "but you're not pregnant anymore."

Magical words, to Diana's patients.

Not only did she have a certain touch, but she also found herself able to perform her work with detachment—something she credited to her father's philosophy that certain things had to be done even if they weren't pleasant. When Diana was eight, for instance, she'd come across some pictures of laboratory rats riddled with big lumpy tumors. She'd been horrified, but her father had explained to her that if we were going to find a cure for cancer ("Remember how sick Aunt Joelle was?"), we were going to have to experiment on rats. It was plain and simple. Period. Given this upbringing, then, when she happened to glance in the bucket after a procedure, she was able to tell herself it was no worse than some of the things she'd seen during her surgical rotation. Even when during a second-trimester abortion she might recognize a body part, still she was able to focus on the women lying on the operating table: women lacking money, lacking partners, lacking the emotional wherewithal to raise a child—that's what Diana focused on, not the bloody tissue in the bucket. Her job, as she saw it, was simply to push the reset button for the woman on the table.

When she found herself pregnant for the first time, a lot of people (Frank in particular) worried that she would find it too difficult to continue her work. But Diana proved them wrong. Just because she wanted her baby didn't mean the patients in her office wanted theirs. Both her parents had taught her that if you believed in something, you didn't let your own personal circumstances stand in the way; the true test of your convictions came when your emotions rose up and threatened to scribble over everything you stood for. Those who let it happen—well, they must never have felt very strongly about things in the first place.

So off she went to work each day, helping her pregnant patients become not pregnant, sending them off with an Rx for plenty of rest and fluids—all the while eating three balanced meals a day, which included plenty of folate and an additional thirty grams of protein to the point where she felt like a slab of beef; and when Frank tried, in his empathetic manner, to broach the topic of how hard it must be for someone in her position to do vacuum aspirations all day long, she waved him away, because people were relying upon her.

All went smoothly, until Megan kicked.

Diana was poised between a patient's knees, inserting the first laminaria into the woman's cervix to start the dilation process, when she felt her stomach rumble. Only no, it wasn't a rumble. Someone was tapping on a drum from within. Diana froze. She'd been imagining this moment since the very start of her pregnancy, but she'd had no idea it could feel so *vital*. The nurse asked what was wrong. Diana rolled her stool back and took a deep breath. The nurse asked if everything was all right, and Diana was about to say no when she caught the look of terror in her patient's eyes—for the girl had immediately inferred that something *was* wrong, not with Diana but with *her*. Diana managed to finish inserting the laminaria, but afterward she snapped off her gloves and told her staff that she didn't feel well and would they please cancel the rest of her appointments for the day. Immediately she went home and lay down on her bed, waiting for another tap on the drum. There it was! And there! And there again! All afternoon she lay with her hands upon her stomach, happily feeling the lump rolling around within, rising up here, nudging her there, all over her broad pink belly.

That evening she told Frank she wanted to take a leave of absence. They discussed the pros (peace of mind) and the cons (her obligations, boredom, money) and concluded they could afford it; and Diana had just gone upstairs to take a bath and relish in the thought of *four straight months to herself,* when the phone rang. It was the local NARAL chapter, informing her that the anti-abortionists were introducing legislation requiring a husband's consent and asking her if she would testify against the bill. No, Diana said emphatically, I'm pregnant, leave me alone, and then she flashed on the recent patient whose boyfriend had told her he would beat the living shit out of her if she ever got an abortion.

"Send me the file," she sighed. She took her bath, but the next morning she went back to work, and the issue of a leave of absence didn't arise again. Not with Megan, not with Ben. If Diana had believed in God, she would have said that God put her on earth for a reason: to give these women another chance.

To push their reset buttons.

She was thirty when she founded her clinic, using a small inheritance she received when her father died. Located on the ground floor of a medical office building, it was three minutes from the hospital, five minutes from downtown, and eight minutes from her house. It was on a bus route. There was plenty of parking. There was a pharmacy on the ground floor where her patients could fill their prescriptions for painkillers. Satisfied that she couldn't have found a better location, she signed the closing papers and thus became the sole proprietor of the Center for Reproductive Choice.

First off, she gutted the office space because the previous occupant (a podiatrist) had set things up like a maze, with narrow halls and tiny examination rooms, and she wanted things different, open and airy, with a pleasant waiting room where you weren't all crammed together side by side amid crumbling dried flowers and back issues of *Smithsonian*. To that end she painted the waiting room a pale shade of salmon, installed a decent sound system, and filled an entire wall with books on women's health. On the other walls she hung framed photographs of simple scenes: a battered window full of geraniums, say, or an empty rocking chair on a summer porch by the sea. She often thought that if she were waiting to have an abortion, she would find it helpful to meditate on the image of oneself alone on that quiet porch, rocking, listening to waves, feeling the cool ocean breeze.

She'd planned on hiring partners, but it never happened; whether this was because of Diana's headstrong nature or simply due to the lack of a good match didn't really matter, because Diana operated happily as a sole practitioner. When her staff reached eight— three nurses, an assistant, two counselors, and two office workers—she stopped hiring. Any larger, and the clinic would be too big. Any smaller, and they wouldn't be able to provide the necessary services. Eight seemed just right.

Over the course of the first decade, Diana had no trouble hiring and keeping the right people. In fact, her folder of résumés grew so fat she had to assign them an entire file drawer. People *wanted* to work at her clinic, not just because they supported what she did but because Diana was known to run a very egalitarian establishment: at the CRC, the receptionist who set up appointments was as important as the counselor who listened to fears, who in turn was as important as the doctor who pushed the reset button.

But when the violence began escalating, the résumé file began to shrink as people shied away from her line of work. On her office wall Diana kept a map of the country, marking the attacks with yellow pushpins. Florida was vulnerable, it seemed. Boston was vulnerable. Maryland was vulnerable; Buffalo, Madison, Seattle, Berkeley— Christ, the whole damn country was vulnerable.

The CRC had its own first real attack right smack in the middle of the holiday season, the year Megan turned three. Diana and Frank had just finished tearing up the house to build an addition for the second child they'd finally decided they wanted. On that December morning Keisha the receptionist went out to get the mail and got her right hand blown off by a pipe bomb. Diana wasn't surprised when Keisha left to take a job answering the phone at an orthodontist's office instead; but she *was* surprised when Deborah, a nurse who had been with her since the start, suddenly took a job over at the hospital in Labor and Delivery.

"Nobody's going to shoot me for timing contractions," Deborah confessed.

No question, they all felt vulnerable these days. Along with success came notoriety, and although there were several other clinics in town, the CRC seemed to be a magnet for the antichoice contingent, especially after Diana testified before the state legislature—this time against a proposed ban on late-term abortions. It was a bad bill, and Diana had spent the morning in uncomfortable stockings and pumps trying to explain that the term *partial birth abortion* didn't even exist in the medical literature and how their particular bill would ban not only those late-term abortions everybody hated to think about but second-trimester abortions as well: cases of shriveled heads with no cranium, for instance, or spinal craters the size of a fist. Diana brought pictures and thought she'd spoken quite reasonably, but on its six o'clock broadcast Channel Four used as its sound bite her statement that the mostly male legislature had no business telling any woman what to do with her body, even if she was eight and a half months pregnant, and they ran it alongside the story of a twenty-six-week preemie who lay fighting for life in an incubator down at Children's, a little alien-looking thing hooked up to tubes and wires, and the implication was clear: if the mother of that preemie had asked, Diana would have scraped and dismembered that baby limb by limb in the interest of the mother's freedom of choice.

"You might as well have said you'd execute a kid for being a pain in the ass," Frank said glumly. "Why'd you have to go and say that?"

Afterward the Center for Reproductive Choice become the bull's-eye of regional hatred. For every bomb threat they received—and there was a time when they were getting one a week—they had to evacuate the clinic, patients and staff alike shivering out on the sidewalk while wild-eyed dogs sniffed through the building. People broke into their offices, dumping files, stealing equipment; and one winter day somebody entered at six in the morning and poured fuel oil all over the floor, and the clinic was saved from arson only by luck when the security guard caught the man washing his hands in the restroom, a cigarette lighter on the edge of the sink. They received suspicious packages in brown paper wrapping—which they knew not to open, of *course* they knew, but which invariably ratcheted up the fear factor.

Finally, upon Frank's insistence, Diana began to take precautions. No shots had ever been fired at her, but she installed bulletproof glass in the windows—not only at the clinic but at her house as well (a decision that would end up doubling the cost of the solarium). She bought a bulletproof vest. She hired two security guards—one to patrol the halls of the building, and one to patrol the sidewalk and keep the protesters the requisite eight feet away from patients entering the clinic.

They were there rain or shine: shouting, singing, holding posters of Baby Mary, Baby Paul, Baby Joseph—grotesque photographs of fetal remains carefully laid out on white towels. They came early and they left late. They came with their toddlers, who waved signs of their own. Often Reverend O'Connell was among them.

One summer evening—Megan was in high school at this point— Diana left the clinic a little after seven and was surprised to find that the protesters had all gone home. Usually a few stayed until she left, politely inquiring how many babies she had murdered that day, but that night a strange silence hung in the air. As she walked to her car, she noticed things she normally didn't: skateboarders in the parking lot, flower baskets hanging on the lampposts. This really was a nice place to live, she reflected. She needed to take a little time off and enjoy it.

Then, as she unlocked her car door, she happened to glance up. Across the street, on the flat rooftop of a small shopping area, a man stood watching her. A worker, she told herself. A roof repairman. But as she got into her car and buckled her seatbelt, the feeling of unease continued to grow. He was just standing there, not doing anything, watching her—and she was sure of it, even from a distance. She thought of a movie she had seen recently, two snipers on two different rooftops, radioing to each other just before one of them fired the shot. As she headed out into traffic, he was still watching her, and by the time she got home, she was so shaken that she poured herself a drink instead of lighting the usual joint, and went into her study and drew the shades.

She never saw the man on the roof again, but from that night on, every single time she left the office she found herself scanning buildings, windows, rooftops—anything that could serve as a stakeout point. The possibility haunted her. She'd been sloppy about wearing her vest, but she began to wear it religiously, and not just to work but to the grocery store and movies as well—even in summer, when the temperature was ninety degrees at nine in the morning. She installed blinds on the windows in the solarium. She got an unlisted phone number. She wondered if Megan and Frank were at risk, and whether as a mother and a wife she owed it to them to stop doing abortions, to protect them.

And so by the age of forty-seven, with her husband at the height of his career and her daughter just off to college, Diana Duprey couldn't remember what it was like to feel safe anymore. She was thinking of hiring a bodyguard, even getting a handgun. She was thinking of moving far, far away. She couldn't fall asleep without a Xanax.

This was not how she had expected to be living her life, at the age of forty-seven.

———————

Sending her one child off to college was nowhere near as traumatic as Diana had feared. That fall, with Megan at the university, she kept waiting for the empty-nest feeling to kick in, but it never did. Instead, she suddenly found herself with time on her hands—time to swim not just in the morning but in the evening as well; time to clean out a few closets; time to think about that book she wanted to write about Ben.

It had been ten years since her son had died, but it could have been yesterday—not so much because of any raw grief, but because sometimes he could still seem so alive, so present. They'd long ago dismantled his room, but some nights she could still smell the lotion she used for his eczema, could still hear Megan cranking the jack-in-the-box for him, or Ben himself trying to sing along with Raffi. She could picture Ben lying on his sheepskin, feet in the air; she could smell the vaporizer, could hear it bubbling gently as a backdrop to his constant rattly breathing in the night.

Diana knew there were some unresolved issues with Frank about Ben, but she'd avoided them over the years by focusing instead on her work and on raising Megan. Yet with Megan off at school now, she felt she and Frank needed to finally tackle some of those issues. They certainly had the time—although as the fall wore on and Frank didn't suddenly change his work habits, she wondered sometimes if he was interested. Frank seemed to have a lot of extra work for a man whose wife was home alone every night. But Diana reminded herself that after twenty years of crabbing at each other about kids and money, they probably shouldn't expect to just fall into each other's arms on a moment's notice and at the same time open up about wounds that hadn't healed right. That, indeed, was a lot to expect.

Things were quiet at the clinic that fall, which is to say that there'd been no bomb threats for a couple of months, and the last demonstration, the one where they spread fresh tar all over the sidewalk, had faded from the press's memory. The legislature had nothing on its agenda, and a kind of monotony had crept in, the kind that you think will set you up for a long, peaceful life but in fact only puts you more on edge.

It was around this time—late October—that Diana got a call from Steven O'Connell. "You have a phone call," Dixie began, and from the sound of her voice (full of dread, as though she had a bad diagnosis to convey), Diana assumed it was Bill Branson calling her again. That guy! Several times a week he called her to talk about

Megan: was she happy at the university, did she like her roommate, was she dating anyone, did she think she'd stay pre-med, did she come home much, how often, and did she ever talk about him? Diana was getting tired of it, but Bill seemed so vulnerable that she figured she better talk to him because the last thing she wanted was one of Megan's boyfriends going suicidal on her. She answered his questions as best she could, but always emphasized that she and Megan had made an agreement that they would treat Megan's college experience as though it were happening a thousand miles away, to which end Diana was not supposed to drop in at the dorm, and Megan was not supposed to bring her laundry home every week.

Go away, Bill, she thought. Get a life.

The last time they'd talked, Bill had reached a new level of desperation. He talked about transferring to an out-of-state school and getting married (even though there was no girl in the picture). He talked about how healthy he felt now that he was working out five days a week. You wouldn't believe my physique, he'd said. (Diana opted not to contemplate that.) He told her he'd decided to go into engineering. (The school didn't have an engineering program.) And then he told her that Megan gave the best head of any girl he'd ever known, and if she wasn't going to be with him he'd see to it that she wouldn't be with anybody no he didn't mean it he just wanted Diana to know how much Megan meant to him he'd never *ever* do anything to hurt her.

I think you need some help, Bill, Diana finally said.

I need Megan.

We've all gone through this, Diana said. It happens to everyone.

I can't live without her.

You can and you will. Bill. Listen to me. You go to Student Health, and you find someone to talk to. You get yourself on medication if you have to. But you forget about Megan.

I can't.

Yes you can. Are you keeping any pictures?

Yes.

Throw them away. Take her off your speed-dial. Delete her address.

I'm such a jerk.

You're not a jerk.

I'm a jerk.

No. You're a kid who's gone through a bad breakup. Just like everyone else on this planet.

Not her.

What?

I don't see anyone breaking up with her.

She's not even seeing anyone.

Yeah, but when she does, I bet he won't break up with her. I bet she'll break up with him. She'll always do the breaking up.

Bill.

Oh god listen to me. I'm such a jerk.

Okay, Diana said. Do you remember what I told you to do?

Yes.

Okay. You go now. Straight over there. They will help you.

I'm such an asshole.

Go.

You're so wonderful, Bill said. God, I'm sorry to lay all this on you. I'm so sorry.

Go.

All right.

Go.

I'm going.

Try not to call me again.

I won't.

But call if you absolutely need to, Diana said. I don't want you sitting up there with no one to talk to. Okay?

Oh god.

Okay?

Fine.

You're sure now?

I'm fine.

Just about any conversation with Bill left her uneasy, but this one in particular had made her wonder if she ought to tell Frank. Being somewhat familiar with the criminal justice system, she knew she couldn't get Bill arrested for merely making threats—but this conversation left her so creeped out that she called Megan and warned her to keep her door locked and make sure she always walked with a friend at night. She decided against telling Frank, though. He was so edgy these days, with that Internet porn case his office had been investigating since the beginning of time.

In any event, the smudge of worry about Bill was always there—so that day in October, when Dixie ended up telling her that it was Steven O'Connell on the phone, Diana felt somewhat relieved: at least it wasn't Bill Branson.

Then, of course, she wondered why on earth Steven O'Connell was calling her.

"Do you want to take the call?" asked Dixie. "I can tell him to call back."

"No," said Diana. "Put him through." For all the things Steven O'Connell said and did, Diana actually did not dislike the man. He was a zealot, yes, but an intellectual zealot, and was known to have steeped himself in heady philosophical literature on both sides of the issue. Ultimately, nothing he read would change his mind, of course, a fact that merely strengthened Diana's conviction that most people were never going to switch sides on this issue.

"Is this a bad time?" asked Steven.

"It's always a bad time," Diana said. "Not only that, but it probably violates the terms of the restraining order. What's up?"

"I need to talk to you."

"I'm listening."

"Not over the phone."

"That would *really* violate the restraining order," said Diana. "I can't meet with you, Steven."

"I'll make an appointment," he said.

"There's no exception for appointments. If I see you, I'll screw things up royally."

"We could meet in Denver."

Diana took a sip of the Diet Coke she had for breakfast every day. "The whole state knows us, Steven. What's this all about, anyway?"

"I'd rather not say, over the phone."

"So it's personal."

Silence.

"How about your house?" he finally said. "Nobody would have to know. And Frank could be there."

Diana picked up one of Ben's many ashtrays that she kept on her desk. This one was shaped like the state of Nebraska, with a big dry chunk taken out of its southwest corner.

"Look, Diana. I don't carry a gun. I'm not going to blow up your house. I just need to talk to you."

"And it's got to be in person?"

"Yes."

Diana went over and closed her door. This was crazy, and she knew it, but there was something in his voice that told her to go ahead, that what he had to say had to be said face to face.

"Come over tonight," she told him.

"Will Frank be there? Because I'll feel more comfortable if Frank is there."

"He'll be there."

"What time?"

"Make it after eight," Diana said. "Park on another street. And use the back door. I don't want the whole neighborhood thinking we're having a fucking affair or something."

―――――――

But Frank, as it turned out, had left Diana a message telling her that he'd be in a meeting until after nine. Following her swim—a brief forty minutes, that night—Diana slipped into a pair of loose pants and a tank top and coiled her hair into a big lumpy knot. In the kitchen she fixed herself a sandwich, then settled on the sofa in front of the television, sorting through the mail as she surfed the news programs. Shortly after eight she heard a light rap on the sliding-glass door. She stood up and went to the door and slid it open.

There stood Steven. Tall and gaunt, he gazed down at her with intense brown eyes. His hair was caught up in the folds of his parka hood, and a full beard covered his face and chin. Diana had always thought he looked more like a hip minister from the 1970s than a conservative and fervent anti-abortionist of the new millennium.

"This is one of the most idiotic things I've ever done," she said, "so come in and let's get it over with."

"Where's Frank?"

"He's working. Forget about it," she said when she noticed the worried look on his face. "His being here or not being here isn't going to make a difference. Unless you plan on blowing up the place," she added. "Ha ha."

Steven grimly removed his jacket and unwrapped the plaid woolen scarf from his neck and draped it over one of the kitchen stools. With the palm of his hand he brushed the rumpled fabric of his flannel shirt. Then he crossed his arms, looked her in the eye, and smiled.

Inwardly she cringed. Steven O'Connell had a rueful, earnest way of smiling, with his head cocked and his eyebrows raised, as though he both understood and pitied you for your sins. She was reminded that while she didn't affirmatively *dislike* him, it was a stretch to say that she actually *liked* him. She felt a moment of sorrow for his four children, who had to deal with that smile all the time, breakfast lunch and dinner, had to listen to him talk about the sanctity of life when all they wanted was to scarf down a piece of meat loaf and get back to shooting hoops.

Definitely not the guy you'd invite to your annual barbecue, Diana thought.

"Better tell me pretty quickly why you're here," she said flatly.

Steven sat on the edge of the stool at her center island. The smile vanished. It was about his son Scott, he told her. Scott, who was seventeen, had a girlfriend, Rose, whom he'd been dating for over a year.

As soon as he mentioned the word *girlfriend,* Diana knew what was coming.

"And Rose is pregnant," she said.

Steven glanced down at his hands.

Be smug right now, she warned herself, and you will have some *very* bad karma to contend with. "How far along?"

"Nine weeks. Has she been in to see you?"

Actually, she had; Diana remembered her well, because she had a tiny rosebud tattooed on her hip. Diana had commented on it as she did the pelvic exam, nothing judgmental except she hoped Rose had gone to a reputable place; but the girl had been embarrassed. In any case, at no point had she mentioned that the father of the baby was anyone related to Steven O'Connell.

"That's confidential information, Steven," she said.

"Well, here's what's not confidential, and that's that Rose's parents want her to have an abortion. Just *listen,*" he said as Diana raised her eyebrows. "Rose herself wants to carry the child to term and then give it up for adoption. We've agreed to take her into our house, to let her live with us while she goes through the pregnancy. But her parents will have none of it."

"This is not your decision, Steven," Diana reminded him.

"I know that," he said. "Which is why I'm coming to you for help. You counsel your patients, correct?"

Diana allowed that she did.

"And if a girl isn't sure about what she wants, you don't perform the abortion, is that right?"

"I'd phrase it differently," she said. "I perform abortions on women who are reasonably confident about their decision."

"On women who want the abortion, you mean."

"No one *wants* an abortion."

"Still, if she has any doubts at all, then you don't do it."

"Probably not right then and there. Maybe later."

"Then here's what I want. I want you to talk to Rose's parents and tell them to stop pressuring their daughter."

Diana was so astonished by this request that for a minute she couldn't say anything. That she might discuss things with a girl and her parents was one thing; but that a third party like Steven would try to step in and tell her what to advise was way, way over the line. Diana suddenly saw a great deal of folly in her decision to let Steven come by. She should have discussed it with Frank. Not even that— she should have flat-out said no. If her lawyer ever found out about this meeting, he'd go ballistic.

Self-consciously she stood up. "You should go," she said in a low voice. She was scared, although she wasn't sure why. "Before Frank gets home."

Steven stayed where he was, on the stool.

"Do I need to call the police?"

"Diana," said Steven, "this is my grandchild."

"Oh stop it, it's not your grandchild yet and besides, this isn't about you, Steven," Diana said. "It's about Rose, and what she wants."

"But she wants the baby!"

"And how do you know? How do you know she's not just afraid of losing Scott, for instance?"

"Because I've talked to her myself," Steven said angrily. "The girl is a Christian, even if her parents aren't. And right now she knows two things: she's carrying a life, and life is sacred. Do the logic, Diana. You want to know what she told me? She told me if she killed her baby, she would never be able to live with herself. You know what she's referring to, don't you?"

Only once in Diana's entire career—which included, to date, thousands of abortions—only once had a patient tried to kill herself afterward. (She hadn't succeeded; and it turned out she'd made several other attempts on her life long before her abortion.) Still, the last thing Diana ever wanted was a patient turning suicidal post-op.

"All I want is that you talk to the parents," Steven said. "Tell them to back off. So they can see for themselves that Rose is sure about this."

"And you think she's sure?"

"I know she's sure." His voice was calm, but his eyes were hot and intense with his mission. Diana fought the urge to step back from the man. She wasn't sure what she thought he might do, but she wished Frank would come home, just in case.

No, actually, she didn't. Frank would totally flip.

"So I talk to them," she said carefully, "and I counsel them to wait, and in the meantime you do what? Sit back with your mouth shut? I don't think that's going to happen, Steven. The way I see it, you're going to use the time to hammer them with pamphlets and pictures. You'll show them movies, like those movies you sent to me."

"I didn't send them."

"Well, someone from your camp did. Anyway, it doesn't matter. You'll simply do everything you can to persuade them they'd be forcing their daughter to make an evil mistake."

"Hear me out," he said. "If you talk to them, I'll stay out of it."

"Like you could keep your mouth shut."

"I promise. I won't say a word. *Unless* they come to me for advice, that is, in which case I'd feel entitled to talk it over with them."

Actually, Diana didn't mind him talking about abortion as much as she minded him displaying his pictures. Steven used some of the most graphic photos available, but what most people didn't know was that the pictured fetuses had been miscarried, not aborted. No matter to Steven. If they could be used to choke people up, he used them.

"Talk maybe, but absolutely no pamphlets or pictures," she said.

"Unacceptable," said Steven.

"Why? You think without them you'll have no case?"

"No," he said. "But with them, let's face it. Few women go forward."

"I know plenty."

"Not after seeing my pictures," said Steven.

"Your pictures are bullshit and you know it. Most of them are miscarried fetuses."

"They still show you what your baby looks like."

Diana closed her eyes. They were reaching the all-too-familiar stalemate, and it was almost nine o'clock, and she didn't want this man sitting at her kitchen island any longer. She decided that what she would do with Rose was no different from what she would do with any patient whose parents were involved: she would advise the parents to step back. If Rose wanted to have the baby, then Rose should be allowed to have the baby.

"Look," she said, "I'll talk to them. Once. But only after I talk to

Rose. And I'm going to make it very clear that a *lot* of women need a few weeks to sort out their feelings. Women who come back and ultimately go through with it."

"Whatever that number is," Steven murmured.

"And absolutely no pictures."

"Fine."

"And no movies."

"Fine."

"And not one word to the parents *unless* they come to you first."

"Fine too."

"How do I know that I should trust you?"

"I am a man of God," said Steven.

Diana rolled her eyes. "Steven, Steven, Steven. Do you really think that would sway me?"

"I believe in divine retribution," he said.

"Christian karma?"

"If you will. If I give my word, I stay with it."

Diana handed his scarf to him. "You say anything about this to anyone and you're screwed."

"Maybe a different phrase?"

"Get one thing straight, Steven," she said, sliding the door open for him. "I say what I want, when I want, and however I want."

Two days later Rose and her parents came into the clinic. Rose, her blond hair pulled up into a tangly knot, was dressed in gray sweatpants and a tight pink tee with the words *Foxy Lady* scripted in rhinestones. Elaine Fries, her mother, was a well-groomed woman in her forties, wearing narrow black pants and a stylishly embroidered denim jacket. Jack Fries was a local attorney. His heavy build conveyed strength rather than sloth, and the permanent laugh lines around his eyes gave his face a kindness and sense of confidence often seen in family doctors: you had the feeling Jack Fries knew what was best for you.

As they squeezed into Diana's tiny office, all three seemed intent on keeping their distance from one another; Rose and Elaine sat stiffly in the two chairs, while Jack stood behind them with his arms crossed.

"Thank you for seeing us," he said. "I know how busy you are. I guess you know the basic facts." Diana nodded. "We've talked with Rose at length about this," he continued, "and correct me if I'm wrong, but I think the general consensus is that an abortion is the only option."

"Rose?" said Diana. "Is that what you want?"

"One thing you might not be aware of," Jack said, before Rose could answer, "is that Rose is a starter on varsity basketball. She's only a sophomore, keep in mind. Most of the varsity players are upperclassmen. Anyway, she has a very good chance at a scholarship—"

"—which we don't actually *need*," added Elaine.

"—and obviously having a baby would interfere significantly."

Rose's mother placed her hand on Rose's knee. "She's been scouted already," she said proudly.

Rose removed her mother's hand.

Diana faced the girl. "Rose?"

Still Jack continued: "It's not that we're upset about Rose having . . . relations, although we would have preferred that she wait. It's that we feel the boy's family is trying to tell Rose what to do. The boy's family—well, I'll come right out and tell you. The boy's father is Reverend O'Connell."

"Steven O'Connell," added Elaine.

"As in, the Coalition," said Jack.

Rose looked out the window and murmured something.

"Rose, honey, we talked about this," Elaine said. "The man is a zealot. He's trying to impose his personal views on you."

"And you're not?" she murmured.

"You never felt this way before," Jack said.

"I was never pregnant before," said Rose.

Her father straightened up, looked at the ceiling, and sighed deeply. "You're fifteen, Rose. You've got your whole life ahead of you. College, basketball, you name it, the world is yours—if you want it. You're too young to have a child. And what about Scott? Do you see yourself marrying the boy? Because I certainly hope not."

"Jack," Elaine said, "let's not—"

"Tell her what a simple procedure it is," Jack said to Diana. "I think she's scared. And that's normal. I'd be scared. Heck, I'd be terrified. But it's really a very simple thing these days, especially if we do it now."

"Physically, yes, it's a simple procedure," began Diana. "But emotionally it can be quite complicated, especially if the mother"—she looked directly at Rose—"hasn't resolved things in her mind."

"I've resolved them," said Rose, jiggling her foot. "I know what I want. I want to have the baby."

Diana looked from one parent to the other and finally shrugged. "You can't force her."

"I'll run away if I have to," said Rose.

"Oh, Rose," Jack sighed. "Rosabella Rose."

Rose flung herself around in her chair to face him. "You think you know what's best for me!" she cried. "You don't know the first thing about me!"

"We know more than you give us credit for," her mother said gently. "We weren't born yesterday, you know."

"Like that helps," said Rose. "You know what? I'm through here. I don't have anything to say to either of you. Or you," she said, looking at Diana. "I know you all think this is one big mistake but it's what I want and it's what I'm going to do, and if I have to go and move in with Scott's family, I'll do that. They want me to, you know. They know how to treat a girl who's pregnant. They have a pregnant girl staying with them right now. We'd share a room. And it's a nice room too. I get a canopy bed and I get my own phone and Mrs. O'Connell knows about nutrition and everything *and!*" she exclaimed, "*and* they'll pay my doctor's bills."

"We'll pay your doctor's bills," Jack said. "It's not a question of money, Rose."

"Well maybe I don't want your money," said Rose. "I told you guys, I'm outta here. I can't believe I missed World History for this stupid meeting." She squeezed through the small space between her mother's knees and Diana's desk, catching one of Ben's ashtrays with her backpack as she passed. It fell into Elaine's lap but Rose didn't stop and so Elaine picked it up and set it back on the desk as Rose stormed out of the room.

Diana had never had such a meeting.

"Well," she began.

"Why didn't you say something?" Jack said angrily. "Why didn't you tell her what a simple thing it was?"

"I don't push women into having abortions," Diana retorted. "I'm here when they've made up their minds. And Rose isn't even ambivalent about it. It's not my role to try to change her mind. I can give you the names of some good obstetricians, if you want."

Jack gripped the back of Elaine's chair and bowed his head. "That's not what we want."

"But it's not a question of what you want," Diana said gently. "It's what Rose wants."

"We have to accept that, Jack," said Elaine, reaching up to touch Jack's arm. Jack shook his head slowly.

"I think it's just that she won't listen to anything we say," Elaine explained to Diana. "Whatever we suggest, she rejects. Maybe if we hadn't suggested the abortion in the first place, she wouldn't be so dead set against it."

"I guess you'll never know," Diana said.

"Well, thank you," said Elaine, rising from the chair. "This must have been difficult for you."

Diana smiled faintly. "I've been in worse situations."

Jack stared out the window for a moment. Then he reached out to shake Diana's hand. "I'm sorry for getting angry," he said. "It's just that this is my daughter."

"I know," said Diana. "I have a daughter too."

"But she's not pregnant, is she," Jack replied.

Diana said nothing but walked them out to the reception area. "Call me if you want the names of those obstetricians," she said.

Elaine Fries glanced around the waiting room. There were two young women there, each engrossed in a different *People* magazine. "This is a nice place," she told Diana. "I've always admired you for what you do."

"As have I," said Jack.

I just push the reset button, Diana wanted to say.

"And who knows," said Jack. "Maybe Rose will change her mind. Maybe we'll be back in a week. She is fifteen, after all."

"Fifteen's a tough age," Diana said. "If she needs me, I'm here."

But Rose didn't change her mind. Diana heard from a teacher at the high school (in for a routine eight-week) that Rose did in fact go to live with the O'Connells. She was getting prenatal care from a well-respected doctor. She was not speaking to her parents despite their attempts to stay in touch with her. It was a sad situation all around, but the silver lining—for Rose, anyway, and for the O'Connell family—was the baby growing inside her.

Diana wouldn't see Rose until December 17, and in fact she was able to put the girl out of her mind as November came and went and fall turned into winter. Sometimes you had to let go. She was letting go a lot at the clinic these days; it was something she'd resolved to do last January and, as with most resolutions, had let slide. But her life was changing, and it was time to reset her priorities. She was forty-seven, her only child was off at college, and she had the rest of her life to consider. She had a book to write—several books, in fact. She wanted to travel. She wanted to go back to school and study art, and music, and literature—the things she'd never had time for during her pre-med college years.

And she had a marriage of twenty years to resurrect. One of them had to take the step to put a little spark back into things, and she didn't think it was going to be Frank. He was still working as hard as ever. Maybe men didn't feel it as strongly when their children went off to college; she hadn't talked to enough people to get a consensus. What she did know was that Frank was like a horse with its blinders on, plodding down the same path as he was twenty years ago. If anyone was going to spark things up, it would be her.

That was the idea, anyway. The trouble was, whenever she looked for matches, she got distracted. There was always housework, bills, car repairs, laundry—and don't forget she was supposed to carve out a little time for herself, according to the self help magazines. So then she'd forget about Frank, and sparking things up; and then she and Frank would bicker over something, and she would think, Why me? Why does it always have to be me who tries to get the ball rolling? I could use a backrub, I could stand to have him take my head in his hands and kiss me long and slow the way we used to kiss, before children; why does it always have to be me? And at that point, even if somebody stuck a love torch in her hand, she wouldn't have known what to do with it.

CHAPTER EIGHT

THE WINTER HOLIDAYS came and went with little by way of celebration. Carolyn returned the day before Christmas, only to learn the day after that her mother had slipped on the ice and sprained her ankle. Again Huck found himself driving her to the airport in a snowstorm. I don't know why my sister can't handle this, she said in the car, but I suppose with two kids and a nanny and a domestic support staff, it's hard to find time to go take care of your own mother. Huck told her she was doing the right thing, though he too wondered why her sister couldn't step up to the plate in a situation like this. That made him feel selfish and small, though, so he reminded her he was going to be working pretty much around the clock anyway.

Megan and Frank stayed on with the Goldfarbs, who canceled their trip to the Caymans to prevent a disastrous scenario from unfolding on Christmas morning with Megan and Frank waking up alone to a joyless, empty house. This warm and welcoming Jewish couple, who had for years denied their three children anything that might possibly have resembled a Christmas tree, went out and bought a sixteen-foot Noble fir for Frank and Megan, along with glass baubles, colored lights, and Mylar tinsel (no small irony since Diana had abhorred tinsel and banned the messy stuff from her own house).

Shock had quickly thickened into grief, and both Megan and Frank found themselves slogging through the dark December days. For Christmas, Megan bought her father an espresso maker. Frank bought her a pink cashmere sweater, which shamed her in light of the fight she'd had with her mother that last morning, complaining as she had that all her parents ever gave her were practical gifts. The sweater instantly rose to most-cherished-gift-ever status, because Megan suspected that not once in her nineteen years had her father gone out and purchased a Christmas present for her. Buying presents was Diana's domain, with Frank's role limited to that of Recipient of Thanks on Christmas morning (often receiving Diana's hastily whispered words about a box's contents minutes before it was opened). So touched was she by the knowledge that her father had driven to a mall, found a parking space, picked something out, gotten it gift-wrapped, and hand-written the tag that she put the sweater on right over her sleepshirt.

"You can return it if you want," her father offered.

Like she would!

The day after Christmas, Frank suggested they drive up to Vail for a few days. This he claimed was simply to be a vacation for them. In fact, however, he had an underlying motive, which was to enable them to wake up in the morning without getting assaulted by yet another daily headline chronicling the latest development in the Duprey investigation.

To avoid a conflict of interest, Frank's office had transferred the case to the DA's office of a neighboring county. One of their first moves was to try to keep the press from reporting the specifics about Megan's photos. They hardly expected to win their motion, given the

First Amendment, but they landed a maverick judge and the story never went to press. Frank's relief that his daughter was not going to read of her fame on Page One was outweighed only by his wish that Internet technology would, for once, vanish overnight. He knew it was only a matter of time before Megan found out about the pictures, but for now, hopefully, she would remain oblivious.

As for the preliminary autopsy report, it had been released just before Christmas, and although the same DA had successfully petitioned to keep it sealed, certain details had been leaked to the press. Thus by Christmas the entire city knew that Diana had been mildly drunk; that she had died of a blunt trauma to the head consisting of a skull fracture and a subdural hematoma; that sometime in the last month she'd taken some kind of amphetamines; that there were traces of semen in the vaginal cavity; and that there were several scratch marks on her arm.

The entire city also knew that both Frank and Megan's fingerprints, given voluntarily, turned out to match those taken from around the house. As Megan would have said, *Well, duh; we live here.* However, it was then learned that Frank's prints matched those specifically lifted from the broken highball glass and the curved chrome handles on the edge of the pool, and with this revelation the public seemed to perk up, to raise a collective eyebrow—even though, as Frank's attorney emphasized, this proved nothing except that Frank had at one point since the last dishwasher cycle held the glass, *big deal;* and that he had at one point since the last house-cleaning session touched the chrome handles, *big deal.* Besides, his attorney noted, there were other unidentified fingerprints on the pool handles too. This sort of mob mentality, he intoned, this "gotcha" attitude, was deplorable.

The community tried not to prejudge but couldn't resist. It was as though they'd suddenly been granted the chance to infuse their collective history with Genuine Tragic Irony: for here was one of their most respected citizens, a family man who did good things for the community, who was handsome and intelligent and kept himself in tip-top physical condition—*and who killed his wife.*

As if the autopsy and the fingerprints weren't enough, people talked among themselves, and it became common knowledge that at some point that afternoon Frank had come across something online that infuriated him. What exactly he saw, the general public did not know. Yet his secretary admitted he had stormed out—she even used the word *ballistic,* much to the dismay of Frank's attorney—and the next person to see him was neighbor Susan Beekman, who witnessed him racing into his house.

"You could hear it clear down the street," Susan declared to a young reporter from the local paper, referring to the ensuing argument. "They were throwing glasses and yelling so hard they woke up my son." Susan Beekman didn't feel much obligation to censor herself. Although she'd borrowed many a cup of sugar from Diana over the years, she'd always looked askance at Frank and Diana's parenting style, especially after she witnessed Megan and Diana smoking a joint on their back deck one April afternoon, which, if anyone was wondering, was why she'd never asked Megan to babysit for young Dylan.

In any event, Susan's garrulous inclinations didn't strengthen any presumptions of innocence for Frank. By Christmas, although no charges had been filed, the lay assumption was that Frank Thompson had killed his own wife. Something he saw on the Internet had sent him flying into a rage, the theory went; he drove home, burst into the house, argued with Diana, and ultimately smashed her head against the side of the pool. Had people known about the threats on the answering machine, or the bundle of letters that turned up at the clinic, they might have focused on Reverend O'Connell and his group; but based on what they knew, people were speculating not who did it but rather whether the charges against Frank Thompson would be second-degree murder or involuntary manslaughter.

Frank found that with some discipline he was able to skim the newspaper articles with enough detachment to keep from coming unglued. Sure, they angered him, but he knew how newspapers worked, knew they were just doing their job. What bothered him far more than his seeing the headlines was Megan seeing them— Megan, who thought if she read something in the newspaper, then it must be true. For the second time in the last year he found himself wishing that she'd gotten into Princeton, just so he could put her on a plane and send her back to school two thousand miles from this nightmare.

This was not an option, however. Nor was his well-intentioned but misguided idea that he could rise at six and stuff the Goldfarbs' paper deep into the trash before anyone had a chance to read it. Or his plan to disconnect the television cable. There simply wasn't any way for him to prevent Megan from hearing or reading what was being said. And so to Vail they went, where they paid astronomical last-minute prices for a one-bedroom condo and skied the velvety Back Bowls for five days straight, retiring to bed each night before the ten o'clock news came on.

On New Year's Eve day they returned to town. It was not an occasion Megan wanted to celebrate—not just because she was mourning her mother, but also because of last year's breakup with Bill, a scene she'd rather forget. She and her father stayed in with the Goldfarbs and watched a movie on their new flat-screen TV. At eleven o'clock Megan stood up and covered a yawn.

"You're not staying up?" her father said.

You and Mom never stayed up, Megan felt like saying; why should it matter tonight? But she was aware of the meanness behind the impulse, and squelched it.

Her father stood up and hugged her. "Okay then," he said. "Good night, honey."

"Good night, Megan," the Goldfarbs echoed.

Nobody wished anybody a Happy New Year.

It was a convenient arrangement, staying at the Goldfarbs', and would have remained so, except that on New Year's Day one of the Goldfarb children called to tell his parents that he'd re-enrolled at the university, and could he and his wife and their two children come and stay with them until they found a place of their own? After hanging up, the Goldfarbs insisted to Frank and Megan that they stay on, but Frank, who'd been raised with a keen sense of houseguest etiquette, concocted a story about how he needed to be able to stay up late without disturbing people. The next day he and Megan packed up their meager belongings and drove to a hotel.

Megan was secretly relieved to give up the Goldfarbs' house for the impersonal confines of a hotel room. Being loyal friends, the Goldfarbs had never shown any sign that they suspected Frank of killing Diana; but with all the talk, all the newspaper stories, how could they help but wonder whether it was true?

Megan herself steadfastly refused to think that her father might be culpable. Her parents fought a lot, sure; but the notion that he might have killed her was not just preposterous but rose from sheer laziness, a complete lack of imagination. People wanted answers, and they wanted them quickly, and she was mature enough to see it as a lynch-mob mentality that sought to pin the blame on the first person who came to mind.

There was, granted, the matter of her father's denial—or rather, his lack of a denial to her. Sometimes, in the dark hours of the night, a tiny malevolent voice nagged at her that he'd never taken her aside and reassured her that of course he hadn't done it. Sometimes doubts began to hum. She turned them off. So what if he hadn't come right out and denied it to her personally? Like the earth isn't flat, right? And do people go around shouting the news through a bullhorn?

Megan was convinced it was one of the anti-abortionists. There was that woman named Eve Kelly who lived outside Denver. It was Eve's voice on the tape they'd found on the old answering machine, the voice saying *You're next,* and when Megan saw a picture of Eve, she recognized her as the woman who'd stood outside their house in subzero temperatures last winter, sandwiched between two black and white posters of fetal remains. She'd worn a long down coat, Megan remembered, and a blue scarf and a silly pompom hat. Sometimes she sang hymns. Sometimes she gave long speeches, to no one. Diana had to get a court order to keep her away.

Megan was sure it was someone like Eve Kelly, and she wondered why the police weren't so keen on pursuing this avenue. Eve was crazy; Eve was a fanatic; Eve knew their house. In moments of impatience she vowed to herself that if the police didn't talk to Eve Kelly pretty soon, she would.

Hoping to avoid the press, Frank had chosen a travelers' hotel on the outskirts of town. But as they walked into the lobby, a gaggle of reporters materialized from nowhere and flocked around them.

"Can you tell us why you're moving into a hotel?" one reporter asked.

"Is it true you've agreed to talk to the police next week?"

"Will your daughter talk too?"

"Does she have her own attorney?"

"Why did your wife meet privately with Reverend O'Connell at your home? What did they discuss?"

"Do you have any reason to think that your wife's relationship with Reverend O'Connell was anything other than platonic?"

Hearing this, Megan gestured at the reporter with her middle finger.

"Ms. Thompson," the reporter called, "is it true you were involved with a teacher at the high school?"

Frank whipped around. "Stay away from her."

But Megan had already stopped.

"Is it true your mother got him fired?"

"No."

"Who did, then?"

"I did."

"Why?"

"He gave me herpes," Megan replied.

Her father grabbed her by the arm and yanked her back. "What are you *doing*?" he said between clenched teeth.

"Giving them stuff to write about." She glanced back at the reporter and shrugged.

"For god's—We're here to register," he told the desk clerk.

The clerk had already printed out a yellow form for Frank. Hastily he signed it and handed it back. Nobody asked who they were. My god, we're famous, Megan thought.

"Lesson number one," her father said as they hurried toward the elevators. "You don't volunteer anything to reporters. Ever. Not one word. Do you understand?"

"We're famous, aren't we?" she said, catching up.

The elevator doors opened. He tossed his bags toward the back and waited for her to get in. When the doors had closed, he turned to her. "Let's get a few things straight," he said. "It's not our goal to be famous. We'll cooperate, we'll be civil, but it's not our role to volunteer information. Regarding the press: not another word. Do you understand?"

"I'm not ten, Dad."

"Then quit acting like it."

"This isn't exactly what I expected to be doing over Christmas break."

"Nor I," said her father grimly. "Roll with the punches, Megan."

Quickly Megan stole a glance at him. In the sallow elevator light, the pads under his eyes sagged loosely, like his skin was one size too big. In a few seconds the elevator jolted to a stop and the extra flesh on his neck quivered. The doors slid open. Megan and Frank each picked up a duffel and headed down the hallway.

"That herpes thing," she murmured. "It was a joke, you know."

Her father hesitated in front of their door and looked at her, and it seemed like he had something important to say. But if he did, he changed his mind. He fed the magnetic key card into the slot on the door and pushed.

If there was one thing she hated, it was having the last word.

———————

Their third-floor suite had two bedrooms, a living area, and a kitchenette. As in all hotel rooms, the air hummed and smelled of disinfectant and electric charge. Megan carried her duffel into the smaller of the two bedrooms. The curtains had been drawn, and in the dim light she scraped her shin on the corner of the bedframe. Angrily she found the light switch. She threw her duffel onto the bed and took out the tops and sweatpants that Sandy Goldfarb had lent her and stuffed them into the bureau drawer.

For the next few weeks, this would be home.

She went back out to the living area, where her father was attempting to set up the espresso machine on the tiny counter in the kitchenette.

"I need clothes," she announced.

"Didn't Sandy give you some of hers?"

"They're huge, Dad."

"What about stuff at your dorm?"

"It's closed until the fifteenth. All I have is these jeans and two sweaters, and that includes the one you gave me."

"I don't have a fortune to spend right now," Frank said. "You happen to know where this tube thingy goes?"

Megan thought it strange that her father was concerned with the cost of clothing. "Are new clothes that I have to buy because our house has been declared a crime scene covered by insurance?"

Frank looked up. For the first time in weeks, his eyes crinkled and he laughed out loud.

"That's a good one, Megan. We'll file it." He tore open a plastic bag and a small part went flying in the air. "Go buy whatever you need," he said, squatting down. He ran his palm over the rug. "Damn thing isn't very simple, is it?"

So that afternoon Megan went out and bought a dozen pairs of underwear, some tops, another pair of jeans, some shorts and a T-shirt to work out in in the hotel gym, and some loose pajama pants. She bought some toiletries and some cheap suede slippers from the drugstore, and while she was there she took a moment and looked up Eve Kelly's phone number. It wasn't listed. Finally she went to the bookstore and bought the Thomas Hardy novel she was supposed to read for the course on nineteenth-century British lit that Natalie had talked her into taking. Leaving the bookstore, Megan wondered what her roommate was doing in California at the moment. Swimming in the ocean? Lounging by the pool? Maybe she was reading Thomas

Hardy. Then again, maybe she'd picked up a *National Enquirer* at the grocery store and was now reading about whether the sperm in Diana's vaginal cavity belonged to Frank or to someone else.

When she returned to the hotel suite, she saw a new laptop sitting on the coffee table. She thought of what her father had said about money, then recalled that he'd had to turn his old laptop over to the police. Megan sat on the sofa and was in the process of logging on to her e-mail when her father came out of the bedroom, yawning.

"Are the reporters still down there?" he asked.

"Most of them," replied Megan.

"Did they ask you anything?"

"Yeah, they asked how my herpes was," she said as she typed in the password to her instant messenger account. When he didn't reply, she looked up. "Don't be an idiot, Dad, it's a joke." She had fifteen new messages. Bill wanted to know if there was any way he could help. Mr. Malone from the high school expressed his condolences. Natalie wrote Are you okay?????? To which Megan replied Be glad your mother is a librarian.

As she was scanning the rest of her messages, she heard the sound of a door creak open. On the screen a message flashed. Billabong has just signed on, it read. That would be Bill. Instantly she regretted signing on.

oh hi, he wrote.

hi, she typed.

can icu?

2 busy now.

w/what?

Megan deleted a slew of e-mails advertising hot horny girls. A pop-up screen presented her with a poll on whether Frank Thompson killed Diana Duprey. She closed that screen too.

i asked u a ?, wrote Bill.

y aren't u w/amanda

i m; want 2 no what wer doing?

no

whats the cops name again?

y

i hv some info

?

yr mthr owed a lot of $

what are you talking about???? 2 who?

a meth dealer

???????????????????????

& hes not a nice guy. I thot the cop wd like 2 no about him

she usd diet pills not meth!!!!!!!!!!!!

If u wnt 2 think that, fine

she ws a dctr!

whtevr

"You want some espresso?" her father asked.

"Sure," she said over her shoulder. get a life, she wrote.

"Here goes," and her father plugged in the machine and pushed the switch. There came the sound of underground water bubbling up. Frank stood back and wiped his hands on a paper towel. "Now *that's* an espresso machine. How did you know I wanted one?"

"Mom said." Megan turned back to the computer and saw that Bill had logged off, thank god.

"Is it hissing?" her father called from the bedroom.

"I think so," she called back.

"Keep an eye on it while I use the bathroom."

He's trying to provoke you, she told herself. Forget about it. She scanned the rest of her e-mail: mostly junk, and she was about to delete it all, when one message caught her eye.

FROM: ALLGODSCHILDREN@HOTMAIL.COM. RE: SINNERS.

Megan glanced over her shoulder, then double-clicked on the message.

YOUR MOTHER DESERVED TO DIE AND YOU DO TOO. DON'T THINK WE'RE IGNORANT. GOD WATCHES ALL.

"I'm going to save so much money with this machine," Frank said, returning from his room. "You know how much I spend at Starbucks on average per week?"

"Dad?"

"What's that, honey?"

"There's a message you might want to see."

Frank came over and stood behind her with his hands on the back of the sofa. He smelled of soap, and she could feel his breath on her scalp.

"Who is it?" she asked.

"I don't know," he said. "Forward it to me, and I'll forward it to the police."

"It's kind of creepy."

The espresso machine abruptly stopped hissing. "Have you ever gotten messages like this before?" her father asked.

Megan decided that Bill's mash notes didn't fall into the same category. "This helps you, though, doesn't it? Like, doesn't it suggest it was someone else? How come the police aren't going after the ant-eyes, anyway? Like Eve Kelly. Remember her? Why aren't they investigating her?"

Frank was inspecting the espresso machine.

"I'd think you'd be totally psyched with an e-mail like this," she said. "How come you're not excited? Something like this should get everybody off your back."

"Wish I could get this thing to unscrew," said Frank, bearing with his shoulder to twist off the cap. "It didn't even make the coffee. There's no coffee in the cup. God damn it."

"Leave it alone, Dad."

"It just pisses me off when you get something new and it doesn't work," he said. "God damn it all."

"Don't touch the lid. We can return it," Megan said. "I kept the receipt."

"Pieces of junk nowadays," Frank was saying, when suddenly the machine exploded with a loud *pop*.

"I told you not to touch the lid!" Megan cried, jumping up. It looked like a small bomb had detonated in the kitchenette, with coffee-colored mud splattered all over the counter and cabinets. Her father had sunk to the floor and was squatting against the wall. He hung his head between his knees like a child. She squatted down beside him and put her hand on his shoulder.

"Did you burn yourself?"

"I'm fine," he said in a muffled voice.

Megan looked around at the mess.

"Want to talk?" she asked gently.

"No!"

"Maybe you should."

"I don't want to talk! I just want a cup of espresso!"

He sniffled and looked up, and they both looked at the mess all around them, and they began to laugh. Megan leaned around him and opened the door of the small refrigerator. She took out a single serving bottle of scotch and handed it to him.

"Better than espresso," she told him.

He stood up and got a glass out of the cupboard and added ice cubes and poured the scotch over the ice and jiggled things around, and then he sat down on the sofa and took a sip. When he finally spoke, his voice was gruff, and he had to clear his throat several times. Megan knew something big was coming.

"She just . . . ," he began, then paused. "She just knew how to push my buttons, you know? All she had to do was turn away. That's all she had to do."

"What do you mean?"

"She just had a way of dismissing the issue. Never listening! All these years!"

"What issue?"

He shook his head. "If you told me twenty years ago that I'd be in this position today, I'd have said you were crazy."

What position? He wasn't making sense. An uneasiness sprouted within her—not quite distrust but something like it. She plucked it like a weed and tossed it aside and waited for him to make more sense.

"But I did love her," he continued. "Believe me. Even though I held a grudge. I didn't even know it was there, to tell you the truth. I'm not the kind of person who usually holds grudges. I thought you'd go off to college and your mother and I would have this second honeymoon. Guess it wasn't meant to be."

Megan felt something take root in her. She went and got another bottle of scotch from the refrigerator and poured it straight up into a glass for herself. She was terrified.

"Dad," she began. "I—"

"But here's the thing," he went on, as though he hadn't heard her. "Here it is January and I'm getting along, I'm doing okay, I manage to get up and go about my day, the sun's out, the sky's blue, the traffic lights are green all the way down Broadway—and then I notice the gloves she was looking for that morning." He gave an edgy laugh. "She'd asked if I'd seen them anywhere, and I ignored her because number one she'd been so crabby and number two it was a pair of gloves and I had other things to think about. But today! There they are! Right there on the floor of my car! Think of the aggravation I could have saved her if I'd noticed them that day." He laughed ruefully. "All day long she wouldn't have had to wonder where her gloves were."

Megan didn't get it.

"My point is," he said, as though he'd read her mind, "marriage is a lot more complicated than you know, Megan." He took the tissue she was handing him and blew his nose. She handed him another one.

Suddenly his face changed. "Hey. Off the subject. We've got the questioning coming up next week. Are you nervous?"

"Kind of."

"Don't be. It's no mystery. We'll go down to police headquarters. We'll meet with those two detectives. They'll ask us questions, and we'll answer them."

"Are we going to be in the same room together?"

"If I have my say, yes."

"What kind of questions will they ask?"

"With you, they'll probably ask what else you know about the threats," he said. "With me, well, that's different."

"Why?"

"Because I'm a suspect."

"Will they ask you if you did it?"

"Probably."

"And what will you say?"

He stared at her as though she had just asked if the tooth fairy was real. Then he gave a derogatory laugh. "Are you kidding?"

"No," she said. "Yes."

"Oh, Megan," he said, closing his eyes. "Megan Megan Megan."

"Did you?"

"No, honey," he said.

Megan took a another deep breath. Her father reached over and tousled her hair. "Jeez," he said. "Megan. Don't even think that way."

She leaned away. She couldn't decide whether he was being condescending or paternalistic or just sucking up to her. She felt herself getting nervous, and she recalled sitting in some Santa's lap long ago where the feeling just wasn't right. She reminded herself that it was just her father here. Same guy as always.

"What were you fighting about that night?" she asked.

"What? Oh good lord, honey, you don't need to know."

"Yes I do," she said, her voice suddenly growing very small. "Why did you throw a glass across the room? What were you fighting about? Me? Money?" She thought for a moment and recalled lying in bed listening to her parents argue about Ben's medical bills. Suddenly a string of unscripted images flashed before her: Ben crawling into bed with her at night, then snoring like an old man; the smell of cough syrup and vaporizers; her mother's stomach right before Ben was born, big and white as the moon.

"Was it about Ben?" she asked. "Were you fighting about him?"

Frank leaned forward on the sofa and rested his forehead against his fingertips. From the back, his shoulder blades poked up like little tents. He cleared his throat.

"When your brother died," he said gruffly, "it was like my skin got ripped off."

She'd been at camp. She and Ben had both had pneumonia that summer, but she recovered, while Ben went from bad to worse. At night she listened to her parents argue about whether she should go, with Ben so sick; her father prevailed and off to the mountains she went. She was nine; Ben was four.

That was the year he ate so much paste he had to have his stomach pumped. The year she taught him to use a pair of scissors, only to have him happily cut holes in everyone's clothes. The year he wanted a trumpet for his birthday, and they gave him a bugle with a kazoo for a mouthpiece, and he woke them up every morning with his high-pitched buzzy whoops. The year he wore a satin princess gown for Halloween.

"So you blamed Mom? And stayed mad at her for the last ten

years? People get grief counseling for stuff like that, Dad," Megan said. "Did you ever think of grief counseling?"

Frank rubbed his eyes with his fingertips. "Oh, we tried. It helped, somewhat. But we still had you to raise. And it wasn't that you gave us a lot of trouble," he said. "You were just like any kid. You tested the rules. You pushed our buttons. The problem is, when you've had your skin ripped off, you don't have a lot left in reserve. And your mother and I had very different ideas about how to raise a child—*any* child, even one without a disability."

Megan had witnessed this. With just about every issue her parents had sat on opposite sides of the table. They even asked her to keep secrets. *Don't tell your father,* her mother would say, *but this is some very high-quality pot.*

Frank rose from the sofa and went and opened up the little refrigerator. This time he chose the clear bottle of gin. He unscrewed the cap and poured it onto the pebbles of ice that remained in his glass.

"Look," he said. "I don't want surprises coming out during the questioning. Your mother and I fought that night, Megan. No question. Knock-down, drag-out."

Megan was suddenly tired and hungry, and she thought her father should have offered to share the gin. "When are you going to tell me exactly what happened?"

"That night?"

"That night."

"I'm telling you now," said Frank. "We fought."

"And you threw a glass at her."

"Yes."

"Did you grab her?"

"Yes."

"Shake her?"

"Yes," he said. "I did."

"And then what happened?"

"I left," he said.

"And where'd you go?"

"Out," said Frank.

"Where?"

"It doesn't matter."

"It matters to me. It's going to matter to the police too. Aren't you going to have to tell *them* where you were?"

"Don't go there," he warned.

"Oh, right," she said. "Keep Megan in the dark. Treat her like Ben. Retardo daughter here."

"Megan."

"Then tell me where you went! Tell me what you were fighting about! Tell me why you threw a glass across the room! She's dead, Dad! Tell me, so I stop wondering whether or not you did it!"

She stopped suddenly, frightened that she might have overstepped the boundaries. Every muscle in her father's face seemed to clench up. Slowly, carefully, he set his glass on the arm of the sofa and sat down again.

"Okay," he said. "You want to know what we were fighting about? Here's what we were fighting about." He leaned forward and hit the mouse pad with his forefinger. Then he typed in a Web address and hit the return key. On the monitor a picture began staggering into focus.

Megan stood behind the sofa with her arms crossed. "What?" she said sullenly.

"That," he said, sitting back.

Color bled down the screen. When she was able to make out the image, she raised her hand to her throat. *The hot night air, cool on her skin. The blanket, soft beneath her. Raising her head to the moonlight.*

"I didn't believe it at first, either," he said. "Then I saw the mole."

Megan sat down on the sofa. Her mind began to race. She *knew* how to work a digital camera. She *knew* how to delete a frame. She knew how to delete *multiple* frames. Each time she had deleted everything. She was positive.

"What bothers me, of course," her father was saying, "is not that these ended up on the Internet but that you let someone take them in the first place. Who was it? Bill?"

Megan stood up. The fury made her shake. She got her jacket from the closet.

"Where are you going?" her father asked.

"Out."

"No you're not," he said. "You sit right back down."

"What are you going to do, Dad? Take away my allowance? Ground me?"

"Sit down, Megan," her father warned. "I do not want you driving in this state."

"I'm *fine*." She had her hand on the door when he grabbed her shoulder. She wrenched herself free but lost her balance, and he grabbed both shoulders and pushed her back into the room, where she staggered against the sofa.

"You can't go driving in this frame of mind," he said.

"You pushed me."

"I didn't push you, Megan."

"Oh my god."

"Megan—"

"I can't believe you just pushed me. Get out of my way," she said, for he was standing in front of the door now, barring her from leaving. "If you don't get out of the way, I will call the police."

"Oh Megan, come on," he began. "You just egged me on a little. I overreacted. I'm sorry."

"Is this how it happened that night?"

"How what happened?"

"*She* probably egged you on. Are you going to smash my head in too?" Not waiting for an answer, she stormed into her bedroom, where she unzipped her duffel and opened the drawers and threw everything—the new jeans, the new tops, Sandy Goldfarb's oversize tunics, everything—into the bag and zipped it shut. She went into the bathroom and gathered up her shampoo, toothpaste, toothbrush. She got the Thomas Hardy novel and zipped everything else into one of the side pockets. Then she went back out to the main room. Her father was still standing by the door.

"Where are you going?" he asked, stepping aside.

"None of your business."

"I can't let you do this," he said. "You're not in any shape to drive."

"You can't stop me," said Megan.

"Don't go."

But Megan stepped out into the hallway. "Oh, and by the way," she said, "I guess I do want my own attorney."

———————

She made it to the small college town up north in just under forty-five minutes. On campus she careened into the parking lot of the squat brick building where Bill lived. Screeching to a stop in the handicapped zone, she cut the ignition and ran into the dorm and up the stairs to the second floor and down the hall to room 213. She stopped momentarily, took a deep breath, and pounded on the door.

Bill's roommate opened it.

"Where's Bill?" she demanded.

"Wow," he said. "Are you Megan?"

"*Where is he???*"

"In the shower." He pointed past the stairwell. "Hey. Chill."

Megan ran down the hall to the door marked "Men." Without knocking, she stormed in, sending the hot steamy air into a roiling fit and startling a barely pubescent boy into frozen panic at the sink. She glanced one way and then another, then followed the sound of shower spray to a stall halfway down the row. She whipped back the curtain, only to catch another boy with a look of astonishment on his sudsy face.

"What are you friggin' doing?" he exclaimed.

Megan dropped the curtain. "Branson!" she yelled.

In the next stall, the water suddenly shut off.

"Megan?"

"Get out here!"

"Just a sec."

"Oh, spare me the modesty," she said, pushing back the curtain. There he stood, hairy and dripping. "Get out of the fucking shower."

Bill stepped out, wrapping the towel around his waist. "What brings you here this evening, Megg-Ann?"

"You fuckhead," said Megan.

"Could you *please* take it down to your room?" said the priggish boy in the next stall.

"You asshole," Megan said. "You fucking asshole."

Bill tightened his towel. "Come on, let's go."

"Don't touch me."

"We'll just go to my room."

"I said don't *touch* me!"

"Fine. Have a cow why don't you." He pushed open the door, and Megan stormed ahead of him and out into the hallway, where she crossed her arms over her chest.

"How much did you get for them?" she demanded.

"For what?"

"I'm going to sue the shit out of you," she said. "You know god-damn well what I'm talking about."

"No, I really don't." He walked down the hall, and she hurried after him. In his room he switched on the light. His roommate had left. Two blanketless cots lined the far wall, and clothing carpeted the floor. Megan thought she smelled skunk.

"Shut the door," she said.

"Relax."

"And put a robe on," she said. "I don't want to look at your fucking chest."

"You have to tell me what's going on," he said, plucking a T-shirt from the floor, "or it's going to be really, really hard for me to answer your questions. Want a beer? Look, we bought a refrigerator—cool, huh?"

Megan kicked a pile of clothes off to the side. "The pictures," she said, pacing in a small circle. "The pictures you took?"

"I remember those," he said. "What about them?"

"They're online."

Bill waited.

"Did you hear me?"

"I heard you. But that's impossible. You deleted them."

"Apparently not all of them. Or maybe your camera's got some kind of recycle bin. Where is it?"

"What?"

"The camera!"

"Home."

"What's it doing home?"

"I don't use it much anymore," said Bill. "It kind of lost its appeal, if you follow my drift."

Megan hugged her chest to stop her shoulders from shaking. They were getting off track. "I just want to know how those pictures made it onto the Internet."

"Well, I didn't sell them," said Bill huffily. "And I resent the accusation."

"If you didn't, who did?"

"Maybe whoever stole the camera."

Megan froze. "What are you talking about?"

"Someone stole the camera," said Bill with a shrug.

"I thought you said it was at home," said Megan. "You're not making any sense."

Bill pulled out a chrome-legged plastic desk chair and sat down. "The original camera, the one we used, got stolen," he said patiently. "I just replaced it with the same model. It wasn't a big deal. My parents' insurance covered it."

"You never told me."

"You think I felt some kind of obligation?"

"When did this happen?"

"I don't know," said Bill. "Sometime in the summer."

"Last summer?"

"The summer before."

"When we were still together?"

"Megan, Megan," sighed Bill. "Can you please not open old wounds?"

Megan began pacing again. She thought again back to that hot night two summers ago, when they'd taken the ecstasy. She tried to remember getting up from the blanket, going into Bill's house, going home—anything!

"Is it possible," Bill asked, "that there were other pictures? Taken by somebody else? Like maybe Mr. Malone?"

It was a good thing there was not a knife available, Megan thought. She looked at him with pure disgust. "Get a life, Bill."

"I take that as a no. By the way, are you sure the pictures are of you and not somebody else?"

"Yes."

"Because people can do a lot with technology today, splicing these digital pictures. Maybe it's your head and someone else's cunt."

"It's me."

"How do you know?"

"I just know."

Bill thought for a moment, then grinned. "Ahhh," he said. "The mole. Well. That clinches it, I guess. Not too many people have a mole right there. How'd you come across these pictures, anyway?"

"I didn't," said Megan. "My father found them. Don't even go there," she warned. "He had a case. It was part of his job."

"Still," and Bill grinned again and raised his eyebrows.

Megan leveled a frigid gaze upon him. "You are slime," she said. Then another thought occurred to her. "Have you been taking pictures of Amanda?"

"Oh no," he said. "Really. Honest."

Megan scrutinized his face. He looked her straight in the eye.

"Honest," he said. "It was only with you."

She didn't know whether to be flattered or insulted. She stood up and headed for the door.

"Why leave now?" he said, rising. "The night is young."

"I don't think Amanda would be very happy to see me here in your room," she said.

"She's very open-minded," said Bill.

"Like I could give a fuck," said Megan.

Seeing that she was indeed about to leave, his eyes grew moist and pleading. "Don't go. Please don't go." He reached out to touch her arm, but she wrenched it away.

"You still don't get it, do you?" she said angrily.

"I can't help it," he said. "I can't stop thinking of you."

"What about Amanda?"

"There is no Amanda. I made it up. I thought I could make you jealous. I can't do it without you, Megan," he said. "We had such a good thing. It was so real. Tell me the truth—did you love anyone else like you loved me? Just answer that. Just tell me I was the only one."

"You need help," she said.

"Just say it," he said. "Tell me there hasn't been anyone since me."

And right then, out of nowhere, she flashed on Huck Berlin. Honest to god.

"And you think that'll help?" she said.

"It'll give me something to hope for," he said. She turned and started walking out of the room. "What about the pictures?" he called after her. "I can maybe help you find out who sold them!"

Megan turned back. "No, you can't, Bill," she said. "Just drop it, okay? We're not going to find out who sold them. Not if your camera was stolen."

"But maybe I can find out who stole the camera! Maybe I can track it down!"

Megan regretted coming up here and involving Bill in this fiasco. There was no point in pursuing it. What did it matter who sold them? The damage was done. The pictures were out there. Her father had seen them. Her mother was dead. What good would it do, to spend her time and energy on finding a guy who made a little money off a few pictures?

She ignored his pleas and walked down the hall, down the stairs, and out into the cold. As she drove west, she made a plan. First off, she had to get back to town and find another hotel to stay in until the dorms opened back up, because she wasn't spending one more night with her father. Not that she suddenly thought him capable of—just because he grabbed her didn't mean   stupid   jumping to conclusions—more like because he had seen those pictures—awful pictures—how could she look him in the eye—

She turned south onto the interstate and got the car up to seventy miles an hour and drove with the windows wide open. Her plan was taking shape. After finding a hotel, she would go to the police. She would make sure they knew about the pictures, so they would understand why her father had been so angry. She would remind them that Eve Kelly lived thirty miles away. And then?

Well, what then?

And the nagging little voice, sensing an opportunity, shuffled right up to her ear. She was forgetting something, wasn't she, it reminded her. Where had her father gone that night? Why wouldn't he account for himself between the hours of five and eight? What was he hiding?

Objectively, anything was possible.

The thought had a smell, like fetid fur. Once thought, it would not go away, and Megan felt raw. But if her father's only story was that he was out for a walk in the middle of a blizzard for three hours, then fine. When you've dealt with your mother's murder—well, it was like the voice said. Anything was possible.

CHAPTER NINE

AT SIX-THIRTY the next morning Huck was at his kitchen table, on hold with the phone company. Actually he was using his cell phone to make the call, the regular phone company having cut off service for unpaid bills, and this irritated him no end, because his cell phone was too small to wedge against his ear even if he cricked his neck real hard, which left him with just one hand to go through the stack of mail on his kitchen table and see what other bills he'd missed.

He was grouchy, admittedly. Carolyn was still in Minnesota, driving her mother back and forth to rehab every day because her sister who lived only ten minutes away just had to go and get the shingles. Carolyn's words, not his, although he shared her frustration, since it meant that here he was, right smack in the middle of another very public investigation and having to take care of her cats and go over every day to water the plants and retrieve the mail, all the while wondering why the friendly father/ex-husband couldn't himself fly out and take care of the mother/ex-wife instead of everything falling on Carolyn's shoulders.

Your call will be answered in approximately . . . five . . . minutes, a voice told him. He switched ears. The excess heat in the house had forced him to crack the kitchen window, which helped, but he couldn't stop feeling like he was in some kind of funhouse, with random pockets of hot and cold air assaulting him right and left. He was about to go open another window when the doorbell rang.

He padded out to the foyer and opened the door. There on his front step, of all people, stood Megan Thompson. She was dressed in a puffy down jacket, bouncing at the knees to keep warm as she focused intently on her feet. Her hair glistened in long inky loops. At the sound of the door opening, she jumped a little, as though surprised to see him.

"Oh! You're here! Can I come in?"

His first thought was to call Ernie. It was protocol, but besides that, for reasons he did not want to articulate—even to himself—he was extremely uncomfortable with the idea of being alone with Megan Thompson in an overheated house at seven o'clock on a cold snowy morning.

"Megan," he said calmly, "what are you doing here?"

She tipped her head and violently batted the mass of curls. "I knew you'd ask that. Can I come in?"

"I don't think—"

"Look, I'm freezing. I just spent the night in my car. I have no place to go right now and my toes are frostbitten and if this is against some rules fine but please," she said, "please let me come in. And then I'll go. I promise."

Huck glanced up the driveway. There was her car, parked crookedly. He pulled the door shut and turned around to find that she had already gone into the kitchen.

"Look," Huck said, following her, "if you're going to come in, I'm going to have to call—hey, go ahead, sit right down."

Sitting she was already, if you could call it that, the way she slouched back in the chair with her legs splayed boyishly ahead.

Huck felt a light sweat break out on his neck. He picked up his phone.

"No!" she exclaimed. "Don't call anyone!"

"I have to."

"Just wait! Just hear me out! I won't stay long, I promise."

"If you've got something to tell me, tell me now, because really," he said, "you shouldn't be here, and if you *are* going to be here, I need to get somebody else over here."

"I do have something to say," said Megan, taking off her shoes. "I tried calling Eve Kelly and guess what? Her phone's been disconnected."

This did not surprise Huck. Eve Kelly had not been pleased to receive a visit from Huck and Ernie last week, and her beatific demeanor had switched to hostility when she realized what they wanted. However, she informed them that she'd been at the restaurant where she worked that Tuesday evening in December, and her employer's records had corroborated her claim.

Huck didn't go into the details with Megan, but he assured her that Eve's disconnected phone was not a problem for the case. Casting him a skeptical look, Megan sat up and pulled off her socks. Her toes were pink and blotchy, and she cupped them in her hands and kneaded them briskly. Again Huck reached for the phone.

"Please," she said, "just hold on a sec. I just want to ask you something, and I don't want a lot of people around right now."

"Quickly, Megan."

Megan glared at him. "Why are you just focusing on my father?"

Huck sighed inwardly. This had happened before, family members taking it upon themselves to solve a case. "Megan," he said, "I think you better leave things to the police."

"Well, you're going down the wrong road. Barking up the wrong tree. Have you gone through the Home Tour logs?"

"We have," Huck said.

"Have you talked to Steven O'Connell?"

"We have."

"You're lying," she said. "Steven O'Connell is out of town."

His neck warmed. "You really shouldn't be here," he told her. "Here. Have some coffee. Warm yourself up, and then go home."

"I have no home," she reminded him.

"I mean your hotel."

"I have no hotel."

"What's that supposed to mean?"

Megan took the coffee and blew on it. "Don't ask," she said wearily, in a way that seemed to cut off everything.

Huck straightened up. You're a cop, be a cop, he thought. He picked up the phone, then remembered with irritation that he had no phone service. He picked up his cell phone and found that the battery was dead. For Pete's sake.

"Megan, it's just not right for someone in your position to show up on my doorstep at seven a.m.," he said. "You know that, don't you?"

"Of course I know that! But I—" She paused long enough for Huck to think she'd lost her train of thought. Then she got a school-marmy look on her face.

"Do you know why my father was so upset that night? Well, I'll tell you why. There's this Web site. There are some pictures. Pictures of me," she added.

Huck cleared his throat. "We know about the pictures."

Megan didn't flinch. "Oh."

"We've known about them for some time."

Megan nodded and blew on her coffee. "How'd you find out about them?"

"Never mind. I don't mean that rudely," he added. "But—"

"Fine. Fine!" she exclaimed, and he looked away, wondering what exactly one should say in a situation like this. Suddenly all his experi-

ence as an officer of the law seemed to vanish, and he had not only
the terrible feeling of losing control but the wholly unexpected fear
that Carolyn was trying to reach him and he was going to sound
guilty as all get-out for no reason at all when he tried to explain how
both phones were dead.

So that when Megan broke the silence, he found himself envious
of her social grace.

"But if you know why my father was upset," she said, "then why
are you still focusing on him? It doesn't make sense. Why would he
take it out on my mother? I'm just throwing this out as an idea. That's
all it is. It's just an idea here. But it seems to me that if he was upset
about some pictures, he'd go and take it out on the person who took
the pictures."

"And who was that?"

Megan cupped the mug to her chin.

"It would help if we knew," said Huck.

The heater fan stopped blowing, and again the house rang with
silence. Finally she said, "It was my boyfriend. My ex."

"Who's that?"

"Does it matter?"

Huck figured he could get the name later. "When did he take
them?"

"A couple of years ago. Look, it was a dumb thing to do. I thought
I deleted them all, and then we broke up and then apparently his
camera got stolen." The color rose in her face. "Is there *anyone* at the
police department who hasn't seen them?"

Huck didn't want to answer that question. Most people at the
department were professional about these things, as the chief had
ordered, but there were always a couple of bozos who had to go and
make wisecracks when no superiors were around.

"So everyone's seen them?"

"Not everyone."

She smiled wanly. He plugged his cell phone into the charger on the wall by the table. "How about a ride somewhere now?" he asked.

She smoothed out the ruffles on Carolyn's placemat. "No," she said. "My car's fine. I didn't know you were married," she said.

"I'm not."

"You've got a girlfriend, though."

"I do," he allowed.

"I'm sorry if I woke her."

"She doesn't live here."

"Why not?"

Huck was not used to people asking questions like this, and he had the uneasy feeling that if he were to leave the room for a moment, this woman, this girl, would manage to find out his bank balance, his medical history, and more. He noticed the reminder postcard from his dentist lying on the counter and slipped it into the silverware drawer.

"Usually I ask the questions," he said gruffly. "Look, finish your coffee. I'll give you a ride over to the station. We can talk more there."

"I don't want to go to the station," said Megan. "If you catch my drift."

"Why can't you go back to your hotel?"

"I moved out," she said crossly.

"Why?"

"I felt like it! God, I'm nineteen—do I have to stay cooped up in a hotel with my father day and night?"

"Where are you going to go?"

"I'll find my own hotel room. Or I can stay with friends. I'll figure something out."

Huck handed her the Yellow Pages. Suddenly very businesslike, she used his cell phone to make a series of calls, ultimately booking a room at a Motel 6 on the outskirts of town. And although it seemed like a sad solution for her to move into a Motel 6, Huck was extremely relieved to have the matter resolved.

Then he noticed Megan staring forlornly at the floor.

"What's the matter now?" he demanded.

"Can't I just go back to our house? I won't touch anything."

Huck marveled at her naïveté. He shook his head. "Can't you find anything other than a Motel Six?"

"Well, there's the Sheraton with all the reporters. And there are a few bed and breakfasts. Cozy and intimate is not exactly what I'm looking for, though."

"Why don't you just go back to your hotel with your father, then? What's the problem?"

"I don't feel like being with my father right now, okay? I've been spending a lot of time with him and I've gotten kind of tired of him, to be quite honest; do you get it or is that something a cop doesn't quite understand?"

It seemed to Huck that there was a lot of conflict going on inside this girl's head, for which he couldn't blame her. Protective of her father one minute, angry the next—it made sense, given the circumstances, but that didn't make him an expert on father-daughter relations. Suddenly he felt his stomach begin to knot up, the way it did just before he gave a speech.

"How about this," Megan said. "How about if I stay here."

"Here?"

"Just until the dorms open."

His heart began to pound. "Out of the question."

"I'll sleep on the sofa," she said. "What, you think people will think we're sleeping together?" Her tone was both defiant and sarcastic, but suddenly her face went blank. Then she gave a sharp little laugh.

"Of course they'd think that, wouldn't they?" she said. "A girl who'd pose for pictures would sleep with anybody."

Huck unwittingly took offense at this.

"Well, you know what?" she went on. "I say fuck 'em. Look, I just need a place to stay. I refuse to go to a Motel Six. I'm so tired," she sighed.

Huck's mind raced as he mentally skimmed through the Code of Conduct. Internal Affairs would have a field day.

Megan, however, didn't wait for an answer. She wandered into the living room, where she glanced around, taking in the blank walls and the curtainless windows. Huck wished he'd taken the time to hang the framed Monet poster Carolyn had given him last fall. There it sat, leaning against the wall. Megan sat down on the sofa. She bounced a few times, then knotted her hair into a loopy red tie and lay down. Huck was too stunned to react.

"I was up all *night*." She yawned, snuggling into herself. "That fucking Bill. He won't let up. Did you ever have that, someone who just won't let you alone? It's like you're always waiting for the bomb to drop. I wish he'd just fire a gun so you could lock him up. Shit," and her voice began to drop off. "I have so much reading to do. How am I ever going to focus?"

And then, within the minute, she fell asleep.

———————

"Get her out of there," said Ernie.

"She's asleep."

"So wake her! Are you nuts? You want to write your ticket out of the department?"

Huck looked at Megan, who was lying on his sofa, curled up with her head in the crook of her elbow. The topknot of hair left her long neck exposed, smooth and mapley. He knew this was against everything he'd been taught, but something told him it was going to be necessary to break the rules here.

"I'll come over," said Ernie. "I'll wake her up."

"No, you won't. She's exhausted."

"Does Frank know she's there?"

"No."

Ernie groaned. "He'll fucking hit the roof, Arthur! Call him. Now. Call him and tell him to come get her."

"Not a good idea."

"Why not?"

"Because if we start passing her around like a kid, she's going to bolt, and she's got some good information. Hey. Do you remember a guy named Bill?"

"I know a lot of guys named Bill," said Ernie.

"A guy her age," said Huck. "Wasn't there somebody up at the house that night? Telling us about Diana doing drugs?"

"Oh."

"Did we ever talk to him again?" asked Huck.

"No, but he's been calling. He keeps wanting to set up a meeting."

"What for?"

"He says he knows somebody who might be upset with Diana for owing him money."

"You think he's credible?"

"Nope."

"Why not?"

"He's looking for attention," said Ernie. "Trying to cash in on the excitement. Why are you bringing him up, anyway?"

"He's the one who took the pictures."

Ernie was silent.

"I'm going to give his name to Peter," Huck went on, referring to a colleague who had been working with the FBI on the child-porn case.

"Fine," said Ernie, "although I wouldn't waste much time on it. Is she awake yet?"

"No, she's not awake! She's sound asleep, and that's how she's going to stay until she wakes up on her own."

"We've got a meeting with the chief at ten," Ernie said. "What are you going to do with her then?"

"I don't know. I'll cross that bridge when it's time. And you don't need to go blabbing about this," said Huck. "In fact nobody at the department needs to know about this."

Ernie groaned again.

"Agreed?"

"Fine. I'm only doing this, you know, because—actually I don't know why."

"You're my friend."

"No, I'm not. You're such a fuckup. I can't believe what a fuckup you are."

"Love the trust," said Huck.

"I'm older than you."

"Age before beauty," said Huck.

"Speaking of which, are you going by Griffin's?"

"What do you want?"

"Toasted sesame with lite cream cheese."

"Getting serious about the weight?"

"Oh, leave me alone," said Ernie.

At nine o'clock Megan remained tightly curled on her side, drooling a little into the crook of her elbow. Huck draped a light blanket over her. In the kitchen he wrote out a note telling her where he had gone, instructing her once again to call her father when she woke up. Then he left.

The chief of police wanted an update on Steven O'Connell: mainly, why did he visit Diana's clinic the morning of December 17?

Why did he and Diana go over to the hospital? Huck let Ernie answer this one; he didn't like to be the one to tell a superior that they didn't have much. Steven O'Connell had taken his family to Costa Rica right after Christmas. All they'd gotten from him before he left was that as a minister he'd simply had a few things to say to Diana that morning about one of his constituents. Yes, they had gone over to the hospital together later that morning. No, he would not disclose what it was about. No, he would not give names.

"I want more. Get a warrant if you have to. In the meantime go talk to the hospital," said Stan.

"Without a warrant they won't give us dipshit," said Ernie.

"Just talk to the nurses. Ask them if they saw Steven and Diana together. Ask them what they were talking about. What's happening with the e-mails?"

"Funny you should ask," said Ernie, "because just this morning Frank forwarded a new one." He told the chief about the message Megan had received from allgodschildren. Huck perked up. He didn't know about this.

"Who wrote it?" asked Stan.

"We're checking," said Ernie.

"That would be nice," Stan mused.

"Don't get your hopes up," said Ernie. "There are probably hundreds of messages out there, and without anything else it's going to be hard to link one particular message writer to whoever took a swim with Diana Duprey on December seventeenth."

"What about that woman who used to picket the house?"

"Eve Kelly. She's got an alibi," said Ernie.

"And the housecleaner?"

"Alibi."

The chief of police shook his head. "So what we've got are the fingerprints—"

"Which are Frank and Megan's," said Ernie.

"And the fingernail scrapings—"

"Which are Frank's."

"And the testimony of the neighbor that Frank came home pissed off—"

"—ballistic—"

"—in the context of his having just seen some fairly disturbing images a few minutes earlier."

"Correct."

"And Frank won't give us an alibi."

"No."

"What's he holding out for?"

"Doesn't make sense," Ernie agreed. "The guy knows he's at the top of our list, but he won't say where he was."

Huck cleared his throat. Ernie and Stan both looked at him. Up until now he'd kept quiet.

"So?" said Stan.

"Am I the only one who thinks we're jumping on Frank too quickly?"

"Want to elaborate?"

"It just seems too easy," said Huck. "For instance, nobody's talked to Piper McMahon."

"The coroner? Why her? Oh. Right. That was ages ago," Stan said.

"I think Huck has a point," Ernie said. "We should at least eliminate the possibility that she harbored some deep-down resentment."

Stan Wolfowitz shrugged. "You want to talk to Piper, it's fine with me. Listen," he said, leaning forward in his chair, "I'm not looking to pin this thing on Frank. I don't hold grudges, and I don't want to see a good man go down on a murder rap. But we're three blind men with an elephant right here in front of us, and it's not the time to go off chasing moonbeams. But hey, talk to Piper if you want. Keep looking into those e-mails. And go to the hospital, pronto. Talk to the staff.

Find out why Steven O'Connell was at the hospital with Diana that morning." He swiveled in his seat and tossed the remains of a muffin into the trash. Huck and Ernie stood to leave.

"I'm not looking to nail Frank," said Stan as they left. "But I am looking to nail somebody."

After the meeting Huck went back to his desk and checked his messages. As he feared, there was nothing from Megan, and when he called home, he was reminded that his phone had been disconnected. There was, however, a message on his office line from Bill Branson, wanting to set up a meeting. Huck told his secretary to arrange a time for Bill to come in, and then he and Ernie headed over to the hospital.

Huck wasn't sure if it was the smell or the bluish glare or simply the banal signs of everyday commerce—balloons, flowers, teddy bears—that made him uncomfortable in hospitals. All he knew for sure was that every time he walked through the doors—and it wasn't infrequent; you couldn't be a cop without being in and out of the emergency room—he wanted to walk right out again.

They did not learn very much from the emergency room staff. One of the nurses acknowledged that Diana and Steven had been in the morning of Diana's death, looking for one of Diana's patients, but when Huck asked who, the nurse reminded him she could not disclose names.

"Where'd they go?"

"We sent them up to Surgery," she said priggishly. "Don't use my name."

The nurse in Surgery was equally reticent. "All I can say is that yes, they were here," she finally allowed. She was a middle-aged woman, with hooded eyes that made her look older and sadder than she probably was.

"Was Diana doing the surgery?" asked Huck.

The nurse pursed her lips. Huck glanced at Ernie.

"You don't have to get specific, ma'am," Ernie said, "but did something go wrong?"

"I can't say that," said the nurse.

"But a lot of things can go wrong, can't they?"

"They can, but they don't," said the nurse. "Not when Dr. Duprey is handling things."

"But if something does go wrong, I guess it can be pretty serious?"

"It can be."

"As in what?"

The nurse looked impatient. "Most often the woman begins to hemorrhage."

"From what?"

The nurse shrugged. "Lots of things. Of course, a perforated uterus is a good place to start."

"And what happens to a patient with a perforated uterus?"

"That depends. At best you recover. At worst you die. In between you might need a hysterectomy."

"Which would make you infertile?"

The nurse smiled bemusedly, as though Ernie hadn't learned eighth-grade biology. Ernie began to nod. "Which would be very upsetting," he said. "Right? And not just for the woman but for her husband as well?"

"Was the woman's husband there?" Huck asked.

The nurse held up her hands and shook her head. "If you want this kind of detail, you'll have to go through our lawyers."

"We're not asking you to tell us who the woman was," Huck said. "But people can get very emotional in an emergency. We're just wondering if this was the case with Dr. Duprey that morning."

"I have no idea."

"But you were there, weren't you?" said Ernie.

The nurse hesitated, then glanced over her shoulder and

motioned for them to step out of the central recovery area and into the hallway. "Look," she said in a low voice, "who do you think most of Dr. Duprey's patients are? They're babies themselves. If they don't have husbands or boyfriends, they've got parents. Do you see where I'm going?"

Mentally Huck began to draft a search warrant.

"Frankly, I was wondering why no one had come by to talk to us," the nurse said. "This has been in the back of my mind for an entire month."

"So the parents were upset," said Huck. "Are we talking verbal exchanges here? Physical?"

The nurse checked her watch and said she had to get back to work. But she hesitated, clutching herself as if cold.

"The father was upset," she said. "That's all I'll say."

That afternoon, while Ernie drafted search warrants to get access to hospital records, Huck drove downtown to the coroner's office. They were taking too long with the full autopsy report, and Huck hoped his presence might inspire them to hurry up. In view of Megan's comment that morning, he also wanted to simply shoot the breeze with Piper. While he doubted Piper was the type to explode with jealousy years after an affair, he felt obliged to substantiate that hunch, if only to be able to assure Megan they'd checked things out.

At two-fifteen Huck walked into Piper's office, only to find Piper leaning face-first into the wall, pushing with all her strength as though holding back a dam. Warm-up jacket, tights, running shoes: she was stretching, and Huck wondered if there was anybody in this town besides Ernie who didn't consider a noontime jog up a mountain a normal way to spend a lunch hour. He pitied outsiders when they visited. If ever there was a way to feel out of shape!

Piper glanced over her shoulder at Huck, then pushed ferociously. "Talk to John," she said to her navel. "It's not my case."

"When is he going to be finished?"

"Any day now."

"Anything new?"

Piper pushed off the wall and dropped her head between her knees. "No. Cause of death was a subdural hematoma, same as always." She stood up, her face beet red, and went over to her desk, where she pulled open the bottom drawer and removed a water bottle and a funnel and a little Baggie of white powder.

"Chief's getting antsy," Huck offered.

Piper funneled the powder into the water bottle. "If he wants a report that'll hold up in court, he's going to have to chill."

"Actually, I didn't just come about the autopsy," he said, watching her shake the bottle. "Can I ask you something?"

"Ask whatever you want. I don't know if I'll answer, though."

"You were friends with Frank," Huck began.

"Yes, I was," she declared.

"Pretty good friends," Huck added.

Piper held his gaze.

"What's your take on his temper? Think he was capable?"

"Any man's capable."

"Help me out, Piper."

Piper sat down in her desk chair and bent over and unlaced her shoes. Huck was afraid she was going to take them off with him right there in the room, and take them off she did, and yes, a woman's feet could smell as bad as a man's.

Then Piper sat up and placed her hands squarely on her thighs. "Let me tell you about the kind of family Frank came from. You know what a Boston Brahmin is? His father was a state senator. His mother ran the Junior Service League. They lived in a town house on Beacon

Hill, and when his father came home at five o'clock, his mother had a pitcher of martinis waiting for him. When one of them got angry, they smiled and walked out of the room. When Frank moved out here, they smiled and never spoke to him again."

"How do you know all this?"

Piper sighed. "Frank and I were lovers, Huck. Okay? Is that really news to you? It was a long time ago. Right after his son died. He didn't know how to grieve and was keeping it all inside, and with me he was able to let some of it out. It's water over the dam, though," she said. *"Capisce?"*

"Did Diana know?"

"Of course she knew. She didn't care, though. Now *there's* a person who could grieve. Boy, could she grieve. Unlike Frank, who just lost weight. Speaking of which." She opened up a foil-wrapped burrito and took an enormous bite, saturating the room with the smell of onion.

"How did it end, if I may ask?"

"No fanfare," she said with her mouth full. "We just stopped seeing each other. And we stayed friends. Good friends. Ever have that?"

"Have what?"

"A friendship with someone you used to love."

"Of course," Huck lied.

"Then you know what I'm talking about. There are a lot of ways to fall in and out of love, don't you think?"

Huck found it presumptuous for her to be giving him advice about love. They hardly knew each other. He flashed on Carolyn, the way she smiled with her mouth turned down.

"I figured you guys would come and talk to me eventually," Piper went on, wiping her mouth. "I figured you'd toss around the theory that I was jealous after all these years. Don't waste your time, Huck," she said, not unkindly.

"When do you think you'll have the final report?" he asked gruffly.

"Any day now," said Piper. "It's not going to have any surprises in it. I know people expect it to, but it won't. And Huck?"

"What?"

"I can see Frank finally exploding," she said. "I can see him throwing a glass across the room. But I can't see him going so far as to do what you think he did."

With a squint, Huck signaled that he would consider this.

"Thanks," he said.

"Don't thank me," she replied. "Thank Frank."

"What for?"

"For putting up with guys like you," she said.

———

It was after seven by the time he pulled into his driveway that evening. Lights blazed from every window, and he could hear the pulsing bass of hip-hop music. Inside he found Megan on the sofa, sitting cross-legged with an open textbook in her lap. She set down her highlighter.

"Hot day on the trail, honey?" she asked brightly.

Huck went directly into the kitchen and turned off the radio and opened the refrigerator and got a beer. He still felt slightly panicked at seeing her here, as he had this morning, but no longer did it have anything to do with breach-of-conduct issues.

"What happened with Eve Kelly?" Megan called.

He came back into the living room. There was no place else to sit besides the sofa, so he stood. "Megan," he said, "leave the investigation to us."

"What about Piper? Did you talk to her?"

"I did, but like I said. It's not your job. And I can't tell you anything."

"Did you know your phone is out of order?" said Megan. "I ended up using my cell to order pizza. Do you happen to have money, though? All I've got is my father's credit card, which I'm only supposed to use in case of emergency. I don't think this qualifies," she added ruefully.

"Did you call your father?"

"No," said Megan.

"You said you would!"

Megan shrugged. "He can call me if he wants."

"Megan, look," said Huck. "You can't stay here. I could lose my job. You must have a friend's house you could go to. You grew up here, you have to have friends."

"They're all off on vacation with their families. My good friends, anyway."

"Then get a hotel."

"Like Motel Six?"

"There's still nothing else?"

"Everything else is booked up with reporters," she said.

Reporters who are going to be showing up here any moment, Huck thought. He wondered why they weren't already here, in fact. He went to the windows and was in the process of lowering the blinds when the doorbell rang.

"There's the pizza." Megan started to get up, but Huck waved her back down. He went out to the hallway and opened the door. There stood a young man with a black woolen beanie pulled tightly over his head.

"Bill Branson," he said, holding out his hand. "I believe we've met?"

CHAPTER TEN

OVERALL MEGAN CONSIDERED herself a calm, responsible, and socially mature individual. Having brokered many a compromise when her parents fought over what she could and couldn't do as a child, she felt she had a knack for dissolving tensions whenever they began to thicken. Which was why she'd ordered the pizza and even teased Huck a little when he walked in the door that night. Granted it was a little manipulative, but she was sure that if she could only get him to relax, then he wouldn't kick her out of his house.

But when Megan looked up and saw none other than Bill Branson standing on Huck's doorstep, she lost it—not only did she cry out in surprise, but the cry itself sounded like the kind of yelp her brother used to make when things didn't go his way.

Peering around Huck, Bill puppeted his eyebrows up and down.

"Why hello, Megg-Ann," he called. "Didn't know you two were on a first-name basis. Can I come in?" he asked, and Huck, to Megan's great consternation, stepped aside and let Bill actually enter his house.

"*Darn* you're looking comfortable," Bill said to Megan. "Hope I'm not interrupting anything. Bill Branson," he said again, clearing his throat, and this time he took off his gloves and offered his hand to Huck. Huck shook it. Cold air lapped at Megan's bare feet.

"It's late," Huck said. "What do you want?"

"I'm here to see you, detective."

Megan suspected that was not the case.

"It can't wait until tomorrow?"

"I can't seem to get ahold of you during the day," Bill said. "You're a busy man. I left you a couple of messages, but you didn't call back. Not that I'm criticizing. I know you've got a lot to do. But I felt it was important to speak with you sooner rather than later. I hope you don't mind that I showed up at your house. You're a hard guy to track down. Here, mind if I shut the door so we don't let all this cold air in?"

Huck obliged him, which infuriated Megan. Didn't he know that once the door was shut, Bill would never leave?

"So what's this about?" asked Huck.

Bill smoothed the new growth of a mustache. "I don't know if Megan should be in on this," he confided.

"Cut the crap, Bill," said Megan.

"Megan can stay," said Huck.

"It's not going to be easy for her," Bill said.

"Just tell me what you came to tell me," said Huck.

"Okay, then," said Bill. "It has to do with Dr. Duprey, of course. Specifically, about her use of recreational drugs." He waved at Megan to be silent. "I have some names, names of people she dealt with these past couple of months. Maybe your department knows about them. Remember that meth lab you guys busted up last fall? Guys had to go in in hazmat suits? Well, sorry, but you only got the lackeys." He handed Huck a piece of paper. "These are the guys who run the show. Plus a few of their customers."

"And how do you know these people?"

"Through a friend of a friend," Bill explained. "See, my roommate and I were talking one night, and he was telling me about this friend who owned a meth lab. And this friend of his had told him he was selling to this abortion doctor. He was getting a real kick out of the fact that here was this prominent lady doctor getting high in the privacy of her own office while everyone in town thought she was such a saint."

"That is so full of shit," said Megan. "That is just *so* full of shit, Huck."

Bill glared at her. "And how many times did you see your mother wearing short-sleeved shirts in the past couple of months? Scary, isn't it," he said to Huck, "these people who have good jobs and live in nice houses and use their remodeled bathrooms for shooting up."

Huck scanned the list of names. "So Diana's name is on this list. So what?"

Bill nodded, as though he'd anticipated the question. "See, I'm at my desk studying one night last fall, and my roommate's friend comes over and he's high as a kite, and he starts talking about all the people who owe him money. People who won't pay up, and what he's going to do to them. And he mentioned a couple of very mean things. And after he left, I found this list."

"It's total bullshit," Megan told Huck. "He's just trying to find an excuse to be with me. My mother wasn't doing meth, you fuckface," she said to Bill.

Bill squinted. "Like you know her so well? If that's the case, how come the two of you talked a total of three times since you left for college?"

"It was way more than three times," Megan retorted, "and besides, we wanted it that way. Don't we have a stalking law in this state?" she asked Huck.

"Megan, Megan," sighed Bill. "Have I ever hurt you? Have I ever done anything really, really wrong?"

Megan's mind raced furiously back through the e-mails. She

thought of the phone calls and the roses and the teddy bears and the way Natalie felt sorry for him and took him out for drinks in September and came back and told Megan he was going to be all right, it would just take time. Had Bill ever hit her? Threatened her? She had no real case, and she knew enough about the law to know that you couldn't get somebody arrested just because you were sick of him mooning over you.

"You seem to know quite a bit about Diana," said Huck.

"Diana was a sweetheart," said Bill. "Look. I'll be honest. I've had a hard time getting over Megan. We were very, very close, if you know what I mean. So when Megan ended things, I kind of went off the deep end. And Diana helped me out. A *lot.* I could talk to her. She understood how I felt. But she also shared a lot with me. I told her meth was an ugly, ugly drug and she should get herself into treatment if she couldn't stop using. She appreciated my concern. We helped each other out."

"He's making this entire thing up," Megan told Huck.

"Talk to the dealer," Bill advised. "You'd be very, very surprised."

"And this is his list?" Huck said.

"It is indeed."

"His handwriting?"

"Indeed."

"Can I keep it?"

"Indeed," said Bill.

"How can I get in touch with you?" Huck asked.

"Here, let me write my phone number down." He took back the list and scribbled his name on it in pencil. Then he handed it back to Huck. "Look. I'm sorry to bother you guys. I didn't mean to interrupt anything."

"See what I mean?" Megan demanded. "He's not here to help, he's here to snoop on me. How did you know I was here, anyway?"

"Maybe you should park your car somewhere other than the parking lot of the firehouse," said Bill. "That is, if you don't want reporters coming by. Well. I hope this helps. You call me if you have any questions, detective. Day or night."

When he was gone, Megan leaped off the sofa. "Oh my god, he's such a *toad*! He's such a *slimeball*! I was out of my *mind* to ever go out with him! Oh my *god*, why can't he just *forget* about me?"

"Megan," said Huck, "you need to call your father."

"I can't!" wailed Megan. "Oh, what is *wrong* with him? My mother just *died*, for god's sake, and he still won't leave me *alone*. I wish he would just drop off the face of this *planet!*"

"Please call your father," said Huck. "You can't stay here. Reporters are going to have a field day with this, not to mention my boss."

"Fine," wept Megan. "Gimme my phone."

She knew he was right, she knew she shouldn't be staying here. Any minute now a reporter was going to see her car and come knocking on Huck's door. The whole thing would look very, very bad.

But she couldn't bear to go back to her father, either. How could she explain her confusion—her fear that her father had done the unthinkable, versus her conviction that he hadn't? What did you do when trust and suspicion were all knotted up in one big family rat's nest?

And so when her father didn't answer either his cell or his hotel-room phone, Megan was relieved.

"Don't fall asleep on me again!" Huck warned as she sank down on the sofa.

"Like I could sleep right now," said Megan ruefully. "I am like so wired I couldn't sleep if you gave me a Valium. And by the way, my mother was not doing meth, I guarantee you."

"Any other drugs that she might owe money on? Because sometimes—well, I know a lot of doctors use. They're up all night, they're busy, it's right there within reach."

Megan flashed on the bottle of Dexedrine her mother kept in the glove compartment of her car. Six years ago Diana had fallen asleep while driving. They'd gotten up at five in the morning for an out-of-town swim meet and were cruising east on a long straight stretch of highway when suddenly a loud vibration startled them both. Megan shouted, and Diana swerved back into the right lane. Shaken, she had to pull off the road to regain her composure, but after that incident she got a prescription for the pills. As far as Megan knew, she only used them to stay awake while driving.

The police didn't need to know this, Megan thought. "My mother smoked a little pot, but she wasn't a speed freak," she said. "I have to go pee."

"Go pee. I'm going to make some dinner," sighed Huck.

"I ordered pizza," Megan reminded him.

"I don't feel like pizza," Huck said.

Megan went into the bathroom, glad for a moment alone to clear her thoughts. She turned on the fan and sat down and peed. For a guy, he kept an awfully neat bathroom, she thought. The towels hung straight, and the counter was free of clutter, and there was even a sprig of dried flowers hanging on the wall behind the toilet.

She got up and washed her hands, then dried them on the little guest towel—surely something his girlfriend put up, she thought. She wondered who his girlfriend was. There were no pictures around, but the flowers and ruffles in the house suggested someone plumpish and nursy. Maybe someone from the Midwest. She reminded herself it was none of her business.

She paused, listening, then quietly opened the top drawer by the sink. There was a hairbrush, an electric razor, a wrinkled tube of ointment "for use on rash as directed," several toothbrushes, toothpaste, a stick of Arrid, Vaseline, Rolaids, Murine, Advil, and Dr. Scholl's foot powder. She opened the second drawer and found a neat stack of washcloths, along with a zippered makeup kit containing pink lip-stick and black mascara and a tube of concealer. Tucked behind this was a box of Trojans. No surprises, no revelations.

Then she opened the bottom drawer, which contained a messy jumble of cords and instruction manuals and loose Q-tips and cotton balls. But toward the back she saw a bundle of something tied together with a blue ribbon. Curious, she pushed aside the cords to remove what was a stack of linen handkerchiefs, each one pressed to a sheen and embroidered white on white with the initials *AHB*. The fabric felt silky soft and cool, like fancy sheets in summer.

From out in the kitchen came the banging of pots. Hastily she tucked the handkerchiefs back and closed the drawer. Not that she'd done anything wrong. Everyone looked in other people's drawers. Still, she had the feeling she'd violated his privacy—not because she'd snooped around in his girlfriend's makeup but because she'd found this gift, this labor of love by someone important in his past, someone who had sent a loved one off into the wide world, secure in the belief she'd outfitted him with the proper essentials.

She flushed the toilet and returned to the kitchen and saw that the pizza had arrived. She'd lost her appetite. Huck was stirring a pot of ramen noodles.

"Call your father," he told her.

Megan dialed the hotel, but there was no answer. She tried his cell but found it still turned off, which now made her feel rejected even though she didn't want to talk to him.

"Noodles or pizza?" Huck asked.

She wanted neither. There was an open bottle of Dos Equis on the table, and without thinking she picked it up and took a swallow. Only afterward did she realize she'd just committed a crime right in front of a cop. Oh well, she thought, at least the jail had beds.

Huck didn't seem concerned, however. He set a bowl of steaming noodles on the table, got a folding stool from the broom closet, and sat down across the table from her. The stool was too high, and his knees bumped up against the table.

"Have some pizza," he said.

"I'm not hungry."

Huck shrugged and slurped his noodles.

"This is a nice little place," Megan offered.

"Thank you."

"How long have you lived here?"

"Five years."

Megan did the calculation in her mind. "So I guess that means you moved in here when I was fourteen."

"I guess," said Huck.

"I'm nineteen now," she added. "So."

"So," he agreed.

"So how old are you?"

Huck eyed her as if to say, You gotta be kidding.

"Thirty?" she asked. "Thirty-one?"

Huck allowed a smile to flicker in his eyes. "I'm twenty-six."

"Where's your girlfriend?"

"She's in Minnesota right now," Huck replied. "Her mother's been sick."

"That's too bad."

"Not really sick," added Huck.

"Oh. Good."

Huck ladled more liquid into the bowl.

"What does she do?" she asked.

"She's a software analyst."

"Must be smart."

"She's smart," Huck agreed.

"Was she the one who put up the dried flowers in the bathroom? I wasn't snooping," she added, noticing his quizzical glance. "They're hanging right over your toilet."

Huck did not reply. What was wrong with this man? she wondered. Did he not know how to carry on a conversation? "So what's her name?"

"Her name," said Huck, "is Carolyn."

"Where does she live?"

"Across town."

"How'd you meet her?"

Huck set down his spoon. "Megan," he said, "you can ask me about the case. You can ask me about police procedure. You can even ask me how I decided to become a cop, if you want. But don't ask about my personal life. Try your father again."

Megan felt ashamed, insulted, and angry all at once. She dialed the hotel again. Still no answer. She hung up and took another sip of his beer, no longer caring that she was in the presence of an officer of the law. Truth be told, she thought he was rude not to offer her one of her own.

"Bet you're pretty curious about me," she said, pausing with the bottle at her lips, "after that little scene with Bill."

"I'm only curious about what Bill might know," said Huck.

"Sure. I'll bet you're curious about the pictures," she said. "Who wouldn't be? What a dumbass thing to do. Talk about doing things on a whim. Did you ever do something on a whim?"

Huck glanced up.

"You should, sometime," Megan continued. "Nothing wrong with a whim. Just don't make it be something as dumbass as posing for pictures with a guy you shouldn't trust."

Huck smiled. "We all do things on a whim, I guess."

"Including you?"

"Sure. I guess. I'm human."

"Can't really see it," she said. Then, in the midst of the ensuing silence, she added, "What's a whim, anyway? Just something you know you shouldn't do, right?"

She looked at him then, and this time their eyes locked. In the next millisecond, they both reached for the beer, and when she felt the dual sensations, the dry warmth of his fingertips mingled with the cold glass bottle, she felt a wild spark shoot up her arm, as though she'd shorted out a wire within. She looked away, not believing what she had just done. And then just as quickly looked back at Huck, who had not broken his gaze at all. For a minute she thought he was angry with her, his eyes were that intense, but then they softened, and he shifted his legs and ran his fingers through his hair.

"Let's not even go there, Megan," he said quietly.

"Right," she said. "Why not?" she said.

"Because I can't."

"Because of her?"

"Because of her. Because of work. Because of a lot of things."

Megan folded her hands in front of her. He was right. She felt her face turn hot as her heart began to pound. She stood up, then, to get her cell phone from her backpack in the living room. But as she passed him, he suddenly reached out and hooked his fingers into hers, stopping her, and before she knew it he'd slid off the stool and pulled her against him. She felt the warmth of his broad chest, the shivery lightness of his fingers on the back of her neck. They both hesitated. He kissed her once, tentatively. And then he kissed her long and deep, and she stirred within, and the only thing she could think was, I've overstepped the boundaries, I've gone where I shouldn't go, and at the same time, I want this, want it and can't stop it. She didn't know who was playing with whom, or even if they were playing at all.

It was Huck who pulled away. Head bowed, eyes looking everywhere and nowhere all at once. He pressed his hands heavily upon her shoulders and finally sucked in a deep breath.

"Call your father," he said hoarsely.

But she could not reach her father. She lied, finally, and told Huck she suddenly remembered a friend who was home. He said okay, sure, that was a good thing. And so before either of them could change their minds, she slipped into her shoes and pulled on her sweatshirt and gathered together her books, her backpack, and her car keys. Outside it was cold and clear and she felt both unshackled and disconnected. On empty streets she drove around for a while, trying to think of someone else from high school she knew well enough to drop in on unannounced at this hour. But she could think of nobody. Finally she drove to her dorm and parked her car and got out and walked around the old brick building. In the back was a dirty basement window to the laundry room. She squatted down on the frozen dirt and pried open the aluminum frame. It opened easily. There was a screen on the inside, which she pulled off. Squeezing through, she dropped down into the darkened laundry room and felt her way to the door, then to the stairs; and with a fist punching her chest she climbed three flights to the safety of her own room, where she was, and he wasn't, and where she could punish herself for all the things she'd done or said that might have tripped things off, making two unsuspecting people want something they simply couldn't have.

CHAPTER ELEVEN

———————

T HE NEXT MORNING Huck managed while shaving to cut himself twice. Then while making coffee he poured a carafe of water all over the counter. On his way to work he ran a stop sign. You fool, he thought. At headquarters nobody seemed to suspect anything out of the ordinary, which gave him some confidence, so that by seven-fifteen he'd taken care of a mountain of paperwork and sketched out a list of questions for Steven O'Connell, whom they were going to interview today. When Ernie came in at a quarter to eight, Huck was able to greet his partner with the wide-eyed grin of a man who has slept like a baby all night long.

"You look like shit," Ernie remarked as he set down a bag of pastries.

Huck realized he'd left the two little clots of tissue on his chin. He peeled them off.

"That girl isn't still at your place, is she?" Ernie demanded.

"No," Huck murmured, in a way he hoped would suggest distraction by more important matters. But he felt Ernie's eyes scrutinizing his face, so he raised his eyebrows and shrugged. "Go see for yourself. She found another place to stay. What's in the bag?"

"Danish," growled Ernie.

"Gimme one."

Ernie handed him the bag, and Huck took out a huge pastry topped with loose streusel which, when bit into, rained crumbs all over his desk.

"You're late," Huck noted.

"One of us has a teenage daughter, and it's not you."

"What's going on?"

Ernie scowled. "Just a boyfriend who's two years older than she is. Do you remember what you wanted when you were eighteen? Yeah. Okay then. And does my daughter comprehend what she is doing when she wears these little spaghetti-strap tops with jeans that don't even come up to here? Does she have any clue?"

"Boarding school?" Huck suggested.

"Don't get me started," said Ernie glumly.

"You know, I didn't lose my virginity until I was eighteen," Huck remarked.

"*That* helps."

"I'm just saying it doesn't always happen when you're underage, is all."

"Well, *I* was underage," moped Ernie.

"Does she know that?"

"Are you nuts?"

"Have you thought of telling her?"

"Why would I do a thing like that?"

"I don't know. Make yourself seem human. You could shed some light on what it was like."

"It sucked."

"See? Maybe if she heard it from you—"

Just then the phone rang. Ernie picked it up. He spoke briefly, then hung up. "Finally. The DNA report's in."

"And it's Frank's?"

"Yup."

"Which we knew, of course," said Huck.

"Yup."

Huck frowned, recalling Megan's initial reason for coming to his apartment.

"What, you're surprised?" asked Ernie.

"No," said Huck, "but I still wonder if we're jumping to conclusions on Frank."

Ernie shook out the newspaper and disappeared. "Guy comes home screaming at his wife and throws a glass across the room and there's enough skin under her fingernails to suggest some kind of a struggle, and you really don't think it was him?"

"It could mean other things."

"Like what?"

"Maybe they had sex."

Ernie tipped his head back and roared with laughter.

"What?" said Huck, wounded.

"Oh, Arthur," said Ernie, "you are just too fucking young sometimes."

"Who says you can't be passionate after twenty years?"

"Ha ha," said Ernie. "Ha ha ha ha ha. You fool."

Huck balled up the greasy paper bag and shot it straight into the wastebasket. "Plus, I got a list from that guy named Bill."

"List of what?"

"Meth dealers and their customers. He claims Diana owed some people some money. Which could give us a motive."

"You think he's credible?"

"I think we have to check it out."

"Fine. You do it," said Ernie.

Huck, who didn't relish the idea of talking to meth dealers, made a mental note to delegate this to the guys over in Narcotics. "What about the voice on the answering-machine tape? Did we get a positive ID yet?"

"Nope. A total long shot too."

"And we still don't know who Diana's patient was in the hospital that morning," Huck pointed out.

"We'll find out. Aren't we supposed to talk to Steven this morning?"

"Eleven o'clock."

"Think he's going to volunteer much?"

"You never know," said Huck.

"You really look like shit, you know," Ernie remarked. "What were you doing last night?"

Having phone sex, Huck wanted to say. "Sleeping. Alone. How about you?"

Ernie sighed. "Wondering how to convince my daughter that it's not normal to go around baring your midriff in the middle of January. You've got it so easy."

Huck stood up and writhed into his sweatshirt. He swallowed the rest of his coffee and tucked a notebook into his back pocket. Walking out, he congratulated himself for putting up enough of a front that Ernie suspected nothing.

Which was how it was supposed to be, given that there wasn't anything to suspect.

———

Shortly afterward, the two men parked their car on the side of a tree-lined residential street and walked up the sidewalk to Steven O'Connell's house. It was a large old house, built of wood and stucco, and it was well kept, with clean-swept eaves and unstreaked windows that neatly reflected the low January sun.

The thing that had always bothered Huck about Steven O'Connell was the fact that he called himself a reverend but had no church. Huck had to wonder about a man who lived so well without an apparent source of income. Exhibit A, the house. Exhibit B, the Mercedes. Exhibit C, the fact that he could take his entire family to Costa Rica. Where did he get his money? As they walked up the steps to the house, Huck struggled to remind himself that a person's independent wealth did not a criminal make.

Ernie knocked. Momentarily the door was answered by Steven's wife, Trudy. She was a small woman with a poodly perm; dressed in gray sweats, she looked tired and puffy, not at all like someone who'd just returned from a few weeks in Costa Rica.

"Steven!" she yelled over her shoulder. "You guys," she said, shaking her head. "Can't you even wait until we've had a chance to unpack and take a shower?"

She led them into the living room, where she removed bundles of leaflets from the sofa to make room for Huck and Ernie. The room had a parlorish feel, like it wasn't used very often; it was painted yellow, with cream-colored trim and brocade drapes in the windows. As they waited for Steven, Huck perused a cluster of family photos on the wall, amused by one of a very young and very long-haired Steven playing a guitar in a geriatric ward.

Then, like a draft of air, Steven himself seemed to materialize from nowhere. He was dressed in khaki pants and a pink button-down shirt.

"Let it not be said that the law enforcement officers in this town are not prompt," he said cheerfully.

"How was Costa Rica?" asked Ernie.

"Stupendous," said Steven. "Although traveling with teenagers has its own challenges. Please, sit down. When we flew in last night," he began, lowering himself into a deep leather chair, "I was hoping

I'd wake up this morning and read in the papers that you'd made an arrest. Tell me where things stand. How can I help?"

Huck reminded himself that Steven was an orator, and orators were actors; so it should come as no surprise that Steven was able to put on a show of earnest cooperation.

"Actually, Steven, we've got a few questions about your relationship with Diana," Ernie said.

"A very intelligent woman," said Steven.

"Yes, well. We understand you met with her the morning of her death."

"I did," said Steven.

"But she's got a restraining order against you."

"That's correct."

"Well, that interests me," said Ernie. "Let's talk about this for a minute. Why'd she need a restraining order?"

Steven's face remained pleasant.

"I'm assuming it had to do with the bubble law, right?" Ernie went on. "Weren't you arrested last summer?"

"I have an ongoing duty to make sure her patients understand what they're about to do," Steven replied.

"Just not within eight feet."

"Correct."

"But you went right up to the door with one woman, last summer."

"She asked for a brochure," Steven said. "I was only complying with her wishes."

"By then padlocking yourself to the railing?"

"Do you want to get into a general discussion of nonviolent protest?" asked Steven. "Because if you do, I've an entire box of literature you might like to read."

"I'm just trying to understand why Dr. Duprey got the restraining order," said Ernie. "Nothing more, nothing less."

"Well, read the court papers, then. I'm a busy man. Thank you, dear," Steven said as Trudy set down a tray of coffee mugs.

Huck sensed Ernie's threshold dropping. He did not want them to blow this interview. "I think what we're trying to get at concerns the morning of Diana's death," he explained. "You showed up at the clinic that morning, which violated not only the bubble law but the terms of the restraining order. We're just wondering why you went."

Steven sipped his coffee. "That's confidential."

"You want to explain how?" Huck said. "Doctor-patient? Clergy-communicant?"

"Doesn't matter, it's still confidential," Steven said.

Now Huck found his own patience wearing thin. It was clear Steven felt backed up against the wall, but Huck wished the man would realize that any lack of forthrightness now wasn't going to make the law go away. He decided to give it one last try. "People at the clinic have said that you were fairly upset that morning," he said. "You want to elaborate?"

"No," said Steven. "As a matter of fact, I do not."

"You were upset, though."

"I said I'm not going to elaborate."

"How about over at the hospital? You were pretty upset there too."

"Look, detectives. My being upset that day had nothing to do with Diana's death. Now—"

But before he could finish, Trudy, who'd just poured some cream into Ernie's mug of coffee, slammed the carton back down on the tray. "You people are *so off base!*"

"Trudy," Steven began.

"They are! Honestly, Steven! When are you going to give up the notion that Jack and Elaine are going to save your ass and come forward themselves?"

Huck took a notebook and pen from his pocket.

"You need to talk to *them*," Trudy told Huck. "*They're* the ones who had the bone to pick with Diana. Don't you guys do your homework? Haven't you talked to the surgery team over at the hospital?"

"Trudy," Steven began again.

"Shut up, Steven. I'm sick of walking around this town feeling like all eyes are upon you and me. His name is Jack Fries," she told Huck. "His wife's name is Elaine. They're the people to talk to. If they haven't left town, that is. And to think that they might have been part of our family at one time! I guess God has his reasons, doesn't he?"

"Jack Fries on the school board?" asked Ernie.

"Yes, and why he has a problem with an abstinence-only program is beyond me. Look what it might have done for Rose," she added.

Steven was glancing into his lap. Only when Huck saw his lips moving did he realize that the man was praying. Immediately he felt his guard rise. Not being religious, he always feared the conversional motives of those who were.

"Rose made her own decisions, Trudy," Steven reminded her.

"Who is Rose?" asked Ernie.

"Jack Fries's daughter," said Trudy. "She's fifteen. She was dating our son Scott. Need I say more?"

Steven cleared his throat. "Rose was with child."

"The man wouldn't even let us have a funeral for the baby," Trudy said bitterly. "As if we had no interest! How some people can be so cruel and selfish and—and—determinative."

"All we wanted was a service," Steven added. " 'For thou didst form my inward parts; thou didst knit me together in my mother's womb.' "

"Scott was devastated," Trudy told Huck.

" 'Before I formed you in the womb I knew you, and before you were born I consecrated you.' " Steven rose from his chair and stood behind Trudy and placed his hands on her shoulders. "It's time for you to leave. Trudy's right. You need to talk to Jack Fries."

"Are you saying you had no role in Diana's death, then?" Ernie asked.

On a side table was a small black Bible. Steven handed it to Huck, then placed his palm upon its cover. "I swear," he said. "I never, ever did anything to hurt Diana Duprey."

"Do you know who did?" said Ernie.

"No," said Steven. "But talk to Jack Fries." He escorted Huck and Ernie to the door. Out on the porch there was a large cardboard box that had not been there when they arrived. The outside of the box showed a picture of a baby stroller. When Steven saw it, his face dimmed.

"Oh, dear," he said. "I thought Trudy had canceled everything for the baby. She shouldn't see this. It's been very rough on her," he said. "She's not handling this well at all." He hoisted the box in his arms and, without saying goodbye, headed for the garage.

Huck and Ernie walked back to the car. "So, do you believe him?" Huck said.

"Not a hundred percent," replied Ernie, "but I'm intrigued." He put the car in gear and headed down the street.

"Who's Jack Fries?"

"He practices family law. He used to coach Little League with me—in fact, I taught his daughter to pitch, back when she was a pipsqueak. If it's the same Jack Fries."

"Slow down," said Huck. "His daughter's how old?"

"Same as Claire."

"Slow down, I said. Is Claire friends with her?"

"I don't know."

"Ask."

"Like she'll tell me. Fine, I'll ask."

"Look out!" Huck exclaimed as Ernie nearly sideswiped a bus. "What's the matter with you?!"

Ernie swerved into the right-hand lane. "Jack Fries represented Leigh's ex-husband, during her divorce," he said. "Screwed her out of their condo at Keystone. I've been waiting for ten years to nail that guy."

For the first time that day Huck laughed. "Small town?"

"It's taken you this long to figure that out?"

"Just drive," sighed Huck.

They found Jack Fries at his office downtown, on the fifth floor of one of the town's few high-rises. Jack was with a client, so Huck and Ernie sat down to wait. Huck didn't mind, actually; it was the first break he'd had all day. He picked up a copy of *People* magazine. Inside was an article on Diana, a kind of post-mortem portrait, focusing on her decision, years ago, not to terminate her pregnancy when she learned at eighteen weeks her baby had Down syndrome. The article included an old family portrait showing the four of them: Diana holding Ben, who grinned out from behind thick lenses; and Frank holding a very disheveled Megan, who looked ready to bolt at a moment's notice. The caption below the picture read, "An Abortionist's Choice."

He didn't have time to read the article, though, because the receptionist's phone buzzed. She stood and led them down an art-filled hallway to Jack Fries's office. Inside, broad picture windows overlooked the foothills, whose knuckled slopes lay bare and grassy to the south, snow-covered to the north.

"Detectives," said Jack, reaching across his desk to shake hands. "What can I do for you?"

"Nice view," Ernie remarked.

"I like it. What brings you here?"

"Your daughter," said Ernie.

Jack Fries tipped his chair back and folded his hands on his stomach.

"What happened when she went in for her abortion on December seventeenth?" asked Ernie.

Jack's face remained expressionless.

"Why'd she end up in the hospital?"

There was a long moment of silence. "Sorry, boys," he finally said.

"Sorry what?" said Ernie.

Jack leaned to pick up his phone, but Ernie stopped him. "Dr. Duprey did perform an abortion on your daughter, didn't she?"

"No," said Jack. "No, she did not."

"You want to set us straight?"

"Nope."

Huck cleared his throat. "Dr. Duprey performed most of her abortions in her clinic. Rose ended up in the hospital. Did Dr. Duprey botch things up?"

"Because a lot of things can go wrong during an abortion," Ernie said.

"Like if the girl starts to hemorrhage," added Huck.

"And needs surgery," Ernie finished.

They waited for Jack to respond. Huck felt his heart beating hard and fast. He and Ernie were bluffing, they were making a lot of assumptions here, but Jack's face had paled and Huck knew as certain as he knew anything these days that they were on to something.

Quietly he said, "Tell us what happened to Rose, Jack."

The color returned to Jack's face as he leaned forward in his chair. "Nothing happened to Rose. Rose is fine. Rose, as a matter of fact, is in school as we speak."

"Gee, I didn't see her playing basketball last Friday night," Ernie remarked.

"Get out," said Jack. "I had nothing to do with Diana's death.

You're a bunch of fools. Not just you two. I'm talking about the entire department here. You fucked up with Templeton and now you're going to fuck up here. You're a sorry bunch. Get your act together."

Huck glanced at Ernie. They stood up.

"I said leave," said Jack.

"We're leaving," Huck said. "But can I suggest something? Hire yourself a good lawyer by the end of the day. Best investment you'll ever make."

Huck and Ernie rode the elevator down in silence. Outside the air had turned warm, and rivers of melted snow trickled alongside the curb. Across the street a hot dog vendor sang his menu. Huck and Ernie drove back to the police station in continued silence. They had a lot to do in the next few hours. They had to update the chief; they had to run a search on Jack Fries (though Huck was doubtful they'd come up with anything); they had to draft warrants. Huck felt primed. For the first time in a month he felt like he was in control. They were going to break this case.

Plus, Megan was no longer staying at his house. Carolyn's sister was almost over the shingles. Everything was coming together.

"It's not an ace in the hole," Ernie reminded him as they pulled into the parking lot of police headquarters. "All it is is a *potential* break. So don't get your hopes up."

"Hell, no."

They got out of the car and walked into the station.

"Guilty as all get-out, though," murmured Ernie.

"Guy's going down," Huck agreed.

———

But arriving back at the department, Huck found a message on his desk. The chief of police wanted to see him immediately. Expecting that he merely wanted an update, both Huck and Ernie went down to his office, only to learn from his secretary that the chief wanted to meet with Huck privately. When Huck asked what about, the secretary merely shrugged and fussed with her mouse.

In another moment the door opened, and Stan Wolfowitz came out. Huck had expected to see Stan. It was Stan's office, after all. He did not, however, expect to see Bill Branson.

"Dude!" Bill exclaimed when he noticed Huck. "Looking well rested, I'd say."

"Thank you," Stan said quietly to Bill. Bill gave a little salute in return and zipped up his jacket.

"Come on in," said Stan. Huck followed him into his office. The chief of police had summitted Mount Everest several years back, so the walls held many blown-up pictures of an unidentifiable human figure, stuffed, bundled, and goggled against a white background.

Huck took a seat in the chair in front of the chief's desk. "What did Bill Branson want?"

Stan leaned back in his chair. "You tell me."

Huck mentally scrolled through the evidence. Had he overlooked something? Missed a tip?

"Okay, fine," said Stan, leaning forward. "I'll make it easy for you. Look, Huck, you're a good cop. And a smart guy. And not a sneak, either. Which is why I am finding this very, very hard to believe."

Huck racked his brains.

"What gets me is that you spent a year in Internal Affairs. You know the Code of Conduct backward and forward."

"Help me out, Stan," warned Huck.

Stan leaned back in his chair. "Fine. It concerns the Duprey girl."

"Megan?"

"Please don't act like you don't know what I'm talking about. Come on, Huck—do you think we'd ever be able to put you on the stand if they knew you'd been sleeping with someone in the victim's family?"

Huck felt like he'd been hit in the chest. A whistling sound filled his ears. For a few seconds he was speechless as he pictured Bill Branson at his front door last night.

Stan's demeanor was incredulous and parental. "What were you thinking? Like, did it even occur to you that there might be breach-of-trust issues here? Conflict of interest? Did you think people wouldn't find out? What in God's name were you thinking, Huck? You didn't even call for assistance when she showed up!"

Too stunned to reply at first, Huck merely stared at his boss, who obviously knew the value of waiting out a silence. He did some fast calculations and figured out that Stan didn't know Megan had been at his house all day; just as quickly he decided not to correct his boss. He shook his head in disbelief. "*This* is why Branson came in here?"

Stan steepled his fingers together and rested his chin at the apex and waited.

"Do you know who Bill Branson is?" Huck demanded. "He's Megan's former boyfriend, that's who."

"He mentioned that, yes."

"Did he also mention that he was the one who took the photos?"

"No," said Stan, "he didn't mention that."

"I didn't sleep with her, Stan."

"What was she doing at your house last night, then?"

"She had a fight with her father. I don't know why she came to me, but she did. And then she left. She didn't spend the night."

"Oh, Huck," said the chief. "Please."

"She didn't!" Huck exclaimed. He started to tell the chief to ask Megan, but he stopped himself, because number one he didn't know where Megan was, and number two he didn't want any more light shined upon Megan, and number three she might mention the kiss—and one kiss certainly did not mean they'd slept together.

Immediately he felt as low and slimy as an old frog, giving himself this kind of wiggle room.

Nonetheless he reiterated his position. "I'm not sleeping with her, Stan. Ask Ernie, if you have to ask someone."

"And he'd know?"

"My best friend? My partner? Please. Ask him. Or not," he said. "Fine. What are you going to do, though? You're not thinking of taking me off the case, are you? You're kidding!" he exclaimed. "On the basis of one allegation by a jealous stalker, you're taking me off the case?"

"Oh come on, Huck, don't make this hard for me," Stan said. "We've got to solve this case, and we've got to solve it without any side issues. The whole damn country's watching. You think I want a concurrent side investigation about members of my police force fucking the victim's daughter? I don't have any choice."

"I don't believe this!"

"Two weeks," said Stan. "We'll see where we are then. I'm sorry, Huck."

"Stan, you gotta know about this guy. He's wacko. He's stalking the girl. He's a lying scumbag who took pictures of his girlfriend and sold them on the Net! Come on, Stan!" His boss said nothing, and Huck decided a different tack was in order. "What good's it going to do to take me off the case, anyway? People are going to think what they want to think. I'm not going to give in to this. By the way, you wouldn't believe what we found out this morning. You know of a Jack Fries?"

"Ernie can tell me," said Stan. "I don't want to hear it from you."

"Oh my god," said Huck. "I can't believe this."

"Go home. Go to Minnesota. Help Carolyn out."

"But we've—"

"Ernie'll tell me," said Stan. "Go home, Huck. Oh, and do me a favor, huh? Stay away from Megan?"

Huck knew at that point it was futile to argue anymore. He unpinned his badge and dropped it on the chief's desk.

"Have it your way," he said.

He left the office and drove aimlessly for a while, out past the reservoir, up one of the canyons, back down into town. He stopped at the liquor store and picked up a six-pack of beer. He drove by the Thompson-Duprey house. The yellow tape was still up, but there were no signs of activity. A dog darted out in front of his car, and he had to slam on the brakes and swerve to avoid it. (The town had a leash law but hey: who was off duty?)

He kept driving. Part of him figured he should simply give in and cruise around town until he spotted the yellow Volkswagen, find Megan, and take her back to his place and do the things with her he'd thought of doing all along. What did he have to lose? What difference would it make? When he was very young, the line between a kiss and something more seemed dark and clearly drawn, and each step you took redefined the whole relationship. Now it seemed that the line was much farther back, that you crossed into that other world simply by holding a certain kind of glance one second too long. By this standard he and Megan were already in deep. And in terms of the public eye, if everyone was going to think he was sleeping with her, then he might just as well.

But Huck drove home. Because the other part of him knew that he had everything to lose, not the least of which included Carolyn. Megan was nineteen. There were seven years between the two of them. She was in a vulnerable state. It wasn't right, and he knew it.

By the time he got home, it was dark. The firemen were outside in the front parking lot, just back from a call. He waved to them and drove down his driveway and cut the engine. Inside he found the heat blasting out of every single duct, so the first thing he did was go around opening windows. He got a beer and propped open the back door to the kitchen, which led out to his small backyard. And as he did so, he heard the rustle of clothing.

Megan stepped from the shadow of the shed into the porch light. She was wearing a dark sweater that hung on her unattractively, with a long ropy scarf that dangled to her knees. Her hair was pinned up, and she wore a pair of glasses.

"I was thinking," she said.

Huck waited, unable to form any words.

"About how you kissed me last night," she said. "And whether it meant anything or whether it was just one of those moments."

"Come out of the cold," he said.

"No," she said. "I'm not going to come in until I understand what it all meant. I haven't been the best person for a guy to get involved with," she said. "For instance, if you asked Bill, he might tell you that I used him. And maybe he'd be right. And maybe I used others too. I don't know what all this says about me, but I want you to know that last night, when I kissed you back, I didn't feel like I was using anybody. That sounds corny, doesn't it? But there wasn't any other reason for my kissing you back, except that I wanted to."

Huck's mouth was so dry his tongue felt like a washcloth.

"Where did you park your car?" was all he could manage.

"Are you worried?"

"I'm worried about a lot of things," he said.

"Like what?"

He managed to tell her, then, what had happened that afternoon, about his being sent home.

"As in kicked off the case?"

"For now," said Huck.

"Because he thinks we're sleeping together?"

"That's right."

Megan glanced down.

"Come out of the cold," he said again.

She edged past him, into the yellow light of his kitchen. He closed the door and drew the blinds.

"By the way, he kicked me out," she told him.

"Who?"

"The dorm guy. That's where I went last night."

"So you still need to find a place to stay."

Megan nodded. She went and stood over a floor duct, huddling into herself. "I hope you're not mad that I came here," she said.

In the bright light, he saw a spattering of freckles across her nose that he'd not noticed before. "I'm not mad."

"And I'll leave, if you want," she added.

"No," he said hoarsely. "Don't leave."

Megan unwrapped her scarf and draped it carefully over the one kitchen chair. He stepped forward and removed her glasses. Her eyes were green on the inside and brown on the outside—again, something he'd not noticed until now. He reached back and unclipped her hair and it fell over her shoulders in unruly curls. He caught his breath as she reached down and lifted her sweater over her head. She wore no bra and her breasts were small and round, the skin very white, like little moons. They were very clearly on the other side of things now, but they had been, he reminded himself, for a long time.

And from that moment on he could think of nothing but being with her, and in her, in a place that up until now he'd dared not allow himself to imagine.

PART THREE

FEBRUARY

CHAPTER TWELVE

_____

LATE IN JANUARY the warm winds began to blow. They raced down over the mountains, rattling windows, prying off shingles, tossing lawn furniture from one yard to the next. They yanked car doors off their hinges and sent eighteen-wheelers wobbling to the side of the highway. They snapped tree limbs, which in turn downed power lines; and they whisked up the waves on the lake near Frank and Diana's house, a lake that served as combination dog loop, athletic track, birdwatcher's haven, fishing hole, and inflationary factor for the surrounding real estate.

According to the local newspaper, the winds were stronger than usual this year, which led to a collective snappiness about town. People were tired of lying awake at night waiting for their roofs to blow off; they were tired of getting up the next morning to find trash cans overturned and litter strewn about the street. Insurance companies were tired of car doors getting ripped off. Doctors were tired of people coming in with grit in their eyes. Lawyers were tired of neighbors blaming each other for acts of God. And the fire department was tired of living in dread of the winds fanning any small fire into an inferno.

As if the winds weren't enough to put people on edge, the Duprey investigation remained stalled. Everyone was waiting for Frank to step forward and either confess or offer an alibi, but he remained silent; and neither the DA's office nor the police were willing to step forward themselves with an indictment or arrest until they were sure they had enough evidence to secure a conviction, which they didn't.

One good thing for Megan was that her classes were in full swing; the dorm was open, and she no longer was compelled, economically, to stay with her father in the hotel suite. Her second semester of biology was living up to its tyrannical reputation, and she had little time for parties or movies or the controlled substances that appeared more and more frequently in Natalie's possession. The frenetic pace did not bother her, however. Though not quite a pariah, she nevertheless felt like she was in a glass box, with everyone wondering what secret knowledge she might possess about intimate family circumstances. She was glad to hole up in the lab.

But as much as her schedule permitted her to avoid the general public, it did not keep her from thinking about what had happened with Huck. There hadn't been a second time, so she tried to write off the incident as just a hookup. After all, he had a girlfriend. But she found herself waking up in the middle of the night, deeply troubled by something she couldn't quite put her finger on. Not her mother's death; that was too obvious. This was something different, something that left a fidgety fear in her stomach. Although maybe it had nothing to do with Huck, she told herself. She didn't know.

For his part, Huck went around trying to pretend it hadn't happened at all. He was allowed back at work (though reassigned to Records) when, two days after they slept together, Megan went to the chief on her own and assured him that nothing was going on between them. This she did unbeknownst to Huck, though he found out about it later, when he returned to work. Although he knew that nonfeasance could be just as bad as an out-and-out lie, he did not correct the chief, something he justified by allowing that what had been, had been only once, and was no more, which was not a lie.

The third week of January Carolyn finally returned home—this time for the rest of the winter, she assured Huck. She found her house full of dust, her cats thin, and her plants drooping, but she was glad to see Huck, and he was glad to see her. They made love twice a night. Whenever the image of Megan's face popped up, he cleared his throat and it vanished. Just like that. It was a new trick, and it worked so well he was surprised it wasn't common knowledge.

Frank himself spent the latter part of the month looking for a new place to live. The hotel bill was mounting on his credit card, and it was clear he was never going to be able to go back to his and Diana's house. Not only was it still a crime scene, but the memories were something he'd never be able to live with. He concentrated on finding a small house in town and was shocked to learn the asking price of a "cozy, turn-of-the-century bungalow" with outdated wiring and rusty plumbing. He kept at it, though, using a realtor who became a kind of confidante for him as they motored from one property to the next. *What do I do with all of her stuff?* he asked, bewildered at the thought of a move. *If the house has two good-size bedrooms, do you think my daughter will live with me?* The realtor had no answers for these questions; she merely listened, and pointed out the proximity of the bike path.

For now, however, Frank remained at the hotel. During the day he went into work, although there wasn't much for him to do. In the evening he drank a couple of scotches and nuked a Stouffer's. He surfed the news programs and tried to stay abreast of current cases. Megan, who had finally shown up three days after disappearing, was cordial with him, sometimes warm even; but he could tell from her eyes that there was still a seed of doubt in her mind. Sometimes they went out to dinner, but this was difficult because the press was always there. More often than not they ordered takeout.

He kept himself busy enough. It was only late at night, alone in the king-size hotel bed, that he could no longer avoid thinking about the growing case against him. He was no fool. Sooner or later he was going to have to divulge his whereabouts the night Diana died. He imagined how he would tell the story, and wondered if it would make sense; he even wrote it down on paper, to test its credibility. He read it over and over, and the more he read it, the less sense it made, and the less convinced he was that it had done any good at all.

————————

The man's name was Edgar Love, and he lived ten miles out of town. Edgar Love was the registered owner of a pornographic Web site called ThePearl.com—a name Frank had thought totally without meaning until some English major on his staff brought in a lurid nineteenth-century novel of the same name. The material on Edgar Love's Web site, however, was purely twenty-first century: high quality, digital, and about as graphic as any medical textbook. There would probably have been no case—it was *Penthouse*-level stuff, within the bounds of the First Amendment—until someone's search turned up pictures of children.

Frank's office had begun investigating the matter a year ago, and when records showed the photos had been sent across state lines, the federal authorities got involved. Normally this would have led to months of squabbling between the two offices, but by some political miracle that probably had more to do with their mutually visceral disgust for the crime in question than with anyone's sudden relinquishment of professional ego, the two offices had cooperated. Working together, they'd seized hard drives—not those of Edgar Love but those of his underlings, full of damning links and out-of-state e-mails. By early December of this year, they were on the verge of an arrest.

Then Frank saw the pictures, and made a mess of things.

Frank was no prude; over the course of the Pearl investigation he'd seen things that sickened and jolted him, images that haunted his dreams at night and sometimes made it impossible to do the things with Diana that a husband and wife are supposed to do. Yet most of the time, as a prosecutor, he was able to maintain a professional attitude about things. He did this by treating the pictures like the pictures he dealt with all the time, as part of his job. These pictures weren't of real-life girls, he told himself; they were simply evidentiary pieces of a huge criminal jigsaw with which they were going to nail this guy.

Then he saw the pictures of Megan, and every drop of professionalism evaporated in the cold December air.

Although he'd never met Edgar Love face to face, he knew everything he needed to know about the man. He knew his address and his Social Security number, the numbers of his bank accounts and what he'd claimed on his tax returns for the past five years. He knew the man's aliases; he knew the names of his wife and son, his sisters, his parents in Massachusetts. He knew where most of his material came from—the Ukraine, Romania. He knew how many hits the site had received since its inception, broken down by hour, day, month, and e-mail address. Based on all this, he estimated that some ten thousand viewers had possibly clicked on his daughter's pictures.

Thinking back on it, he wished he could say that he had acted out of a sense of duty. He wished he could say that he simply wanted to preserve his daughter's honor. But that wasn't really the case, because his duty was to let the wheels of justice take care of men like Edgar Love, and his daughter's honor was a quaint but irrelevant concept in this day and age—something he had no control over whatsoever. Besides, the pictures of his daughter remained out there in cyberspace.

No. What motivated him after the argument with Diana was

merely this: one man's wish to snap his fingers and have another man vanish.

Twenty-four years in Cañon City, or the rest of your life on an unnamed island. You choose.

In early January the federal authorities had gone to arrest Edgar Love at his house in the mountains. There was nobody at home. There were dirty dishes in the sink and a basket of laundry at the base of the stairs, as though the family had just run into town for a doctor's appointment. But the plants were drooping and the fountain was dry and a quick peek in the refrigerator released the putrid smell of bad meat. Edgar Love and his family were gone, and no one knew where.

Except Frank.

———————————

The strong Chinooks that hit the town in January melted most of the snow that had fallen during December's blizzard; by the beginning of February, the lawns in town lay bare, brown, and matted down with November's grass. Tiny weeds sprouted, along with the nubby tips of crocuses and tender green lettuce curls in garden beds throughout this homegrown town.

At Susan Beekman's house, the melted snow exposed a moonscape of pocked holes and booty. This was the work of their dog, Rudy, a Siberian husky who roamed the neighborhood in search of anything he could get his teeth on, which he then carried back to their yard for leaner times in dogville.

On the first Sunday in February, Susan Beekman woke up in a bad mood. Her house was a mess, groceries sat in bags, toys were scattered, and her husband's dirty socks lay *on the kitchen counter for chrissake*. She felt a little overwhelmed by it all. Then she looked out and saw the litter in her yard, and it struck her that here, at least, was a manageable project. At the very minimum, she could accomplish *something* that day.

And so she locked Rudy in the garage and, armed with a shovel and a large trash bag, went out to work in the yard. Within half an hour she had unearthed a headless Barbie, a rocky loaf of rye, a bag of candy canes, a half-dozen split tennis balls, a stiffened black sock, a ham hock, and a chewed-up Tupperware container. Nothing seemed salvageable, except for the yellow and green sprinkler head lying close to the fence separating her property from Frank's. Without giving it much thought, she figured it was Frank's and tossed it over the crime tape. Close by was a brown leather glove; figuring it was also Frank's, she tossed that too over the tape.

At ten o'clock, noticing her husband and son in the kitchen window, she put down the bag and took off her gloves. She surveyed her yard. No longer did it look like white trash. Not bad, for an hour's work.

————————

One brown leather glove, soft and pebbly, cashmere lined, size medium: by noon on Monday Ernie had it tagged, labeled, and Ziplocked into evidence. He sat at his desk pondering its significance. Where had it come from? How had they missed it? Which is not to say that he wasn't delighted to have something new. The cashmere lining would yield skin cells, which the lab could test for DNA. Of course, if it turned out to be Frank's, it wouldn't add much to their case; a husband's glove provided no new link to the death itself. But if it was not Frank's, then they would have their first lead in a month.

Wishful thinking, he cautioned himself.

That Monday morning Ernie leaned back in his chair and stared out his window. Water poured from a gutter, and sun glinted off the puddles in the parking lot. He needed Huck and cursed his friend for putting himself in a position where Stan had had to stick him down in Records. Ernie never asked Huck what had gone on with Megan, and he didn't want to know; still, he was angry with Huck for making things look bad at the very least. Now, because of Huck's possible indiscretions, he, Ernie, was having to work with Detective Marcus Stoner instead. This was a bad thing, not just because Marcus was new and told off-color jokes but because he didn't have a whole lot going on up there. He always focused on the wrong thing. When first reviewing Diana's file, he focused on her medical history ("Was she ever suicidal?"), her use of swim goggles ("Maybe she couldn't see where she was going"), whether she'd eaten in the last hour ("You can get a cramp swimming is what my mother always said. Did anyone think of that?").

"Yowsers," Marcus had said at the end of his first day. "This could go on forever, couldn't it?"

With Marcus on the case, Ernie might as well be working alone.

He spent the rest of that Monday in early February conducting more interviews. Already three people had verified that Jack Fries had indeed been playing squash at his health club from five to six-thirty on December 17. And several nurses vouched that he'd been at the hospital from six-forty-five until nine, with his daughter, Rose. It looked like Jack Fries was off the hook. Piper McMahon too; she had been at her daughter's second-grade holiday concert.

Which left Frank.

Ernie went home early that evening and made love to his wife, wondering how all this was going to affect his midyear review. Over dinner he picked at his food and argued with his daughter over whether the shadowy area four inches below her navel constituted the beginning of her pubis or not. He ended up falling asleep in front of the television.

Around four he woke up. Stiff and achy, he climbed the stairs and slipped into bed beside Leigh, but couldn't fall back asleep. He feared that this case would drag on forever, another black mark on the police department. He racked his brain. An intruder? No evidence. Jack Fries? Tight alibi. The anti-abortionists? Of course, but who? Without more, it was like finding a needle in the haystack, there were so many of them.

Then suddenly, for no apparent reason, he recalled the meth dealer that the Branson boy had mentioned. He'd talked to Narcotics back in January, but Narcotics had no record of the man, and Ernie had let the matter slide. Now he realized that had been a mistake. The man might have been using an alias. Maybe he'd been over at Diana's house that night, demanding money, and dropped a glove on the way out.

It was a long shot, but what else was he going to do?

Two rooms away electronic music shattered the dark: five a.m., time for his daughter's two-hour grooming routine. Ernie rolled over and covered his head with his pillow. If only he could sleep until seven, he thought, then surely he would break the case.

CHAPTER THIRTEEN

WHILE ERNIE LAY in bed wondering how he was going to salvage the case, Frank himself lay in bed drafting his letter of resignation. It had taken him a month, but he'd finally accepted what was now so obvious: that what mattered was clearing his name, even if it meant revealing where he'd gone that night. At five-thirty he got up and, after making a cup of espresso, sat down with his laptop and began to write.

This letter will serve to inform you of my resignation from the district attorney's office, effective immediately.

Rage was too weak a word to describe how he'd felt after seeing the online pictures of his daughter. But even as he confronted his wife by the side of the pool, even as the bitter, blame-soaked words spilled from his mouth, Frank knew he was taking it out on the wrong person. Looking back on it, he rued the fact that his only good decision that night—to leave the house before worse things were said—was the very reason why his wife was now dead. Had he stayed, she would be alive today.

Grimly he thought of how clear things could be, in hindsight.

The obstruction of justice was regrettable but necessary.

After leaving the house—and his wife, wet and dripping and stunned by his accusations—Frank made one quick stop at a travel agency. Then, with snow pelting his windshield, he headed up into the canyon. The main road had enough traffic to keep the snow from sticking, but the side road had a foot of untouched powder and his car immediately began snaking from side to side. Engaging the four-wheel drive, he gripped the wheel and slowly made his way up a series of steep, exaggerated hairpin turns. Finally the road leveled out into a high country basin, and as he coasted silently along, he thought how beautiful and appropriately terrible it all looked: dark and snowy and cold; a place for wolves, for predators.

He drove on. In 4.2 miles he came to Edgar Love's mailbox. There he pulled into a small driveway and parked between a pickup truck and a giant SUV. Outside it must have been ten degrees colder than in town. A path had been shoveled from the driveway to the house. Golden light shone from the windows.

Frank zipped his jacket and turned up his collar and stepped out of his car. He had been up here before and knew the property. Edgar Love's house was built from salvaged wood and glass, and looked like it had evolved over time, with rooms added on every which way. Solar heating panels rose ominously from the roof. Tonight a child-size plastic shovel lay abandoned on the walkway. Frank stuck it into the snowbank, then trudged up the steps and knocked on the door.

In seconds he found himself face to face with Soren Love (née Hildebrand, age thirty-five, one previous marriage, no priors). She was a small wispy woman, dressed tonight in a loose denim workshirt over a pair of magenta tights, her light brown hair messily knotted up with a pair of chopsticks. She did not seem surprised to find a stranger at her door and, assuming he was stuck, asked if he needed a phone.

Frank told her no, he was not stuck; he was here to see her husband. Immediately her demeanor changed.

"At six-fifteen on a Tuesday night? I don't remember you calling."

"I didn't call," said Frank. From upstairs came the high-pitched sound of vocalized artillery.

"Who is it, Soren?" A man had materialized at the base of a wrought-iron spiral staircase, upstage left.

"Mr. Love," said Frank. "Good evening." He knew he did not need to introduce himself; most people in this town knew their prosecutors.

"Let him in, Soren," said Edgar Love.

"We're about to eat, Ed," Soren pointed out.

"Then invite him to dinner," said Edgar quietly.

Soren looked irritated but told Frank to take off his shoes. Frank obeyed, neatly aligning them with a dozen other pairs against the wall. He glanced about. The house had an artsy feel, with chiseled beams and a stone floor with random mosaic inlays. On the wall by the door hung an ethereal tangle of blown glass threads, red and blue and purple. Risky art with a child around, Frank thought.

"Soren works with glass," Edgar explained as he descended the last three steps. He was a slight man, clean-shaven, with short brown hair and funny elfin ears. He wore a black turtleneck with the sleeves pushed up and loose khaki pants, and he was barefoot. "That piece there has a remote lighting system."

"Impressive," said Frank.

There was a brief silence while Frank and Edgar assessed the sculpture. Then Edgar said, "Sor?" kind of flicking his glance upward, and Soren looked at him in astonishment; they had a deal going here, Frank could tell, and Edgar was breaking it somehow, but Soren must have decided not to escalate the issue. She squeezed past him and climbed the stairs.

Edgar headed into the kitchen. "You're nuts to drive in this weather," he remarked over his shoulder. "Watch your step. Another piece by Soren." He indicated a large, red, somewhat drunkenly shaped plate hanging on the wall. Frank followed him past the kitchen into a glassed-in seating area filled with plants and graced by a tall pyramid-shaped fountain made from slabs of blue slate. A small Christmas tree sat on a table in the corner, lit up with tiny white lights. Flute music played in the background, and loaves of bread sat cooling on the counter, and a large cast-iron pot simmered on the stove. "I trust you've got four-wheel drive."

He sat down on a small sofa and gestured for Frank to do the same, but Frank leaned against the counter that separated the kitchen from the living area.

"Obviously we don't need any introduction," he told Edgar, "although you must be wondering why I'm here."

Edgar waited—well coached not to volunteer anything, Frank noticed.

"I wanted to talk to you about something I happened to come across online this afternoon," he said. "I think you might know what I'm talking about."

Edgar smiled. "I run an online hardwood business," he said. "Am I correct in assuming this has to do with tropical hardwoods?"

Frank said, "It does not."

"How odd," said Edgar Love. "I have heard—although I can't ver-ify it—that the Justice Department has been investigating the indus-try for price fixing. In which case it might not surprise me to be questioned about certain conversations I did or did not have at cer-tain points in time. Assuming you people work together," he added. "Possibly not a fair assumption?"

"I'm not here to talk to you about meetings or conversations you might have had with other wholesalers."

Edgar slapped his thighs definitively. "Well then! If you're not here to discuss business, then I suggest you leave before the snow gets any worse."

"Oh, I'm here to discuss business," said Frank, "just not the business you think."

Edgar asked what business that might be, and Frank told him. Edgar smiled at his hands. Then he rose from the sofa and went into the kitchen area. He filled a teakettle from a water cooler. He put the kettle on the stove and used a match to light the gas flame. Then he opened a drawer, took out a tin box, and set two mugs on the counter.

"I get my tea via mail order," Edgar remarked. "There are so many more varieties, and it's much better quality. Not that I'm a snob. Now this"—he held up the tin—"*this* is green tea." He pried off the lid and took out what looked like a bonbon, artfully wrapped in white paper. "If you like a somewhat grassy flavor, you will like this."

"We've seen your photos," said Frank.

Edgar unwrapped one of the lumps and sniffed it. "Though it's something of an acquired taste," he went on. "Soren, for instance, does not like it."

"Not just the legitimate ones," said Frank. "The others too. Did you think we wouldn't know what link to click on?"

"Funny you should come up here by yourself," remarked Edgar. "Wouldn't you want to bring someone else from your office?"

"I'm not here for the reason you think I'm here," said Frank.

Edgar dropped the half-dome of pressed tea into a small iron teapot. "The thing about green tea is, you cannot let it steep more than three minutes or it becomes bitter," he warned. "A lot of people make that mistake. They think that the longer you steep it, the better the flavor."

"You posted the wrong photo, pal."

"But!" Edgar held up his finger. "What most people don't know is that you can rebrew the same tea several times. One of these nuggets makes three pots of tea."

"Do you get their legal names, or pseudonyms?"

Edgar fussed crumbs off the counter before turning to face Frank. "What are you getting at, Frank? I have other things I could be doing tonight. I have a son upstairs. I have books to read. I have a wife to fuck. Help me out here."

"You posted my daughter," said Frank.

"How old is your daughter?"

"Nineteen."

"Of age, then."

"Not when the picture was taken. You're looking at twenty-four years in federal prison, Edgar."

The teakettle whistled, and Edgar turned the burner off. He waited for the boiling to subside, then poured water into the pot. "See how the leaves uncurl, how they writhe about? The Chinese call this a state of agony. I find that quite poetic, don't you?" With a clink he set the cover on the teapot, draped it with a small white towel, and upended a small sand-filled timer. "Shall we?"

Frank reached into his breast pocket and took out the oblong envelope he'd picked up at the travel agency an hour ago. He set it on the counter, next to the teapot.

"Going somewhere?" asked Edgar.

Frank imagined an X-Acto knife: how it would feel, making that first decisive cut into a man's chest.

"Take my daughter off the Web site," he said, "and the tickets are yours."

"I beg your pardon?"

"You're welcome to call your attorney. Maybe he can explain it better than I. Ever heard of a Judge Robie, down in Denver?"

"A good man," said Edgar.

"And very loath to accept a plea in these kinds of cases."

Edgar removed the tea basket from the pot and set it, steaming, on a small plate.

"Look, Frank. I've got a kid upstairs with a fever of a hundred and two. I appreciate the work you guys are doing, but you have the wrong person."

"I don't think so," said Frank, and he pulled out another piece of paper, this one a printout of Megan with Edgar's domain at the top. Edgar glanced at it briefly. He opened a cupboard and began searching for something.

"One-way tickets," said Frank. "Three of them. Wherever you want. Just take my daughter off your site."

"And then what?"

"I put the case on the back burner."

"No deal," said Edgar, "unless you close the case."

Frank shook his head. "Back burner's the best I can do. I can't tell the feds how to run their investigation."

"This looks very much like blackmail," said Edgar. "Is that your policy at the DA's office these days?"

Frank shrugged. "Take it or leave it, Edgar. It's up to you. Oh, did I mention that Judge Robie has twin daughters? Freshmen in high school?"

"Photogenic?" Edgar winked, then rolled his eyes. "Oh, lighten up, Frank, it's a joke. But tell me. Why should I trust you? Who says you're going to hold up your end of the deal?"

"Sometimes you've just got to make that leap of faith."

"Your case is full of shit," said Edgar.

"Want to test it out? Fine with me. No, thank you," he said as Edgar moved a mug toward him. "Too late in the day."

From upstairs came the sound of feet slapping across the floor, followed by sustained shrieking. Frank glanced at the ceiling. "Sounds like he's not so sick anymore. Ready to travel, even."

Edgar stirred his tea methodically, the spoon tinkling against the glass. Frank waited. He was used to this. Silence never bothered him. He could wait all night, if he needed to.

"Fine," Edgar finally said. He reached for the tickets, but Frank picked them up first.

"Take her off now," said Frank, slipping the tickets back into his breast pocket. "While I watch."

Edgar turned and padded into a small room off the kitchen. Frank followed. The room was set up with a desk and a computer and a couple of file cabinets. On the screen was a child's computer game, fish chasing fish chasing fish.

Edgar sat down at the computer. Frank watched as a series of images crossed the screen. When Megan's came up, he turned away.

"Same as the printout?" asked Edgar.

"Yes."

"You're sure?"

"Yes."

Edgar made a few keystrokes.

"She's gone," he said.

"Let me see," said Frank. Edgar moved aside, and Frank leaned over the keyboard and began a new search on Edgar's Web site. He tried it again. He tried it a third time. Then he stood up and took the tickets out of his pocket and handed them to Edgar.

"You realize that the image has probably been downloaded by any number of people," Edgar said. "It might even have made its way onto any number of other Web sites. Cyberspace is pretty huge."

"But there's nothing I can do about that, is there?" said Frank. "This I can do. Just remember. If she ever pops up on your site again, we'll find you."

"Go home," said Edgar. "We're done here."

"Do you get it?"

"I get it."

Frank went back out to the kitchen then and relit the burner. He took the picture of Megan from his pocket, held it over the burner, and watched the blue flame lick its way up through the folds. When the paper was engulfed, he dropped it into the sink. Then he went out to the entryway and dug his heels into his shoes and zipped up his jacket.

It is highly probable that Mr. Love's whereabouts can be traced, and I will cooperate fully with state and federal authorities to locate him, to bring him back to the United States, to hold him accountable for his actions.

Outside the snow was blowing harder, but by remaining in second gear, he made it safely down through the hairpins. In town the plows were out, and he drove along the main artery acutely aware of how brilliant and beautiful the Christmas lights were this year. He was a lucky man. Lucky for a lot of things—lucky that apologizing came easy for him, so that he could go home and apologize to Diana for the things he had said. Lucky he had the relationship he did with his daughter, that he would be able to put this behind him and forget about it. Everyone has a few youthful indiscretions, he reminded himself. Let's hope this was her only big one.

It was light when Frank finished his letter. The espresso sat like thick mud in his cup, and he was tired of room service breakfasts, so he left the hotel and drove to a diner and ordered as much meat as possible: bacon and ham and pork chops and sausage, causing the waitress to smile, as though she'd been waiting years for such an order. While his food sizzled on the griddle, he bought a newspaper and skimmed the headlines, then turned to the op-ed page—something he rarely did these days, knowing there would be at least one article about his wife's death.

Today there were two. One, a tangential piece by a Denver fellow (of dubious intellect, in Frank's view, a man who would spend his life writing for local papers while trolling for the one story that would land him a limp book deal), opining that a recent bill before the state legislature to expand the bubble law lacked teeth because it failed to provide for stricter penalties. And another, this by a more intelligent writer, that chastised the police department for getting rid of the one detective who might have proven useful in solving the investigation.

"Speculation that the detective in question may have engaged in unethical conduct remains unproven, a red herring at best and a witch hunt at worst," the woman wrote. "Let's not lose sight of the fact that a killer remains at large."

Frank closed the newspaper as the waitress set down his plate of cholesterol. Perhaps now, with Edgar Love behind him, he could focus more rationally on helping the police find the killer. He could speak out and make those impassioned pleas the public craved. Perhaps it was naïve of him, but he felt he would be forgiven for doing what he did—by anyone who had children, at least.

"More coffee, Frank?" the waitress asked.

Megan was right; he was famous. "Please," he told the waitress. If only Diana were here now, he thought. She would be proud.

CHAPTER FOURTEEN

———————

T HAT MORNING HUCK looked at his face in the mirror and was
shocked at his appearance. The corners of his mouth pointed
down in a U. His skin was doughy, and his eyelids were fat. The
ancient scar on his chin appeared recently snipped. He looked like
his father used to look, he realized: old, worried, slightly dented.

Heat poured out of the vent in the bathroom, and from his
kitchen came the sounds of Carolyn stacking dishes. These days she
was always up earlier than he. She'd been back for almost a month
now, and he had yet to level with her about Megan. At first he was
going to tell her right away. Then he thought that would be a bad way
to spend their first night together. The next day—her first day back at
work—they had lunch together, and he was going to tell her then,
but she thought she was coming down with the flu, and he couldn't
bring himself to say anything. You total shit, he thought afterward.
Then, when she decided it was just a cold and not the flu, he told her
what Bill had told the chief of police, and, full of loyal assumptions,
she rolled her eyes and shook her head and said what a dickhead the
chief was; and Huck didn't have the gumption to tell her the truth.
And that was where things stood, with every day of silence another
frayed thread between them.

Thank god it had only been one time.

No. Not thank god. Because what disturbed him above all else was that in a small dark corner of his mind, he kept thinking of Megan coming over that night, kept replaying the exact same scenario over and over. And it made him feel bad, once again, when he wanted to feel good.

You coward, he told himself.

"Hey you," Carolyn said through the door. "Coffee's ready."

He finished shaving, dried his face, and turned out the vanity lights. Without them his face didn't look so bad, he decided. He dressed and joined her in the kitchen. She was still in her robe, sitting at the little table reading the newspaper. She'd gelled her hair and combed it straight back, like a greaser.

"Here." She straightened the paper and stood up. "You sit. I'm finished."

"I've really got to fix that other chair," said Huck.

"I'll bring one from my place," she said.

"Good," he said. "Then we can sit here together."

"Oh Huck," she said. "You are so cute."

She kissed the top of his head and was about to leave the room when there was a knock at the door. "Sit still," she said. "I'll get it."

She went to the door and opened it. He heard her say, "Yes?" Then he heard a man's voice say, "I'm looking for Huck, actually.

"Dude!" Bill Branson exclaimed when Huck appeared in the little entry foyer. "I didn't wake you, did I? Here, I brought you a latte."

Huck crossed his arms. "It's quarter of eight in the morning, Bill."

"I'll take the latte," Carolyn said.

Bill handed the cup to her. "Sorry—I didn't mean to barge in. But I have the cell phone numbers of the guys I told you about."

"Who is this guy?" Carolyn asked Huck.

"This is Bill Branson," Huck said.

"The Bill?"

Bill held his hand out to her, but she just blew on the latte.

"Get a life, kid," she said, heading back to the kitchen.

"Ooh." Bill winced intimately at Huck. "Not exactly a morning person, is she? Man, it's cold. How about I come in?"

"How about not," said Huck.

Bill murmured something about two nonmorning people. "Anyway, I'm on my way north," he said. "I thought you'd like to have these phone numbers."

"Take them to headquarters," said Huck. "Give them to Ernie."

"I can't," said Bill. "It'll take too much time, and I have an exam at ten this morning."

Huck realized he wanted Bill out of his house as quickly as possible. "Fine," he said. "Just give me the list."

Bill glanced at the paper. He took his gloves off and retraced a few sloppy digits with a pen.

"And who are these guys again?" Huck said.

"Dealers, suppliers. I told you. People who might have been upset with Dr. Duprey. If I were you, I'd start with Trigger here. Trigger's real name is Owen Capshaw. Wonder why they call him Trigger, huh?" Bill let a snarky grin slide across his face. "Owen's a Gulf War vet. He likes his peace and quiet, likes to make a little easy money and doesn't like it *at all* when people owe him. Hey: *Owen— Owe-him!* Wow."

Huck folded the paper and tucked it into his pocket. He guided Bill outside and shut the door behind them. They stood together on the stoop.

"Look, Bill," he said quietly. "I don't like you. Stay away from my house. If you have something for the police, go to the police. Don't come to me. Don't come here."

Bill frowned. "God, I was just trying to help." He glanced over Huck's shoulder at the door. "Did you see the op-ed today?"

"Thank you, Bill."

"Or I guess the question is, did *she* see the op-ed?"

"I said thank you, Bill, now—"

"Does she know about you and Megan?"

"Excuse me?"

"That's not nice," said Bill, "sleeping with two people at the same time. Megan did that to me, and I know how it feels. She was sleeping with her English teacher! And then she'd come home and fuck me blind! I thought that was really low."

"Get out of here," said Huck.

"How *is* Megan these days?" Bill asked. "Do you think she's moving on? Getting over her mom's death? What a tragedy. She was my virgin, you know. Guess who taught her how to give a good blow job?"

Huck couldn't stop himself; before he even realized it, he'd slammed his fist into Bill's face. Along with the smack of skin and bone came a grunt from the boy's chest as he staggered back.

Huck loomed toward him. "If you ever," he said, "and I mean ever, show up here again I will beat you to a bloody pulp. I will beat you so bad your mother won't recognize you. Am I clear on this? I want to be real clear, Bill, because I really don't want that to happen."

Bill spat blood onto the walkway. He wiped his mouth. "She'll fuck you over, you know. She'll bust your balls, and then she'll dump you. You think she actually feels something for you? You think you're better than me? She's a cunt," he said, spitting another bloody glob at Huck's foot. "A cunt who uses anyone she can get. Hey man, all the best." He backed down the walkway, holding out his hands, preacherlike. "Gimme a call in six months, you can fill me in on where things stand. Joke's on you, asshole," and he hitched up his collar.

"Try a video camera," he called just before sliding into his car. "I never got that far myself, but I bet she'd really get off on that." He slammed the door and revved the engine and spun his tires in the muddy slush as he backed up Huck's long driveway. Then, giving a long honk, he drove off.

It took Huck a good minute or so to regain his composure. When he finally went back inside, there was Carolyn, buttoning her coat.

"Needs a little anger management therapy, doesn't he?" she remarked. "Did you ever ask him why he came up with that story?"

Misery clawed at Huck's heart. "What good would it do?"

"I guess I'd just want to confront him," Carolyn said, "knowing he'd said that about me. Well, I'm off. Are we having dinner here or at my place tonight?"

"Yours," he said, but before he could kiss her, she'd already gone out the door. A minute later she came back in and tossed a pair of gloves into the basket by the door.

"He dropped these," she said.

Huck closed the door. With a morning like this, things could hardly get worse. He went into the kitchen. There on the table lay today's newspaper. He sat down, picked it up, skimmed the headlines, then turned to the op-ed page.

————————

At five o'clock that evening, after a day of doing nothing, he walked into a quiet, staid jewelry store downtown and picked out a ring. He paid by check, then slipped the black velvet box into his pants pocket and walked outside. People looked at him differently, he thought. He found himself smiling back. He stopped at a florist and bought a dozen red roses, tightly budded. Then he went home. He showered, shaved, and put on a clean shirt. At six-thirty he drove across town to Carolyn's and let himself in. He hung up his coat on the coatrack.

The cats rubbed at his leg, and he fed them and then waited for her to come home.

At seven o'clock he heard her key in the lock. She wasn't surprised to see him. Nor was she surprised when he handed her the flowers; she exclaimed and fretted over them while setting her bag down and taking off her coat. Huck reached into his pocket and fingered the velvet box. She seemed like a stranger to him right now, something he attributed to the thing he was about to do.

"You wouldn't believe the crap that's going on," she told him, taking the flowers into the kitchen, where she unwrapped the cellophane and began hacking off the stems. "John's been talking to these people in Texas about a buyout and Al's mad because of some figures John made him adjust last year and he's afraid everything could come out with an audit."

She filled a vase with cold water and plunged the flowers into it. The whole thing looked sloppy and artless.

She went on: "And Al gave me this huge new project, like I don't have other things to do. That Al. If he didn't like what John was telling him to do with the books, why'd he do it? If it were me, I would have just said no."

Then she turned to him and put her arms around him and laid her head against his chest. Huck felt a sudden terror that she was going to feel the box. He pulled back. It was, after all, to be a surprise.

He asked if she'd talked to her mother today.

"Oh!" she exclaimed. "And that's another thing! My sister just got back from Hawaii, and all she keeps saying is she needs to get away from the kids. Why do people have kids when they don't want to spend time with them?"

"Well," Huck said, "I don't know."

"Don't you think it's selfish?"

"Maybe," said Huck, "although—"

"It's so selfish," she declared. "When I have kids, I'm not going to farm them out to somebody else."

Her chatter annoyed him. Suddenly he felt like a supreme fraud. He excused himself and went out to the car and put the ring in the glove compartment. Back inside, he suggested that they go out to dinner. She said she'd eaten a huge lunch and wasn't very hungry. He suggested takeout. She said she'd eaten too much takeout in Minnesota. Huck ended up cooking a pot of ramen noodles for himself, but couldn't eat for the darts ricocheting off the wall of his chest.

He had *grossly* underestimated the trouble he was in.

In the meantime Carolyn had changed into sweats and was now settled on the sofa. Her heels were cracked, and she dug at the skin while moisturizing them. He dumped the noodles down the disposal and rinsed his dish, and as he loaded things into the dishwasher, he was struck with the awful feeling that he knew all there was to know about this woman. Finally, after polishing every available surface of her kitchen, he walked into the living room.

"Carolyn," he said, sitting on the chair that faced the sofa, "we have to talk."

She was not surprised. In fact, her calm acceptance of his revelation bothered him somewhat, which in turn added to his misery. She asked a few questions. Did he want to call things off? What did he want from her now? Huck didn't have any clear answers. That didn't surprise her, either, and Huck wondered if her lack of drama signified that she'd been through this before.

"I don't think I want you here tonight," she told him finally.

That was fair.

"And don't call me tomorrow," she added, which struck him as unfair, but he was not in a position to complain.

On his way home that night he asked himself, if she had done this to him, would it have been harder, or easier?

———————

Early the next morning he called Ernie and told him to stop by on his way into work and pick up Bill's list.

"Another list?"

"Cell phone numbers."

"Why can't you bring it in?"

"I'm not coming in."

"Sick?"

"Yeah."

"You don't get sick."

"Well, I'm sick today," said Huck. "Come pick it up."

"If you're sick I don't want to come into your house."

Huck sighed.

"Oh fine," said Ernie.

Ten minutes later Ernie pulled up in his Subaru station wagon.

"Where's Carolyn?" he asked when he came in, looking around.

"Already at work," said Huck. "Here's the list."

Ernie made a face as he took the piece of paper. "Guy's kind of a lameass, isn't he?" He opened the refrigerator and ducked inside. "He ever say anything about the pictures to you?"

Huck thought back to Bill's last comment about using a video camera.

"No," he said.

Ernie took out a jug of orange juice but found it empty. He put it back. "Frightening," he said, straightening up. "The things kids do now for kicks. Megan ever explain it to you?"

"No," said Huck.

"Every time I hear about something like this I think, it could be Claire. You know what scares me the most sometimes? Being one of those parents who later says, 'But I never dreamed my kid might be doing blankety-blank.' So I make a genuine effort to dream up everything possible—and then Claire says I don't trust her. You can't win." He shook out a handful of Frosted Flakes from the open box on Huck's table. "Ever think about where things are going with her?"

"With who?" said Huck, startled.

"Carolyn!"

"I do," Huck allowed.

"She's a nice gal," said Ernie, using a word that Huck knew would make Carolyn wince. "If you're going to be in my shoes sixteen years from now, you might as well be there with someone like Carolyn. What's the matter?" he said when Huck didn't reply. "You don't really want my advice right now?"

"That's right."

Ernie perused the list. "Why'd you sit on this all day yesterday?"

"I was busy."

"Down in Records?"

"It gets busy there. How's Marcus doing?" Huck asked.

"Useless. What do you eat this shit for? It's pure sugar. What's wrong with you, anyway?" He poured himself another handful. "Well, off to the races. You don't look so sick, by the way." He zipped up his jacket and started out but then happened to glance at the basket by the door.

"Hey. Where'd those come from?"

Bill's gloves were still on top of the pile, where Carolyn had dropped them the day before.

"They're Bill's. Take them. If he turns up at the station, you can give them back to him."

But Ernie was frowning. Huck knew the look. Ernie knelt down, and Huck squatted beside him. The gloves lay nestled together, cold and flabby and curled. One was plain black, the other brown with little pinholes.

"What's the deal?" he asked Ernie.

Ernie didn't reply. From his pocket he took out an exam glove and pulled it on, then took out a plastic bag and put the gloves into the bag and sealed it shut.

"Are you reasonably certain these are Bill's?" he asked.

"Yeah. So what?"

"That's what you get for being down in Records. We've got a glove."

"From where?"

"Frank's backyard."

Huck looked at the plastic bag. "And one of those is the mate?"

"The brown one. What's Bill been doing, hanging around their house?"

"Well, he and Megan were going out," Huck offered.

"But they broke up over a year ago," said Ernie. "And the glove we found has sure as shit not been sitting out in the elements for a year. I'd like to talk to the fellow. Where did you say he is?"

"Back at school," said Huck.

"Well, you know what? I think I'll give him a little call," said Ernie. He picked up Huck's phone and unfolded a piece of paper from his pocket and dialed a number. He paused blankly, then abruptly started pacing. "Yeah, Bill, this is Detective Vogel calling back. Yeah, sorry it took so long. Got a minute?"

Feeling too fidgety to listen to a one-sided conversation, Huck fussed about the kitchen. He tied up the trash bag and took it outside to the Dumpster. He checked his mailbox, even though it was still early in the morning. When he returned inside, Ernie told him they were going up north, pronto.

"And we're taking Megan," he added.

Huck hiccuped loudly, clumsily. "Why?"

"Because Mr. Bill here is suddenly getting cold feet. Says he'll only talk to us if he can talk to Megan first."

"Not a good idea, Ernie," Huck said, feeling the heat rise in his neck. "The guy's been stalking her. He's wacko. No way should they be in the same room together unless it's at headquarters."

"I already called campus police," Ernie said. "They're going to meet us at Bill's room. Why? What's the matter?"

"We shouldn't take her up there. He's dangerous. Call the chief. Get his okay at least."

"Hey. Who's handling this case?" When Huck didn't reply, he went on: "We'll even get the local police there if it'll make you feel better. Where's Megan right now?"

"How should I know?"

"You really want me to answer that? Get your coat, Arthur. We're going to go find her, and then we're going to take a ride up north and hear what this guy has to say about Diana Duprey."

"I'm not on the case," Huck reminded him, pulling on a sweatshirt.

"As far as I'm concerned, you are. I want a psych eval on this guy," Ernie said as they headed out to his car. "What do you know about him, anyway? How'd he get past our radar?"

Huck climbed into the front seat of Ernie's car, tossing candy wrappers and empty water bottles into the back to make space for his feet.

Ernie jammed the car into reverse and twisted around to back up. "When did he break up with Megan? How much contact has he had with her since then? What's his relationship with Diana?"

"Slow down," said Huck. "Let me tell you about obsession," he began.

CHAPTER FIFTEEN

B Y SHEER LUCK they found Megan on the broad front steps of the campus library, talking with a group of students. She was dressed in gray midcalf sweats, along with a skimpy purple top with little mirrors that caught the sun when she moved. No coat, no hat, no gloves. Not having seen her in the last few weeks, Huck lagged behind as Ernie approached her. Ernie spoke briefly. Megan turned in mid-sentence and looked at Huck.

Huck dug his hands into his pockets and in a rare moment wished he were not a cop.

"I told you, my mother wasn't doing meth," Megan said breathlessly as they hurried back to Ernie's car. "Listen. She smoked pot, and she kept some speed in the car for when she got tired. That's it."

"Good," said Ernie. "That helps us."

"But this is such a wild-goose chase! There's no way she was in trouble with some meth dealer!"

"Keep saying that," Ernie said. "Huck, pick up the pace."

Huck had been trailing behind. They hadn't seen each other since their night together last month, and he felt like Megan was handling it a lot better than he was.

As if sensing his thoughts, Megan looked over her shoulder. "I thought you got kicked off the case, Huck."

"I did."

"But for right now, he's back on," said Ernie.

"How's Carolyn?" Megan asked.

"She's fine," said Huck.

"And her mother?"

"Doing pretty well."

"Good. Shotgun," she said as Ernie unlocked his car. Then she looked at the two men and colored. "Habit. You can sit in front," she told Huck.

"No," said Ernie, "you sit up front, Megan. Huck, you're in back."

Megan slid into the front seat. "A siren. Cool. Your car didn't have a siren," she said to Huck.

"That's because Huck has a weenie car," Ernie said.

Megan grinned, and Huck was grateful for Ernie not knowing anything, so Ernie could make fun of Huck like this, and he and Megan could pretend everything was up-front and normal.

They sped out of town and headed north through corn-stubbled fields, Ernie for the most part keeping the conversation light by telling Megan about his daughter Claire and their continuing arguments about the clothes she wore.

"Any advice for an old geezer?" he asked her.

"Ignore it," said Megan. "Even if you forbid it, she'll just change her clothes as soon as she leaves the house." She dug through her book satchel and found a water bottle and drank. "I get the feeling this isn't about any meth dealer," she said after a while. "What exactly do you want from Bill?"

"Just a little information," said Ernie.

"Has he done something?"

Ernie glanced in his rearview mirror. Huck was glad it was Ernie who had to invent excuses right now, and not him.

"Why don't you just tell us a little bit about the guy," Ernie began.

"Like why I let him take the pictures?"

"That's telling us about *you*," Ernie said gently. "I'm more interested in Bill. Start with when you broke up. When was that, anyway?"

"A year ago. New Year's Eve, in fact."

"Whose decision was it?"

"Mine."

"And how did he take it?"

Megan pulled up her knees and clasped them to her chest. "He's like, Oh, no, you're the only one I love, blah blah blah. I figured he'd stay bummed for a week and then move on."

"But?"

"Oh, you know. Roses in the locker. Chocolates. Weird e-mails."

"What'd the e-mails say?"

Megan was silent. Huck wondered if she would have been more forthcoming had he not been sitting in the backseat. Ernie seemed to grasp this as well, for he didn't press the matter.

"We can come back to that. Anything else?" he asked.

From his view in the back Huck couldn't see her face, but he could see that she was holding her head very rigid, as though her hair were made of spun glass. An eighteen-wheeler shuddered by, going ninety five. To the left was a slashed-up hillside for off-road vehicles, empty today. Megan murmured something.

"Excuse me?" said Ernie. "I didn't catch what you said."

All Huck heard was something like ". . . crap he did in my room." Then she fell silent, and finally she turned around to look him square in the face. "I really wish you weren't here, Huck," she told him.

"I'm sorry," he said.

"Me too," she said.

Ernie's eyes flashed at Huck in the rearview mirror. Just one second too long, so that Huck would understand that Ernie now grasped the full complexity of the situation here in the car. Huck shrugged, and Ernie refocused his glare on the road ahead. Huck did not envy Claire, being genetically obliged to report to this man.

"You want to finish with this later?" Ernie asked Megan.

"No," she said. "I might as well tell you now. I had a job last summer. I was out of the house all day. He had a key, and he'd let himself in and go up to my room and get himself off. Ever hear of that happening?"

"Sure," said Ernie, though he spoke for himself, and definitely not for Huck.

"There's probably not much you haven't heard of," Megan remarked.

"Not a whole lot."

"Well, it grossed me out," said Megan. "It was like a dog, coming in to mark his territory."

"Did your mother know?"

"No. She would have flipped. I washed everything before she got home. Here's the thing, though," she continued. "He was an asshole, and it was a disgusting thing to do, but I should have tried to be a little more understanding throughout it all. I wasn't very sympathetic. I didn't know what it was like! Nobody ever dumped me, and I just didn't think about what he was going through. I could have been a little more human."

"I'm sure he got all the compassion he needed from others," Ernie assured her.

"But it wasn't like he committed a crime or anything," she went on. "He just felt . . . rejected. And so he got a little weird. He got a little desperate. I really wasn't very understanding. You really can't tell me what you want to talk to him about?"

"We just want to chat," said Ernie. He turned off the interstate, and they headed through flat open farmland with wheat poking through patches of snow. For a long time nobody spoke as they drove.

Huck wondered if she had any clue about why they were going to talk to Bill. He also wondered how much more he should have argued with Ernie about bringing Megan.

But there was no opportunity to talk with Ernie about this, with Megan right there in the car with them, and soon they were approaching the outskirts of the small college town. With Megan navigating, they drove toward campus, and she directed them to Bill's dorm, a nondescript brick building with an army of bicycles out front. There were also two police cars, campus and town. Ernie parked his car, then turned to face Megan.

"I want you to wait here with Huck," he told her. "I'll be back in a couple of minutes. Don't go anywhere."

"Like I would," Megan murmured, glancing out her window. When Ernie had disappeared into the building, she turned to Huck and sighed. "What's going on?"

"Nothing. Bill may have some information about the case. But he wants to see you too. Ernie's gone up to make sure the place is safe."

"He uses e-mails, not guns."

Huck studied the carpeting. There was a large dark blot on the floor by his foot, something he wouldn't have wanted to touch without a glove. They sat in silence. Megan applied Chapstick. Huck's stomach rumbled. Neither laughed at the sound.

Fortunately it didn't take long for Ernie to come back down and signal for them. They got out of the car and headed into the building, where a cold dankness enveloped them, a combination of stale beer and unwashed laundry and last summer's refrigerant. As they climbed the stairs, their footsteps echoed off the cinder-block walls, and Huck flashed on a drug raid a few years back where they'd found a nest of dead squirrels under a pile of clothes.

"Now, I want to prepare you," said Ernie when they reached the top. "It's not just Bill in the room. There's a campus police officer, along with someone from the local force."

Megan laughed nervously. "He's really not dangerous."

"We're just following procedure," Ernie said. He pushed open the door to Bill's room. There he was, sitting on his bed, dressed in shorts and a green T-shirt with a parks-and-recreation insignia. His cheek was purple and swollen where Huck had punched him the day before. Two uniformed men stood off to the side. Wall-to-wall clothes covered the floor, clean as well as dirty. Bill must have just burned something in the microwave, because the little door was open and the room smelled sour and tinny.

Without saying hello, Bill glanced from one man to the next, eventually letting his heavy-lidded gaze fall on Megan.

"What are we now, a groupie?" he said to her.

"What did you want to talk to me about?" she said coldly.

"Nothing, really. I just wanted to see you."

"You scumbag. My mother wasn't doing meth. What is wrong with you?"

Bill ignored the question. "Did you get in touch with Trigger?" he asked Huck.

Megan laughed sharply. "Oh, Trigger, that's good. Is he another one of your inventions?" Suddenly she turned to Ernie. "Do these two other cops have to be here?"

"For now," said Ernie.

Megan turned back to face Bill. She closed her eyes but simultaneously raised her eyebrows like she was using them to tug her lids back up. "Look, Bill. I know I wasn't the most sensitive person in the world when we broke up, but you're living in a fantasy world if you think my mother was doing meth. You're also living in a fantasy world if you think that spreading rumors about my mother is going to get back at me."

Bill gazed at her. "That's cute, Megan," he said. "Are we taking psychology this semester?"

Ernie stepped forward. "Actually, Bill, you don't seem to have much more of substance to say to Megan, and we've got a few things we'd like to discuss. You agreed to this. Megan, why don't you go back down to the car and wait. The officers here can escort you."

"I'd rather not, actually," said Megan.

"Yeah," said Bill. "Why can't she stay here? You already frisked me; I'm not going to hurt her. What's the big deal?"

"That's right," said Megan. "You don't need to treat me like a child, you know."

"Because she's hardly a child," Bill added.

"Fuck you, Bill," said Megan.

Bill closed his eyes and shook his head in reproach. Then he crossed his arms and looked at Ernie. "If she goes, I don't really feel like talking to you anymore."

Huck wanted to call the whole thing off; they didn't need a confession, certainly not right now. But Ernie seemed to have come up here on a mission. "Fine. Megan can stay. Megan, take a seat over there, please." He indicated a chair near the door. Megan sat down.

"Okay, then. This has to do with Diana," Ernie began.

"Of course! Who else?"

"You and Diana."

Bill shrugged.

"You want to tell us a little about your relationship with her?"

"Do I have to answer that?" Bill said, grinning.

"No," said Ernie. "You don't have to answer any of these questions, remember?"

"Well, it wasn't sex-shu-al, if that's what you're getting at," Bill said, winking at Megan.

"Not exactly," said Ernie.

"That was a joke," said Bill.

"Not really the time for jokes, Bill," Ernie reminded him.

Bill nodded—a little too earnestly, Huck thought. "Sorry. Diana was an amazing woman. More like a mother to me than my own mother herself. Very sympathetic."

"About what?" said Ernie.

"This is going to get personal," Bill warned.

"We're all friends," said Ernie.

Huck folded his arms over his chest. As much as he and Ernie acted like peers, they weren't. Ernie had ten years on him, and at times like this it showed, for even though Bill had managed to get his way by having Megan here, he hadn't come close to tipping the balance of power. Whereas Huck feared there were some people out there, Bill quite possibly among them, who could twist things around on him before he realized what was happening.

"Continue," said Ernie.

"Okay, then," said Bill. "I don't know what Megan has told you, but I had a hard time when we broke up." He bit his lip. "A very hard time, if you will. I had high hopes for the two of us, see. I saw us getting married. Having kids. All that stuff. But then Megan wanted out. I kind of fell apart. It was a bad time for me. I couldn't let go."

"And Diana?"

"She took me out for coffee a couple of times," he said. "At my request. And she told me about her own experience, how when this one guy broke up with her in college, she completely fell apart. Dissolved. Didn't know who she was anymore. Even tried to kill herself."

"More bullshit," Megan told Ernie, but he held up his hand to silence her.

"And that's how she was sympathetic?"

"Sympathetic but firm," Bill insisted. "She advised me to throw myself into hard physical labor. So I did. I got a job doing yardwork for the summer. Hot sun. Sweat. So tired I was asleep by eight o'clock at night. It helped. And then this fall, moving up here. That helped too. And of course meeting Amanda."

"More bullshit," said Megan.

Bill wagged his finger at her.

"You said there wasn't any Amanda," she said.

"Well, I lied," said Bill. "I lied that I lied." He winked, which caused Huck to feel sorry for Megan, right then.

"When was the last time you saw Diana?" asked Ernie.

Bill pursed his lips and thought hard. "August," he finally said. "Right before I started school. We met for coffee one last time. She gave me a going-away present. An itty-bitty address book. Kind of corny. Nobody uses an address book anymore, you know? But that was the last time," he said. "August twenty-fourth. August twenty-fifth I moved up here. August twenty-sixth I started classes."

"So you had no contact with her after that?"

Bill's face grew intense. Then he shook his head. "Nope."

Ernie looked over at Huck, who knew the routine: wrap it up, bring them in for questioning later. Huck nodded back. Ernie gave a shrug. "Okay, then. But hey. One thing. We'd like to get a hair sample at some point, if you wouldn't mind."

It was the kind of cop moment Huck loved—seeing the color drain out of a person's face, or even just watching them begin to fidget. Bill simply sat there with a blank look on his face. Then he straightened up and yawned. "Sorry," he said. "A what did you say?"

"A hair sample."

"Weird! But sure," he said. "Now?" He reached up to pluck out a strand.

"No, not here," said Ernie. "And not just now. Why don't you come back to town with us, though. It's totally up to you, of course. But we can take care of it this afternoon. Bring you back up here tonight. You don't have classes, do you?"

Bill glanced at Megan. Huck did too: she was staring at Ernie, and for the first time since he'd known her, she looked truly perplexed—as though she'd switched on the radio mid-story and heard the word *assassination,* or *smallpox.*

"Detective Vogel?" Megan asked.

"Yes, Megan?"

"Why do you need a hair sample?"

"It's routine," Ernie replied.

"No, it's not," said Megan. "My father's a lawyer. Plus I watch cop shows."

Huck caught Ernie's eye. Picking up on his partner's message, he moved across the room and gently touched Megan on the arm. "Catch some air?"

Megan ripped her arm away from him. "This is why we came up here? This is what you guys wouldn't tell me?" She began shaking her head in disbelief, coupled with what Huck saw as a sense of betrayal. She stared from one man to the next, all enemies at the moment, her gaze finally resting on Bill. "They think it's you," she said with incredulity. "Was it?"

"Huck," said Ernie, "if you can—"

"Did you kill my mother?" Megan asked Bill.

Bill's face remained expressionless for a few seconds, and then his eyes crinkled up, and he nodded and smiled broadly, as though finally understanding the theory of relativity.

"That's what you think?" He looked at all of them and shook his head. He gave a long sigh. "Oh my god. That's what you think. Oh dear sweet Jesus," he said.

"Did you?"

Bill shook his head. "Oh, Megan," he said, closing his eyes. "Megan Megan Megan. How—"

"*Bill.* Did you kill my mother?"

Outside a magpie swooped in and perched on the window ledge. It flicked its blue-black tail twice, then flew off. The heater fan started blowing. Down the hall a door slammed. A burst of male laughter.

"Tell me the truth, Bill."

One by one, Bill began to crack his knuckles. "You don't know what it's like to really—"

"Quit beating around the bush!" shouted Megan. *"Did you kill her?"*

The room fell silent again.

"Yes," said Bill.

For Huck, it was always a shock when someone actually confessed, no matter how certain you might have been of his guilt. It was like opening the gift you wished for but didn't really expect, or getting an A on a test you hadn't studied for. And here, today, having woken up in the morning with not only no expectations but no wishful thinking as well (he was, after all, working down in Records), he found himself listening to Bill's words in part as though they were a distant news story, someone else's scoop, for which he didn't deserve any credit at all. In the end he would probably get that credit, along with Ernie; there would be praise, recognition, maybe awards and promotions as well.

Still, he would see his role in this case as more personal than professional, and this would always keep him grounded, whenever he started to think too highly of himself.

As he spoke, Bill mostly just sat hunched on the edge of his bed, letting his hands dangle between his knees. Sometimes his voice was barely audible. Sometimes he paused.

"But how could you?" Megan would whisper, whenever this happened.

And Bill of course would not reply. Huck could have told her this would happen. Rarely did anyone in this business know how or why they'd done what they'd done. Most of the time it just happened—to a wife, a friend, a lover, a business partner; over love or money, usually. Anyone who could explain it—well, they were a different breed, the ones you had to be truly afraid of.

When Bill was finished, there were still many unanswered questions about Diana's day. But that would come. Hour by hour it could all be accounted for now—either by Megan, or by Frank, or by Steven O'Connell, or by Jack Fries. It was, in the end, simply the story of a long and complicated day, just like any other of Diana's long and complicated days, only this one had an unfortunate end.

"But how could you?" Megan asked once more, when he was through.

And the room simply rang with silence.

CHAPTER SIXTEEN

O N THE MORNING of December 17 Diana woke to the sound of the shower. Frank had slept in the guest room the night before; he'd said he was coming down with a little something. Or maybe he had gas. It didn't matter. She slept better alone.

At 6:20 Diana herself rose. Dressed in her robe, she went downstairs and made coffee and got the newspaper and defrosted some bagels. Having slept well without Frank's presence, she was upbeat; although she had a busy schedule that day, darned if she wasn't going to find time for a little Christmas shopping in the afternoon. Frank was determined to give Megan a new set of tires for Christmas, which made Diana equally determined to buy her something frivolous on her own.

Just as she sat down with her coffee and the newspaper, she heard footsteps on the stairs, and Frank appeared. "Hey," he yawned, setting his hand on her shoulder. It was cold and weighed heavily, like a gel pack.

"Hey yourself," said Diana. "There's coffee."

"Half decaf?" asked Frank.

Diana nodded. Actually the coffee was as leaded as it could get. It wouldn't kill her husband to get a little buzz once in a while.

"Don't cook for me tonight," he told her. "I've got racquetball with Richard, and then we're having dinner."

Again, Diana didn't mind that he would be gone; she liked having the house to herself. She would swim, make a salad, read a book.

"Hey—isn't Megan almost finished with her exams?"

"Tomorrow," replied Diana.

"It'll be nice to have her around, won't it?"

"Don't get your hopes up," Diana said. "She's going to be much more interested in hooking up with friends than hanging out with us."

"I hope you don't mean Bill," Frank said darkly.

Diana sucked air with her teeth. "Bill's out of the picture."

"I wonder about that."

"Give it up, Frank. Trust me. He's gone."

"I trust you—it's him I don't trust. By the way, have you given any thought to what limits we're going to set while Megan's here at home? I don't want to start waiting up for her all night again."

Diana looked up from the paper. "She's a freshman in college, Frank."

"Who can respect our needs."

Your needs, she thought. I like staying up late.

"Never mind, we'll cross that bridge later too," said Frank. He swallowed the rest of his coffee and put the cup in the sink. "But we should figure out a policy. Don't forget the bills, by the way."

"Cup goes in the dishwasher."

Frank opened the dishwasher and placed his cup in the center of the top rack, where it took up more space than necessary. "You always jump before I have a chance to do anything."

"That's because I know you, Frank. You were going to leave it in the sink for me. I've lived with you for twenty-two years, and you were going to leave it there because you know I'll put it in myself since it bothers me and not you to have dirty dishes lying all over the kitchen. Did I leave my gloves in your car, by the way?"

Frank shook his head without giving it much thought. He gave an audible sigh as he put on his coat. Then he picked up his briefcase. "What's on your agenda today?"

"I don't know." She'd woken up in a good mood, and now she was in a bad mood. "Maybe I'll bite somebody's head off."

"You would, too," murmured Frank, on his way out.

Diana showered and dressed, putting on a tank top and then a shirt. Layering was crucial at her age; she could go from normal to feverish within seconds and needed to be able to strip down quickly. She loaded the rest of the breakfast dishes into the dishwasher, found the stack of bills Frank was talking about, went into her office to find stamps, pawed through her top drawer and resolved to go through all those raspy answering machine tapes she was hanging on to because one of them had Megan's voice saying something cute and she wanted to save it; she found the stamps in the back of the drawer, tore off a dozen, grabbed the mail, and left the house.

By the time she got to the clinic, it was snowing hard. Already picketers had gathered on the sidewalk; today being Tuesday, it was the group from the Baptist church with their posters of Baby Luke. Thursday it was the Catholics with Baby Jessica; Friday it was the mothers with Baby Mary. Today because of the snow the picketers wore heavy jackets and coarse knitted hats and held steaming cups to their mouths. They nodded to Diana, and she nodded back, grateful for the mood—today, at least—of mutual acceptance. She drove around to the rear of the building, parked the car, and turned off her windshield wipers.

The back door of the clinic was unlocked.

Usually she was the first person at the clinic in the morning, but today a set of fresh footprints led up the walkway. Diana turned off the engine. She wondered if she should call the police. Then she recalled that she'd called them just four days ago, when the electricity went out. They'll think you're hysterical, she told herself. Maybe you forgot to lock the door last night. Maybe the security guard had to get in for something. Maybe Dixie just came in early.

She gathered her things, locked the car, and walked up the path to the back door. She pushed it open. The hallway was dark. Warily she switched on the lights. Slushy footprints led down the hall to her office.

"Hello?"

No answer.

"Hello!"

Still no answer. Involuntarily Diana touched her chest; she hadn't worn her vest today because she'd tweaked her shoulder reaching for something, and wearing the vest aggravated the pain. She reached into her purse for her cell phone and turned it on. It beeped and went dead. Now her eyes scanned the hallway; the nearest phone was a wall unit ten feet away. She took a step forward, and the floor gave a loud creak.

Just as she was about to turn and run, the door to her office opened and a silhouette appeared in a panel of light.

It was Megan.

She noticed Diana's face and stared back. "What's the matter?"

"Are you *crazy,* breaking in like this?"

"I have a key!"

Diana pushed past her daughter and went into her office, where she took off her coat and dropped it onto a chair. "Honest to god, Megan—you could have gotten yourself shot! Where's your head?? How old are you??"

"I thought we could have breakfast together," Megan said in her soft morning voice, trailing Diana. She was puffy-eyed, and her hair was disheveled. "I brought muffins."

Diana glanced at the oil-blotted bag sitting on her desk. Usually when Megan brought something, she wanted something in return. "Don't you have an exam today?"

"Biology, and it's tomorrow," said Megan. "I've got all day to study. You want a muffin or not? If you're not hungry, I'll take it back to Natalie."

"No, I'll have one," said Diana. "That's very sweet of you, honey. You just scared the shit out of me."

Megan opened the bag and took out two giant sugary muffins. She handed one to Diana and greedily peeled the paper off the other.

"So," she said. "I saw the group out front."

"The Moroni case is coming down in January," said Diana.

"Which way do you think the court will go?"

"I'm not worrying about it right now. I've got six procedures this morning and Christmas shopping this afternoon."

"Speaking of Christmas," said Megan. Diana looked up, her mouth full of muffin. "Well, I had an idea for a present."

"We're giving you a new set of tires," Diana reminded her.

"But you usually get me something fun too."

Diana looked at her watch. "You know, honey, I've got a lot on my schedule this morning. If you—"

"That's the thing," said Megan. "We have to buy the tickets by Friday."

"What tickets?"

"To Mexico."

"Who's going to Mexico?"

"Me! I mean, I want to," said Megan. "I was thinking you guys could give me a ticket for Christmas."

Diana peered closely at her daughter to make sure she wasn't joking. "Are you joking?"

"A lot of people are going."

"Always such a strong argument."

"I'd really really like to go," said Megan.

"So would I. God, I haven't been to Mexico in twenty years. We already talked about your big present, Megan," said Diana. "Good tires cost a fortune."

Megan murmured something.

"Or not," said Diana. "You could show a little gratitude, you know. You weren't even going to have a car this year until your father found that car for sale."

"A nineteen-seventy-five Bug with a heater that doesn't work?"

"So sell it," Diana said. "Take the bus. Walk."

"I never ask for anything," said Megan.

"Oh please."

"What have I asked for lately?"

"Try a college education? A new laptop? Brand-new bedding for your dorm room? Books? Room and board?"

"I saved you so much money by going in-state," Megan said. "It's all I want for Christmas! I need to get away from here! I need to have something to look forward to!"

"So do I," said Diana. "Maybe we'll all go to Mexico."

Megan shifted tactics. "You have no clue why I'm asking you to do this," she said haughtily, and Diana forced herself not to laugh, for her daughter now sounded like an old biddy wanting to be begged.

"Okay: why?"

"I can't tell you."

"So how can I have any kind of a clue at all?"

"You just have to trust me. It's a big deal."

"I'm sorry, Megan, but you've got to be a little more open with me."

"Okay," said Megan, and she took a deep breath. "It's Bill."

Diana felt the hair on her neck rise.

"He keeps calling me. E-mailing me. Telling me he wants to do stuff to me."

"What kind of stuff?"

"Bad stuff."

Diana brushed muffin crumbs from her lap. She thought about Bill's repeated phone calls to her, his pleas for advice over the past year and especially this fall. Threatening to kill himself. Or asking if she'd seen the movie *Cape Fear*, because that's what he felt like, Robert De Niro with a bone to pick. She wondered if he'd gotten the help she'd advised him to get. Probably not.

"He's a talker," she told Megan. "Best to ignore him."

"How do I know?"

"I know his type. Plus you can't do much legally, unless he actually does something to you."

"But I *could* go to Mexico."

"You want to explain the connection?"

"Oh, you are *so selfish!*" Megan shouted. "Never mind. I'll go stand on a street corner and earn the money." She glared at Diana sullenly. Diana realized her daughter had run out of steam, and with the pressure suddenly off, she began to wonder why she'd vetoed the idea so vehemently.

Megan buttoned up her jacket. "I'm sorry I even came."

"We'll talk about it tonight," said Diana. "Have dinner with me. Your father's going out."

"No, Mother, I have to *study* tonight," said Megan, roping her scarf around her long thin neck. "I'm in *college*, remember? I have *exams*. Forget I asked. Forget I said anything. In fact, forget I exist."

"Megan—"

Megan turned, hoisting her backpack. Then she glanced back. "Have fun killing babies today," she remarked. And without another word she flounced out, slamming the door behind her.

Through her window Diana watched Megan trudge off through the snow. Again she regretted having said no right off like that. The ticket probably wasn't more than three or four hundred dollars. They had the money. And it could have been that frivolous gift she'd been planning to buy. But no, she'd had to go and veto the idea without thinking. Like Frank, she thought. What's wrong with me?

And what about Bill? The guy did need some professional attention. She decided that she had to talk to Frank about this. Tonight, when he got home. He had a right to know, even if he got upset. Maybe it was time to call Bill's parents, too, or even go to the police. Frank would know what to do.

———————

Her morning was a hectic one, as usual. Depending on how far along they were, Diana's patients came in one or two days ahead of the actual abortion, at which time she inserted a thin stick of seaweed into the woman's cervix, which would start the dilation process. The woman then went home and returned the next day, either for another laminaria insertion or the extraction itself. Inserting the laminaria took only seconds, but the extraction process took more time, depending, again, on how far along the woman was. On a good day Diana usually saw six to eight women throughout the course of the morning.

Today she managed to stay on schedule, so that by late morning she had started four women on their dilation and taken care of three who were back for the second-day extraction. By keeping busy, by staying on schedule, she managed to keep her mind off the argument with Megan. When Frank called around eleven-thirty, she decided not to mention it to him.

"Sorry if I was a little testy this morning," he began.

Diana squelched a sigh. Again, as with Megan, there was probably an ulterior motive here; usually if her husband called during the workday, it meant something was wrong. Was it? she asked.

"No! I just wanted to apologize. And see if you wanted to have lunch with me. We never do that anymore. We said we would when Megan went off to college, and now we don't."

"I'm way too busy," she said, thinking of the Christmas shopping she wanted to do.

"Oh, come on, Di," said Frank. "Take a little time off. We need to do things together again."

Diana rearranged the trio of Ben's ashtrays on her desk. Hadn't she herself pledged to make more time for their marriage? It wasn't often that either of them reached out to the other for something as ordinary as having lunch together. There was still a week until Christmas; there was plenty of time for shopping.

"Fine. Where?"

"How about Walt's? One o'clock?"

It sounded so much like a date that she hung up slightly amused. And hopeful too, she had to admit. She and Frank had issues, but who didn't after twenty years of marriage? They'd lost a son. A lot of marriages fell apart over something like that. A lot of marriages fell apart over *nothing*.

She was about to scrub up for her last extraction when Dixie buzzed her. Steven O'Connell was out in reception and wanted to see her.

"No way," said Diana.

"He looks pretty upset," ventured Dixie.

"Too bad. If he doesn't leave, call the police." She hung up and went out into the hallway and reviewed the patient's chart as she headed toward the procedure room. The woman was fourteen weeks pregnant, a mother with three children, thirty-five years old, and under suicide watch in connection with a serious depression. She had been in the last two days for successive laminaria insertions;

today Diana would administer light sedation and scrape out the fetal tissue.

She was about to enter the procedure room when she heard a scuffle out in the reception area: raised voices, a bump against the wall—and then suddenly Steven O'Connell came barging down the hall toward her, followed by Dixie, who was trying without success to grab his arm as he kept wresting it away.

"Get your hands off me!" he exclaimed. "Diana—thank God—I need you—"

"Get out of here, Steven," Diana said calmly.

"Hear me out, Diana!"

She caught Dixie's eye and nodded at the alarm.

"Wait!" Steven cried. "It's about Rose!"

Disgusted with the man's assumption that his needs took precedence over all others, nevertheless Diana motioned for Dixie to hold off.

"I have a patient in this room who's had to endure a lot of waiting at this point," she told Steven. "You can wait half an hour."

"Not Rose!"

"What do you mean?"

Steven dropped to his knees and began banging his fists on the floor. Honestly. "Cut the theatrics, Steven, and just tell me what's going on."

Steven clutched at his face and breathed in deeply, then raised his head and clasped his hands in a pose that so resembled a Renaissance painting that Diana fought the impulse to make a joke.

After a few seconds, he slumped. "Rose did something to herself. She's over in the hospital. I need your help."

Calmly, Diana asked, "What did she do, Steven?"

"I don't know!" he cried. "There was blood, a lot of blood! She's over at the hospital now. Please, please come and help," he begged.

Diana glanced at Dixie, who was looking on incredulously: Steven

O'Connell asking Diana Duprey for *help*? Diana turned back to Steven. "I will take care of my patient," she told him in a steady voice, "and then I will go over to the hospital with you and see what I can do. Go back to the reception area and sit down and wait. Don't leave. Don't make a scene. Just go and wait."

"How long?"

"If all goes well," said Diana, "half an hour."

For the next thirty minutes she worked under the bright lights, seated on a stool between the woman's legs. Her name was Julia, and she cried when Diana injected the anesthetic into her cervix, but as Diana scraped out the raw bloody tissue, Julia lay still. Finally Diana rolled her chair back, snapped off her gloves, and stood up. She smoothed Julia's hair back, then rested her hand upon the woman's dampened forehead.

"You'll be okay," she told her.

"I know," whispered Julia.

"It's just hard right now, I know."

Julia nodded.

Diana squeezed her hand. "I'm going to leave now. Mary will take good care of you. You rest. I have to run over to the hospital, but I'll be back to check on you in an hour or so."

The procedure finished, Diana didn't bother changing out of her scrubs but hurried out to the waiting room, where Steven leaped to his feet. Diana told him to fill her in on the way over to the hospital. They hurried outside into the dizzying storm. The snow was light and fluffy, but the cold wind burrowed deeply into her chest, and she began to trot. Steven struggled to keep up.

"She did it herself," Steven panted.

"Where?"

"In the bathroom."

"What did she use?"

"Chopsticks. And a bicycle pump."

Good god, thought Diana. "Was she conscious?"

"No," he said. "I called nine-one-one. They took her to the hospital."

"Do her parents know?"

"I called them," said Steven.

"And Scott? Does Scott know?"

"No," he cried. "Scott's in school. Is she going to be all right?"

"I don't know," said Diana. She now questioned her judgment in making Steven wait while she took care of Julia. Faced with the man's hysteria, she'd operated on the assumption that whatever the problem, the doctors on call could take care of Rose. Now, though, she flashed on a worst-case scenario. Not every doctor could sew up a perforated uterus, and a half hour could make all the difference in the world in a case such as this.

"I just don't get it," said Steven. "How could she do this?"

Diana glanced at him. He has no clue, she thought. She pictured Rose at the O'Connell house, waking up every morning to their happy expectant faces. Grace before meals. Prayers before bed. She imagined them feeding her, weighing her, measuring her belly as it grew. "She's fifteen, Steven. She's a sophomore in high school and scared to death."

"She wouldn't have had to raise it," Steven said. "I would have adopted it myself."

Diana stepped out into the street and stopped traffic with her hand. "It's not an art project, Steven," she told him as they crossed over to the hospital. "It's not something you just make and then hand over, like an ashtray. Look," she said when they reached the curb. "It takes a certain kind of person to give up a baby, and maybe Rose wasn't one of them."

"I consider that a character flaw, then," Steven said.

She looked at the man standing beside her—another member of the human race but a different species altogether.

"For you, it's really black and white and nothing in between, isn't it?" she marveled.

"I call it clarity."

"And you know what I call it? Personal fascism." She didn't care if her words were extreme; nothing was ever going to open this man's eyes. She sorely regretted now that she hadn't made more of an effort to talk to Rose and find out what was really going on in her mind; if she had, maybe she'd have been able to foresee Rose's change of heart before Rose locked herself in the bathroom with a bicycle pump.

They entered through an unmarked door that led directly into the emergency room, where a group of medical staff were clustered around a central desk watching one of the doctors juggle a hacky-sack with his heel from behind. When he saw Diana and Steven, he sent the little embroidered ball flying high and caught it in his left hand.

"She's up in Surgery," he told Diana gravely.

"Howie's taking care of her," added one of the nurses.

Howie Weinstein was the hospital's chief gynecologist, an arrogant man who didn't like anyone second-guessing his decisions—which, since his decisions were usually right, often infuriated her. Frank's take was that she didn't get along with Howie because they were cut from the same cloth, two blunt and outspoken doctors with robust egos. (Robust being Frank's word, carefully chosen not to offend his wife.)

"Is he a good doctor?" Steven asked as they rode the elevator to the second floor.

Diana sighed. "He's a great doctor, Steven. If anyone could take care of Rose besides me, it's Howie Weinstein." She didn't mention that Howie Weinstein was always faxing her articles on new developments in late-stage abortions, FYI, or that when his son was accepted to Yale, he handed out cigars to everyone at the hospital, including

Diana, who'd just that morning mailed off the deposit for Megan's space at the university. No, Howie was great.

The doors opened, and they hurried down the hall to Surgery—where they were met by Howie Weinstein himself, still in his scrubs, two little round marks on the bridge of his nose where his glasses had been.

"You're too late," he said, wearily putting his glasses back on.

"Don't tell me," Diana warned.

"I had no choice."

Diana slammed her fist against the wall.

"It was like Jell-O, Diana," he said. "There was no place to suture. It's a miracle she even got pregnant, with a uterus like that."

"Why didn't you page me?"

"There wasn't time."

"I'm right across the street!"

"She would have bled to death. Besides, you couldn't have done anything. Trust me, Diana. There was nothing else to do. What are you doing here?" he asked Steven.

"I'm the grandfather," replied Steven in a shaken voice. "What does this mean?" he asked Diana.

"He took out her uterus," Diana told him.

"Whose grandfather?" Howie asked. "Rose's?"

"No," said Steven. "I'm the baby's grandfather."

Diana could see Howie's mind working, and in a way she could never have imagined, she found herself feeling protective of Steven O'Connell—as though he had every right to be there and call himself the grandfather of the child that never was. Alliances were shifting by the minute. She felt like Alice herself, stepping back and forth through the looking glass.

"Do Rose's parents know?" she asked Howie.

"Yes," said Howie.

"How'd they take it?"

"How do you think?"

"Where are they now?"

"They're in with Rose," he said. As though guessing what Steven was about to do, he added, "I wouldn't go in there if I were you."

Diana took Steven aside. "He's right," she said. "Let me go. There's a room down the hall. Wait there."

Steven gazed at her with a lack of comprehension that she knew all too well from her years as a doctor, when there was bad news to give.

"Rose is alive," she reminded him. "That's the important thing."

Steven nodded hungrily.

"Go wait. I won't be long," she told him.

———————

In the dim light of the recovery room, Diana approached Rose's bed, which was surrounded by a dizzying array of IV poles and tubes. Amid the electronic jungle stood Rose's parents. Jack's tie was loosened, his shirtsleeves rolled up. Elaine looked tired with no lipstick.

Rose lay sleeping under a white cotton blanket. Wisps of hair strayed from the edges of her blue surgical bonnet. As Diana approached, Jack glanced up; his face stiffened, and he turned back to Rose. Elaine covered her face with her hands.

Diana glanced at the green lines blipping on the monitor and scanned a roll of data coming from the printer.

"I think she's waking up," said Elaine. "Her eyes kind of opened. She's so pale, though."

"She lost a lot of blood," said Diana.

"And every so often the line wiggles around," Elaine said. "There. See?"

"That's normal too," said Diana. "Did Dr. Weinstein explain things to you?"

Elaine reached out and tucked a wisp of hair back into the bonnet. "She can't have children," she whispered.

"He tried very hard to save her uterus," Diana said. "It just wasn't possible. She's lucky to be alive."

"Lucky," Jack murmured.

"But he did save her ovaries," Elaine noted.

"Her ovaries are fine," said Diana. "So technically she can still have children."

Again Jack said something under his breath.

"Using a surrogate," Elaine added.

Diana nodded. She took Rose's wrist in her hand and just held it, feeling the pulse. "And you won't have to be thinking about hormone replacement," she went on. "Still, I'm so very sorry."

Jack looked up. "*Lucky*. Not exactly the word I would have chosen. You should have listened to us back in October."

"Jack," said Elaine.

"All it would have taken was a few well-chosen words," said Jack.

"Honey," said Elaine, "don't go there."

"I'll go wherever I want right now," said Jack, leveling a grim look at Diana. "You should have listened to us. We knew what was best for her."

The clarity of hindsight, Diana wanted to say. But she knew better than to argue with a father holding vigil at his daughter's bedside.

"Are you going to give her the happy news when she wakes up?" Jack said. "Or shall we?"

"Jack, don't. I'm sorry," Elaine said to Diana. "He's so upset. We both are."

"What kind of an abortion doctor are you," Jack asked, "that you would let a fifteen-year-old girl go ahead with a pregnancy?"

"I don't counsel people to have an abortion if they don't want it," said Diana.

"But she did want it. She was brainwashed by that family. You should have known. I could sue the shit out of you," he said.

Of all the hurdles she'd faced as an abortion doctor, none had been as difficult for Diana as cultivating restraint. After the fresh tar incident last year, for instance, she'd wanted nothing so much as to hurl her gooey-soled clogs at the protesters. But she didn't; prudence and professionalism prevailed; she walked on by without a word. After twenty years in the business, she'd learned a few tricks that helped her maintain her composure—to turn the other cheek, even if it was against her nature.

But there was something in Jack's voice that made her prickle and flush. The day had started off badly, and things were still headed downhill.

Chill, Ma, she heard Megan warn.

"And you think you'd prevail?" she said.

"I don't care. Because I could certainly make your life very, very unpleasant," he said. "I could ruin your practice."

"Jack, honey," said Elaine.

"Did he pay you or something?" Jack asked.

"I beg your pardon?"

"Steven O'Connell. Did he pay you not to encourage Rose?"

"Is that a joke?"

"Or maybe there's something going on between the two of you?"

"Excuse me," said Diana (*Ma! shut up!*), "but who goes around with his dick hanging out every year at the ABA conference?"

Jack sprang up and grabbed Diana by both arms and snapped her head back. "You should have *done* something!" he shouted. "You're supposed to keep girls *safe*! Our daughter almost *died*!" And with that he kicked a nearby chair over and stormed out of the recovery room.

Diana stood there, shaking. After a few moments she straightened her shoulders and glanced at Elaine, who had begun to weep.

"I'm sorry," Diana said. "That was out of line."

"You must take a lot of pleasure in hurting people," Elaine said. "Do you treat your own family this way? Making comments like that? I feel sorry for them," she said.

"Look," Diana began, "I think we're all—"

"Here our daughter's just had an emergency hysterectomy, and you dare to talk to my husband like that. Do you have any sense of humanity at all? Oh my god," she said. "You are a monster."

Diana swallowed. She had been accused of being a monster many times before, but only by the zealots on the other side of the issue. Again everything seemed topsy-turvy. Frank, Megan, Steven, Rose's parents, herself—nobody was behaving the way they should behave. Was she losing her mind?

"You get out," Elaine said. "I don't want you in this room. Dr. Weinstein is taking care of Rose. We don't need you here. You're just making things worse."

Diana backed away. The degree of truth in Elaine's words stung. She *was* making things worse. And for a moment all she could focus on were her mistakes—not just as a doctor but as a wife, a mother, a person. She had failed to sense Rose's change of heart. She had failed to be honest with Megan about Mexico. She had failed to nurture along a marriage that might have come alive again. Even her decision to have Ben fifteen years ago seemed now like a horrific failure.

"That's right," said Elaine. "You can leave now. You can go. You can disappear off the face of this earth, for all I care."

It was at that moment that Howie Weinstein came in. He glanced at the monitor and looked at the chart and put his hand on Elaine's shoulder. "Everything looks good. She should be waking up any minute now."

"Get her out of here," Elaine murmured, holding Rose's hand.

"Who?" asked a confused Dr. Weinstein.

But Elaine didn't have to explain, because Diana had already fled the room.

She didn't remember that she was supposed to have had lunch with Frank until she was already in the pool, by which point it was four o'clock. The light was dim, but many houses in the neighborhood were already ablaze with gargantuan Christmas displays. Each year they got more and more ostentatious, to the point where Diana felt their neighborhood had become a suburban Las Vegas. She herself hadn't put up any lights this year and didn't miss it. Sometimes she wished she were Jewish so they could just do away with the Christmas hoopla.

She tugged at the bottom of her dark green suit and lowered herself into the water, which was cool and foamy and sent a shiver up through her neck. A steel bar jutted out from the front; Diana took hold of it, braced her feet up against the edge, and bounced lightly, stretching as the jets pummeled her chest. Slowly she felt herself begin to relax. She had poured herself a couple of shots of scotch when she got home, knowing it wasn't the wisest thing but figuring that after the day's events, even a swim wouldn't calm her nerves. She knew it was against all rules but didn't care. She was forty-seven and she knew her capacity for alcohol and she wasn't going to drink enough to drown.

After a few minutes she let go, and began to swim.

In her mind she was always swimming to France. She imagined the choppy waves of the English Channel, the gray sky, the sound of the boat next to her. *Shall we keep going?* they would shout, and she would shout back, *Keep going!* because what they would not know was that she felt like she could swim forever, not just to France but to Egypt and India and the barren shores of Australia.

She turned up the speed, swimming straight into the wake of an unseen boat. Within minutes she was in machine mode, hands cupped, arms pulling down and around, legs *whuffing* steadily behind her as she lost herself in the rhythmic expulsion of bubbles through her mouth. Sometimes while swimming she heard music. Sometimes she composed letters to old high school friends. Sometimes she went back to the lake house of her childhood, the choppy water, the smell of hemlock, the fat yellow spiders drooping on their webs beneath the rickety dock.

Today, however, she simply swam. Maybe it was because of the scotch. It didn't matter. She became numb. Her arms turned like water wheels. Her legs kicked. Her mind went blank.

Suddenly the jets stopped. Unable to react in time, Diana shot forward, scraping her knuckles on the front edge of the pool. Pushing back, she found her footing and squinted through her goggles. Oh. Frank.

She lifted her goggles and sucked the blood from her knuckles. "Don't do that."

Frank loomed above her. "Get out."

"Sorry about lunch," she said. "You wouldn't believe my day."

Frank picked up the highball glass she'd set by the edge of the pool and flung it across the room at the ficus tree, glass shattering against the green tiles. "If you are at all interested in saving any thread of this marriage," he said, calmly gazing at the mess, "get out of the pool."

Diana couldn't help but stare at this uncharacteristic behavior. "Jesus fucking Christ, Frank," she said. "Where do you get off, talking to me that way?"

Frank squatted down. He laced his fingers and let his hands dangle between his legs and continued to gaze at the ficus tree. She rarely saw him like this, wound up and tense and ready to spring. "Go get a drink, Frank."

But her words seemed to float past her husband. In what seemed like a trance, he swished his hand in the water. Then suddenly he grabbed her arm. "What is your problem!?" she exclaimed, wrenching it away.

"Get out. We need to talk."

Diana hoisted herself, dripping, onto the edge of the pool, making sure to keep an arm's distance between the two of them. She picked at the rags of skin hanging off her knuckles. "What the fuck, Frank."

Frank cleared his throat. "I used to wonder," he said, lightly splashing water against the side of the pool, "whether I was wrong all those years."

"Wrong about what?"

"Wrong to let you get your way all the time."

"I have no idea what you are talking about. And this isn't the best time to bring up heavy-duty issues, by the way. You have no idea what kind of a day I had." There was water in one ear and she shook her head to the side. His fingernails had left three little pink smiles on her arm.

"Never any consequences," he went on. "You let her talk back to you. You let her break curfew. You gave her beer and pot. 'She's going to do it anyway,' you said. 'She might as well do it in the safety of our own home.' How old was she when you put her on the Pill?"

"I never put Megan on the Pill!"

He held up a round pink case. "Then how'd this get in her bureau drawer?"

"There are other doctors in town, Frank. Honest to god."

"Do you remember," he continued, "the open enrollment debacle?"

During open enrollment at the end of fifth grade, Diana had insisted on letting Megan make the choice as to which middle school to attend. To Frank's dismay, Megan chose the unstructured arts school over the more academically oriented neighborhood school. Diana viewed the decision as a sign of maturity. Then in mid-September they got a call from the principal informing them that Megan was floundering: she needed more structure, he said, and he advised that she transfer back to the neighborhood school. Frank was unabashedly bitter and smug.

"Of course I remember. So what?"

"And how long did she last?"

"What's your point?"

"She was ten years old! And you insisted that *she* should be the one to make the choice. *We* should have made that decision! But no, you wanted to give her autonomy, just like you wanted to let her set her own bedtime and decide what to eat for dinner."

"This is what's bugging you so you have to come home and beat me up?"

Frank rubbed his eyes. "My point is you were never willing to impose any limits."

"Oh. That again." They had been over this issue so many times before—or had they? Diana suddenly realized that many of their so-called discussions on this matter had actually taken place inside her own head, whenever she was angry with him for something else. She tried to remember a real, face-to-face confrontation.

Frank continued: "Now. Fast-forward a few years. Remember that drawing class she took in tenth grade?"

"At the college," said Diana. "Figure drawing."

"With twenty-one-year-olds. Did you ever speak to the instructor? Did you ever make any effort to find out what might be going on?"

"Did *you?*"

"Don't change the subject. Did it ever occur to you that they would have live models for the class? That they'd pay you to model? That Megan was into her clothes fetish at that point? Remember how much a shirt from Abercrombie cost?"

Diana threw her head back. "Spell it out, Frank!"

"In one evening she might have earned enough for two shirts," said Frank. "But of course it probably never occurred to you to tell her there might be some limits here."

"So you think she might have posed nude for a class. So what? Haven't you ever taken a drawing class? Everybody poses. And it's not about sex, in case you're wondering. It's about the human body."

Frank held up a finger, the know-it-all teacher. "Maybe for those who are truly drawing. But what if your motive is something else? What if you're carrying around a camera?"

"And who would do that? You are so paranoid, Frank. Can't you for once assume that people are normal? And don't play lawyer with me," she snapped when he didn't reply. He would do this in their arguments, and it drove her crazy, this legal gamesmanship that depended on one of them waiting out a silence. "What are you getting at, Frank? Cameras in an art class—Megan—nude photographs—" Then suddenly she stopped. Her mouth soured.

"The Pearl investigation?"

"Yes indeed," said Frank.

"Pictures of Megan?"

"Yes indeed."

"How do you know it's her?"

"Do you want to see them for yourself?"

"No," said Diana. "Oh my god."

"Oh my god is right, Diana," said Frank.

Diana began to shiver. She stood up and put on her robe and slipped her feet into her flip-flops. "So what you're saying is that

Megan posed for the class, and someone took pictures and sold them to someone else who you're investigating for this case?"

"You want to tell me how else they might have gotten online?"

She crossed her arms and began to pace. "Maybe they're not really of her. Maybe they're of someone else and they just superimposed her face on them."

Frank cocked his head, as though listening to a flimsy excuse from a wayward child. "They're Megan," he said. "Right down to the mole on her stomach. Besides, what would it matter? If it's her face, it might as well be her." He stood up and, as was his custom during most of their arguments, headed out of the room. Diana flip-flopped after him.

"Don't walk away on me, Frank Thompson!" she shouted, grabbing his arm. "Don't come in here in the middle of my swim and dump a load like this and then walk away! Why are you looking at me like that? What, you think it's my fault? You just got through telling me I don't control my daughter, and now you're telling me I do?"

"I hold you responsible," Frank said icily.

"Oh!" Diana crowed. "Oh! Don't you *dare* pin this one on me! Come back here!" she shouted, following him down the hall. "Son of a bitch, don't walk away on me!"

Frank wheeled around and grabbed her arms and shook her once, hard, so that her neck snapped back. It was the second time that day someone had done this to her. She pushed away and rubbed her neck.

"By not giving her a little guidance once in a while, you're now responsible, yes, I'm saying that," he said. "But there's more here. I'm talking about our marriage in general! Everything you wanted, you got! You got to raise Megan the way you wanted! You got to decide where we went on vacation! You got to get the kitchen remodeled when I wanted to just move into another house! You got that stupid pool, for chrissake!"

"You want to turn this into a money issue? We can talk about your Range Rover, if you want. Or your river trips."

Frank tossed his head with disgust. "You're completely missing the point."

"Or that Emilio what's-his-name suit you had to have," she went on. "How much was that again?"

"See? You haven't heard a word I said. You're getting what you want right now, just by not listening."

"I heard everything you said. You're telling me it's my fault if Megan made an error in judgment—"

"Wow, a miracle. You listened."

"—and if she went and posed for these pictures, I'm somehow responsible. You blow me away, Frank."

"Fine with me. At least I've gotten you to stop and think and hear my point of view. Because you know what? I don't think you've considered my point of view since the day we were married."

Diana laughed loudly; that was so untrue.

"No," said Frank, "I take that back. Let's date it a little later. Since the day we found out about Ben."

The nasty smile drained off her face.

"That's right," he said. "You stopped listening then. You were going to have Ben regardless of how I felt. Isn't that the truth? You had to go and prove you weren't just a heartless baby killer Oh *no*, you were the great Dr. Duprey, the abortion doctor who decided *not* to abort her retarded child. Great way to refute the pro-lifers. Hey, it's a matter of choice, see? What a photo op."

Diana felt her knees weaken. By bringing Ben into this, Frank had ripped off an age-old Band-Aid, and with it an enormous scab. *Ben, her baby boy, her beautiful, happy, heartache of a baby boy.*

"You loved him," she whispered.

"Of course I loved him! How couldn't I? But did I ever really have any say in the matter?"

"I listened to you," said Diana. "I knew how you felt. There wasn't a whole lot of middle ground in this issue, you know. How could we have compromised?"

Frank dropped his head and ran his fingers through his hair. He closed his eyes and shook his head. "Fourteen years."

"Of what?"

"Of shutting myself down."

"And this is why you wanted to have lunch?"

"No." He gave a mean laugh. "This morning I actually had this delusion that we could become close again. Maybe I thought we could finally talk about this and heal things up. Then again, maybe I'm delusional now. I don't know. God, I just don't know."

"Are you saying you want a divorce?" she asked.

"I don't know. I'm tired. I'm tired of everything right now. I'm tired of my job. I'm tired of people who lie and cheat and steal. I'm tired of scumbags. I'm tired of people who sell pictures of children. I'm tired of making excuses for everyone."

"Are you tired of me?"

She needed him to look at her then, but instead he lifted his gaze to the ceiling and closed his eyes. "I need to get out of here," he said. "I'll be back. I don't know what I feel. I don't even know if I mean what I'm saying right now. I'm going out. Go back to the pool. Finish your swim." He turned and started climbing the stairs, leaving her in the front hallway. "Go on," he said. "I'm going to change my shirt and get out of here. I have to do something. Go on." Wearily he toiled up the stairs.

In a daze, Diana walked into the kitchen. She sat on a stool at the kitchen island, staring numbly at a catalog for outdoor gear. She felt sickened by his accusations but knew there was a measure of truth in his words. She *had* gotten professional mileage out of her decision, even if it wasn't her intent. Someone had even written an editorial in the local newspaper about Ben: "The Doctor Makes a Choice," they'd titled it. After that the clinic received a large bequest from an anonymous donor, which they'd used to add on the recovery wing.

But to say that she'd made the decision *just* to get professional mileage? She couldn't believe he'd said that. She put her head down on her arms as memories of Ben came flooding in. They'd gotten the news that he was carrying the extra twenty-first chromosome on a Wednesday afternoon, and by dinnertime she'd made up her mind. To Frank it was going to be simple, she knew; it would be a matter of putting sound medical knowledge to use. But as she stood by the island watching him chop tomatoes, she knew she would never be able to abort this child. She needed to carry him to term and push him into this world; she needed to see his face and look into his eyes and hold him and nurse him and rock him, just as she had done with Megan.

They'd argued, through the night and for an entire raw, ugly week. He told her it wouldn't be fair to Megan. She said they would *make* it fair. He told her he was afraid of raising a retarded child. She said he might be only *slightly* retarded. He told her she was letting her hormones make the decision. She said nothing then, merely leveled a stony gaze at him until he looked away. After a week he gave in.

"He could be severely retarded," he said.

"I know."

"He could die in his first year too."

"Yes," said Diana, "he could."

"I couldn't take that, Diana," Frank said.

His voice had caught, and Diana, who up until that point had not wavered in her conviction, suddenly faltered. For the first time in a week she really looked at her husband. His eyes were getting pouchy, with that little flap of skin beginning to droop over his eyelid. And for some reason the mere sight of that little flap started unraveling everything in her. He was a good man. Who was she to subject him to the possible heartbreaks this baby might bring? Maybe he was right;

maybe they were getting in over their heads. Maybe only IVs and slobber and a tiny pine casket lay ahead of them. Why introduce pain and grief? Why complicate their lives?

At which point she'd had to look away. She'd envisioned a wisp of smoke: sharp and well defined but always rising out of sight, the baby that never was. No. She couldn't.

Ben was born on a warm spring day when the mountains were melting and everywhere, it seemed, you could hear the sound of rushing water. The hospital staff was ready for them. There was apprehension in everyone's eyes—who was this child, and what would he be like?—but Diana focused instead on the normalcy of it all, the nurses' subdued excitement as they hooked up the fetal monitor, with Frank bowing his head in somber concentration, and Diana cheerful and upbeat as her belly tightened rock hard, chatting away until the real contractions suddenly bore down, breathing in and out like Darth Vader until the urge to push overwhelmed her and she gave two long vein-bursting screams and delivered her second baby into the hands of the waiting obstetrician.

He had round, wide-spaced eyes and a head the size of a grapefruit. His trebly cries tore at her heart, and she held him to her breast, but he was unable to suckle. Her breasts stung as he batted his head against them.

"He's so beautiful," she whispered.

"They always are," the nurse replied.

She recalled Frank lifting him from her chest, taking the flannel blanket from the nurse and wrapping Ben in its soft folds. There was nothing wrong with him, she had thought as Frank took him away. Nothing. Nothing at all.

But there was, of course.

She lifted her head. The kitchen seemed foreign and disorganized, and she felt like she was in someone else's home. After a while she heard Frank come back downstairs. She heard the front door open and close, and noticed the Beekmans' lights turn off. Nosy bitch, she thought. Numbly she wandered back to the solarium, where she switched off the lights and sat on the edge of the pool. They should have faced things a long time ago, she told herself. It was true. Ben had blasted a hole in their marriage. Even more than that: the whole experience of waiting for Ben, and loving Ben, and losing Ben had triggered such a tectonic split in their marriage that after Ben died they'd been living on separate coastlines. And no matter how hard they tried to carry on with their lives, that sea of loss had always been there, cold and gray as the North Atlantic.

Had she really railroaded him into doing everything her way?

For a long time Diana went back and forth like this: hating Frank, hating herself, hating Frank again. So engrossed was she in this debate that at first she didn't hear the knock on the sliding-glass door. But whoever it was knocked again, and this time she glanced up.

There on her back porch stood Bill Branson, wearing a bomber jacket that was lightly dusted with snow. With great agitation he motioned with his hands, and for a second she felt like an exasperated young mother again, *No, it's not time to come in yet, go build an igloo, go sledding, I'll call you when dinner's ready.*

In any case, the mere sight of the boy sucked any remaining resolve out of her, and she couldn't help but wonder what she'd done to deserve a day like today. She wouldn't wish a day like today on her worst enemy. She started to get up to unlock the door, but Bill had already given it a tug and the door slid open, and she recalled one more thing on her to-do list that remained undone, calling a locksmith.

Snow flurried inside, and a gust of wind chilled the room. "Whoa-whoa-whoa!" she exclaimed as he started forward. "Don't you dare come in here with wet boots!"

Bill bent down and removed his boots and left them outside on the porch. Then he slid the door shut. He slipped off his jacket and pulled off his gloves, dropping everything in a heap on the scuff rug. It was, for Diana, the last of the last straws.

"Your timing, Bill," she said wearily, "is just stellar."

Bill padded over to the pool and squatted down and stuck his hand in the water. He sniffed loudly and ran his hand up over his nose and wiped it on his pants.

"Oh god," Diana murmured, for she could see that he had been crying, and knew it was about Megan.

"I'm freaking out," he wept.

"Bill. You've got to stop this."

"I can't," he said, sniffling. "Every day it just gets worse and worse."

Diana was so tired, so drained from everything else that she was afraid not only of snapping at the boy but of ridiculing him as well. She flashed on what she'd said back in the hospital, to Jack Fries. She closed her eyes and willed herself to keep her mouth shut for any but the most benign words of support.

"I've tried dating," Bill was saying. "I've tried counseling. No matter what I do, I can't stop thinking about her."

"Oh Jesus, Bill," said Diana, "do you know—"

"You think I'm crazy," he said. "I know. *I* think I'm crazy." He gave short staccato laugh. "You wouldn't believe the things I think of doing to myself. It just seems so hopeless. Like why go on? Everybody I meet feels sorry for me. They can tell. I don't even have to say anything. They look at me and they say to themselves, Yup, there goes another loser."

"Bill, we've all—"

Bill jumped up. "Don't tell me we've all been through this!" he shouted. "You haven't! Nobody's been through what I'm going through! Don't you get it? Don't you see what the obstacles are? You want me to spell them out? Fine, I'll spell them out! First, I have to get over her, which I can't do. But even if I could, then I'd have to meet someone else—which isn't going to happen since nobody's going to want to talk to a loser." He began cracking his knuckles. "And even if *that* happened, we'd still have to *like* each other! What are the odds there, huh? Why don't I just kill myself today and save my parents the cost of feeding me for another fifty years?"

Diana knew how futile it could seem; after breaking up with her college boyfriend, she'd been convinced that entire galaxies would have to align for her to ever find love again. Then she met Frank, and everything changed in a day.

"You'd be surprised—" she began, but Bill cut her off again.

"I don't want to hear it. My mother says that all the time. 'You never know what's just around the corner.' Buncha crap. Besides, I don't want anybody else. I want Megan."

Diana fought to stay calm. "Bill, listen. I'm saying this as a doctor. You're obsessed. You're completely obsessed. This is not normal. You need to see someone about getting some medication."

"You're saying I'm crazy?"

"No, I'm—"

"Because you're right!" Again that staccato laugh. "I'm crazy! I'm nuts! I'm absolutely completely off my rocker!"

"You're not crazy," Diana said calmly. "You're just obsessed. A doctor could help. I have a lot of names, you know."

Bill's face hardened. "I don't want names. I want Megan."

Now her patience had completely vanished. They were going in circles. He wasn't even listening. Suddenly she wanted to vaporize this boy who just wouldn't go away. She pictured Indiana Jones shooting the native in exasperated disgust and felt capable of a similar deed.

"You want Megan?"

"Yes, I do."

"Well, guess what, Bill," she said meanly. "You can't have her."

"Oh yes I can," he said.

She almost laughed, he sounded so childish. "How?"

"You're going to help me."

Hearing these words sent a chill down her spine, as though he'd suddenly brought out a gun. She wished Frank would come back. She bent over and turned on the jets and slipped into the pool, letting herself sink up to her neck in the foaming wrath.

"Look, Bill," she said, gathering her hair into a ponytail. "I've had a day the likes of which you can't even imagine. You are pushing me over the edge. I have no patience whatsoever for you right now. Now listen. I've been available to you for an entire year. It's over with my daughter. There is nothing you can do to get her back. And I certainly will not help you."

"Look." Proudly he reached into his coat pocket and brought out a small velvet box. "I bought her a ring."

If Diana had previously thought she'd been at the end of her rope, then she hadn't known how long it was in the first place. It always amazed her, how much you could pull out when you needed it. "Don't show me," she said calmly. "I don't want to see any ring. Put it back in your pocket and return it to the store. Leave her alone. Leave me alone. If you can't do that, we'll get a restraining order."

Still, Bill seemed not to have heard. "I have tickets to Cancún too," he went on. "The rest of our lives would be like this. I'd give her anything she wants. I'd get down on my knees for her."

Without responding, Diana lowered herself and swam into the jets. Bill tapped her shoulder. She ignored him and continued to swim. He tapped her shoulder again. This time she found her footing and lifted her head.

"Don't ignore me," he said.

"Bill. Pick up on the social cues. Time to go."

"But what about my plan?" he exclaimed. "You don't get it, Diana! This is my last chance!"

The rope was gone. The reserves used up. She had nothing left inside. The banality of the situation astonished her.

"Oh, Bill," she said wearily, "would you just . . . quit . . . *groveling*." She ducked her head underwater, and when she came back up, she saw Bill with his jaw hanging open, like Ben's, only goofier.

He licked his lips. "What did you say?"

She sculled away from him. "I said quit groveling. Jesus, you're nineteen—"

He reached out and grabbed her ponytail and whipped her around so that she was facing away from him. "Groveling?"

Diana reached up in pain. She thought she told him to let go, but wasn't sure if the words made it out of her mouth. "Hey. Bill. Let go," she said again. But he yanked her back again. Now her neck was in genuine pain, and when he loosened his grip for a moment, she found her muscles had locked up.

"You think I'm *groveling*?" He gave her neck another snap, this time with enough force that the back of her head hit the edge of the pool. "That's how you see it? You bitch." He yanked her head back once more, and now hot searing pain flooded her field of vision. She felt herself begin to flail, but he pushed her head down and held it under water like a toy. Her neck felt like someone was cutting it with sharp scissors. You little twerp, she thought, and she felt a sudden burst of energy that allowed her to lash and writhe about in an effort to escape his grasp. But she wasn't strong enough, and he held fast; although she managed to surface briefly, he shoved her down again. Pain stomped on her chest as she fought for air. Finally she managed to reach up from behind and grab his wrists, but he, with his more leveraged position, was able to wring his hands free and in one split second managed to cross both her wrists behind her and lift up, and she felt something rip across her chest. She surfaced and gasped and tried to kick off from the wall, but felt another burst of pain rip through her shoulders as Bill hung tight to her wrists.

"I don't grovel," he said. "I make a lot of concessions but I don't *grovel*." Holding her wrists with one hand now, he grabbed her ponytail and snapped her head back against the wall once more. He kept her facing away from him, but as he yanked, again and again and again, small chips of his face darted in and out of her vision. "I may be an asshole some of the time but I do not *grovel*; I do not *lick anyone's feet*."

Once more she tried to twist out of his grasp, to kick off with her legs, but there was nothing left to work with. Her legs floated away from her. Her arms dissolved. Bullets sprayed from her eyes as he yanked hard, one final time.

The last thing she saw was the water, sparkles above her head, the color green, columns of bubbles rising away from her.

———————

She was floating on her stomach, and he pushed her away.

"Hey," he said. Diana didn't move, and he gave her another push. "Hey. I'm sorry. Diana." He reached into the water and pulled her by the arm and rolled her over. Her eyes were open, and still she did not move. He shook her gently, then hard. "Diana. Hey."

His heart began to pound as it became clear to him what he had just done. Hastily he wiped his hands on his jeans. Panicked, he looked from one floor-to-ceiling window to the next, but saw only the black reflective shine of the night beyond. He looked at Diana one more time and then suddenly and clumsily bolted toward the sliding door, grabbing his coat and gloves, bunching them in his hands and using them to slide open the door because of course he couldn't touch anything with his bare hands; he was a criminal now. He loved a girl, and he killed a woman because he loved a girl. Nobody would understand.

Outside he stamped his heels into his boots and lumbered off through the snow into the dark void beyond the fence, kicking things into a mess behind him to cover up his footprints.

———————

But as for any footprints, he needn't have worried; by the time Frank got home from his visit with Edgar Love, it had snowed another four inches, blurring Bill's bootsteps, leaving at most a dim line of vague impressions, themselves to be smoothed over by a few strong gusts of wind.

Next door Susan Beekman let her dog out one last time.

In his small overheated house Huck Berlin forlornly opened up his Chinese takeout.

And across town, in her cinder-block room at the university, Megan and her roommate Natalie cut the second green tablet in half.

CHAPTER SEVENTEEN

ONCE UPON A TIME Huck believed that when the time was right, he would make not only a good husband but a good father as well. He saw himself settling his family in one of the outlying developments, maybe on a cul-de-sac where kids could ride their bikes. He'd fix faucets and clean the gutters, perhaps tackle a home project once a year, like the playhouse Ernie had built for his daughters when they were young. He envisioned himself like the fathers he saw in the video store, renting five, six, seven movies at a time on a Friday evening, arguing over ratings but caving in on the giant boxes of Red Hots, because he liked them too.

Now he wasn't sure.

Never would he have guessed that something that had been so clear in December could have grown so indeterminate by the end of February. And it wasn't because of Carolyn, either. Carolyn was willing to forgive him and move on. It was all inside him. Doubts the color of smoke. He fought them, he denied them, he opened his heart to let them fly away—and still they settled in each morning, unwilling to bargain.

It was over.

He'd blown it.

Big time.

The first weekend in March Carolyn came over to collect her belongings from his house. There wasn't much, which surprised them both, for they assumed they'd woven their lives together with enough physical objects to require a day's worth of sorting to unravel things. But apparently not. For the most part, everything she wanted she fit into a liquor box. Clothes, makeup, a few CDs. The Monet print that he'd never gotten around to hanging.

"Oh—the placemats," he said. "Don't you want them?"

"You can keep them," she replied. "They were never my favorite."

Ernie was kind, and did not berate him for his folly, although he did allow that it made things awkward for Leigh at work. "They'll get over it, though," he said. "They're big girls."

Fate was kind too, for not allowing him to run into Megan. He heard from a friend over at the DA's office, who'd heard from Frank, that she'd thrown herself into her studies. Possibly she was considering spending the next year in Honduras, or Nicaragua, volunteering as a medical aide. That was good, he thought. From the same person he heard that Frank himself had taken an extended leave while the U.S. Attorney's office down in Denver considered whether to file charges against him. The house was up for sale.

Huck assumed that with Bill Branson's confession, the general public would allow the Duprey case to recede into its collective archives. But while national interest waned, local interest remained acute; having been fed a daily diet of sexy news, the town had developed an addiction, which it was unable to shake in the absence of something equally sexy to take its place. The newspaper didn't help at all. Front-page articles detailing Bill's arrest, his bond, his preliminary hearing—the headlines screamed for weeks. And then there were the spin-off articles: "Is Your Child Being Stalked?" in Sunday Lifestyles, for instance. It was an election year, and Huck wished they'd turn to politics.

One day in mid-March—three months to the day after Diana's death—he stopped at a neighborhood coffee shop for a bagel. It was almost nine, but the tables were still crowded with scruffy laptoppers and sweatshirted fathers with their fleece-bundled babies and marathon runners all sinew and bone in their breezy nylon shorts. The girl at the espresso machine slammed her levers this way and that, and the pungent aroma of rich dark coffee, combined with steam and cinnamon, provided sharp contrast to the dry windy air outside.

Suddenly there was a lull in the general din, and Huck glanced up. Standing in the doorway were Robert and Sarah Branson, Bill's parents. Their pictures had been in the paper enough so that if you hadn't known them before, you did now; Robert was tall and broad-shouldered, a former football star for the University of Southern California, while Sarah was a diminutive woman with a sharp jawline and hair so thin on the scalp, it worried you a little.

Valiantly ignoring the silence, the Bransons took their place in line, and soon the noise levels rose to a happier level. But after Huck got his bagel, he turned, and in exiting he had to walk right past them. The last time they'd seen each other was in court for Bill's preliminary hearing. Now as their eyes met, Huck felt well-contained sorrows begin to leak.

Robert Branson nodded. "Detective," he said.

"Good morning," Huck said politely.

Sarah Branson stared up at him from behind a spare fringe of bangs.

"Going to work?" Robert asked.

"I am," replied Huck. He didn't like this situation one bit and was eager to leave, and to that end he wished some car in the parking lot would back into another so he could excuse himself and tend to a simple fender-bender. "And you?"

"No," said Robert. He did not elaborate.

"Well, then," said Huck. "Off to work." He toasted them with his coffee, giving a goofy smile.

"Mr. Berlin," said Sarah.

"Yes, ma'am?"

"How old are you?"

Huck did not expect this question. "I'm twenty-six, ma'am," he replied.

She nodded sagely, as though his age explained everything for her.

"Two decaf lattes," Robert told the boy at the counter. "Honey, you want a scone?"

The woman knew something. She wouldn't let go of him with her eyes. It made him nervous, and he wished more than ever that he'd eaten a bowl of cereal at home that morning.

"To you this is just another case, isn't it?" Sarah said.

"No, ma'am, I—"

"Just another day on the job. Do you have any idea what it's like to put the two people together?"

"Which two people, ma'am?"

"The boy who killed Dr. Duprey with the boy who wanted to be Michael Jordan for Halloween five years in a row?"

"Sarah, honey," said Robert.

"Allegedly killed," Huck pointed out.

"Whatever," said Sarah. "No, you don't, do you? How could you? You don't have children."

"I imagine it's probably one of the worst things a parent could go through," said Huck.

"Yes. It is. But it's one thing to imagine it, and another thing to go through it."

"Sarah, let the man go," said Robert.

"Just one old woman to one young man," Sarah Branson said. "Who knows what he'll be dealing with twenty years from now."

Robert gave her a nudge then, and Huck stood back to let them exit, even though he'd been the one on his way out before they were even served. He noticed that several people at nearby tables had been listening, and now they quickly dropped their heads back to whatever they were reading. And as Sarah and Robert left the coffee shop, he thought to himself, not for the first time, that it would be a lot easier to be a cop in a place where everyone didn't know everyone else.

He plodded through his days at work. The chief had put him back on Investigations, and any minute things could change with the commission of a new crime, but it seemed that day after day the people in this town woke up with the sole ambition of obeying the law. He chastised himself for wishing for tragedy. It was a lousy profession, he thought.

––––––––––

In mid-March a single room opened up, and Megan took it. She and Natalie had stopped speaking to each other at the end of February, over issues of music and alarm clocks and Natalie's habit of borrowing even the most intimate articles of clothing without asking. Midterm examinations gave Megan a 3.9 GPA, which pleased both her and her father. They ran together daily now, rain or shine, three miles up into the canyon and back. He suggested they train for a marathon, and she was game. There was nothing quite like pushing yourself to see what you were capable of.

On the surface she was doing very well. She started seeing a school psychologist to explore the unresolved issues with her mother. She slept soundly at night and took vitamins and learned the *Ujaii pranayama* method of breathing as a means of relaxing herself when other methods failed. If she had any free time on the weekends, she helped her father sort through her mother's papers; they made plans to publish a collection of her essays, the profits to be donated to a new clinic that was opening up in town.

Then, the third week in March, she ran into Huck, and everything around her shattered.

She was on her way into the grocery store to buy laundry detergent, and he was coming out with a cartful of groceries. Both slowed, and they stopped about ten feet from each other. He was wearing a baggy sweatshirt and carried a newspaper under his arm. To see him in the flesh made her want to stop and stare and run away, all at once. His eyes seemed to cut straight through her, blue lasers aimed at her heart.

"Hello," he said.

Not one night had she gone to sleep without recalling the warmth of his body next to hers. Not for long; she knew it was unhealthy to dwell upon something that had happened only once. Still, if you'd asked her to recall the curve of Michael Malone's shoulders, she'd have blinked and come up with nothing. If you'd asked her to recall not only the curve of Huck's shoulders but the slope of his belly and the muscular hardness of his thighs as well, she'd have been able to take a lump of clay and mold the exact likeness, right down to the knuckles on his hands.

"Hello," she said in return.

And in those few seconds when their eyes searched for answers to questions no one dared ask, she marveled at her foolhardiness for believing she could simply sleep with this man and then walk away as if it had never happened. For the first time in her life she wanted to talk to her mother about this, wanted answers to simple questions: *How do you know?* and *What do you do about it?* and *How do you forget, if it's not meant to be?*

Then Huck's eyes broke into pieces, and he smiled at her.

"How are you?" he asked.

"I'm okay," she said. "What about you?"

"I'm okay too," he said.

What bores they were!

He asked her, then, what she was going to do over spring break.

"Not Mexico," she said.

The trip, obviously, had gotten shunted aside following the death of her mother; at this point Megan would have felt out of place dancing naked on sunny beaches in throngs of coconut-oiled bodies.

"I'll probably help my father. He's still looking for a house."

"You're good to him," he said.

"He's all I've got," Megan reminded him.

He didn't mention Carolyn, Megan noticed, and she didn't ask, for fear that he would tell her they'd gone and gotten married in the last month. She did notice, however, that the newspaper under his arm was folded open to the want ads.

"What are you looking for?" she asked.

He glanced at the paper. "Oh. A dog," he said.

"A dog! That sounds homey."

Huck grinned.

"What kind?" she asked.

"I don't know. Maybe a mutt. I was going to go to the Humane Society and take a look."

"Oh."

"Do you want to come?" he asked suddenly.

The question flustered her. She had laundry to do, a big lab to write up, a paper to draft, a run scheduled with her father that afternoon.

"Okay," she said.

"Okay?"

"Sure."

"Now?"

"I'm free," she said, an entire vocabulary re-forming in her brain.

"Well hey," he said. "Let's go."

"I'll follow you," she said.

"Still the VW?"

"A hundred and thirty-five thousand miles," she told him.

"But no defroster."

Megan smiled. "Still no defroster."

They walked across the parking lot. A car drove by, windows open, music blaring. It was spring, and even in a sea of asphalt you could smell mud, and puddles rippled, and the Girl Scouts hawked their cookies, and purple crocuses poked through their leafy mulch, and buds swelled, pregnant with chlorophyll. And in a cement kennel a few miles away a litter of puppies, brown and black and gray and definitely not of one lineage, squirmed over one another in their efforts to simultaneously stay warm, and break free.

ACKNOWLEDGMENTS

I am deeply indebted to the following readers for their comments on the manuscript: Detective Jack Gardner of the Boulder Police Department; Patricia Bosak, RN, CNM, of the Boulder Valley Women's Health Center; Professor Marianne Wesson of the University of Colorado School of Law; and Lisa Halperin, M.D. A huge thank you to my agent, Molly Friedrich, who just recently came into my life with all of her energy, warmth, and infinite wisdom; and to my editor, Jordan Pavlin, for her confidence and enthusiasm. I'm extremely grateful to Young Audiences of Colorado, for their continuing support over the years. Thanks to Kate, Zoe, and Nick, for unknowingly offering me a window into the teenage mind when my own memories failed. And Pierre: thank you for consistently vetoing alternative careers. You are the love of my life.